DEAD MAN'S BADGE

DEAD MAN'S BADGE

ROBERT E. DUNN

© 2018 Robert E. Dunn

All rights reserved.

No part of this book may be reproduced, stored in a retrieval system, or transmitted in any form or by any means, electronic, mechanical, photocopying, recording, or otherwise, without express written permission of the publisher.

ISBN: 0997832363
ISBN 13: 9780997832365

Published by Brash Books, LLC
12120 State Line #253
Leawood, Kansas 66209

www.brash-books.com

ONE

Nothing is easy—not even dying. At least for me it wasn't. The half hour spent digging my own grave in the glare of headlights and the cold of a desert night was literally the hardest work of my life.

A man digging his own grave in the movies makes a perfect, squared-off hole. He digs it deep too. The reality is that you gouge out a ragged hole in the ground that measures in inches, not feet. Self-dug graves are always shallow. Also in the movies, the men digging are resolute. They either accept their fate or work confidently on escape. Real men will scream or plead, cry or beg. Always there is bargaining.

Hope. It's a bitch. It'll keep you shoveling, and it's the only thing that will.

The three of us digging were past making bargains. Four of us began the exercise of moving our own dirt. One man couldn't take it. The two men holding guns on us, the quiet one and the one who laughed at everything, called the fourth man "maricón."

In east Texas, where I grew up, we would have said "faggot." I've used the slur many times. Hearing those two hateful killers denigrate another man with superiority in their voices made me ashamed of my own failing to be a better person.

When they shot him, he was on the bare dirt crying like a child. He begged, not for his life but to be again in the arms of his mother. Being the man he was, being a maricóne, had nothing to do with his tears. Those were falling because he had been beaten for sport and mocked in his despair.

Sometimes, when that bitch hope leaves us, the only thing that can fill the hole is tears. I couldn't find it in my heart to think less of him for crying. At that point I was certain I would be doing the same soon.

"Trabajar más rápido; no quiero perder toda la noche matando estos hijos de puta," said the one closest to me. "Work faster; I don't want to spend all night killing motherfuckers," or something like that. He was the one who didn't seem to be enjoying the job. His partner seemed to be in no hurry.

Neither was I.

"¿Quién va a enterrarel el maricóne?" the second guy asked. He wanted to know who would bury the man they had already killed.

"Haga que el Yankee haga un agujero más profundo. Pueden compartir," the one with his gun on me answered. I was the Yankee. I didn't have a perfect translation for that, but I knew it came down to me digging a bigger hole to share.

The shovel I used was old, and the handle had broken off. It terminated into a ragged point that ate my skin. Every scoop of dirt jammed my fingers into crevasses that pinched or splinters that pierced my palms. The dry wood was tracked red with my blood.

For some reason, I'd been cursing the instrument rather than the men who held guns on me. I heard a preacher say once that we're all born in the middle of a ladder. From the first breath, we start climbing. Every choice is a rung up or a rung down. That put me one step above a broken shovel and two from a dirt hole and at the bottom of my personal ladder. I wasn't arguing the point. Good people rarely end up where I had. Life is a series of choices that always brings us to the same place. The only difference in lives is how you feel about it at the end. I was feeling pretty fucking bad.

I put my palm on the end of the shovel and jammed the rusty, blunted blade into the soil. When it struck, a bit of the fractured end broke away. A long splinter sliced into my hand.

"Damn it." I pressed the cut to my mouth. The second bastard laughed. I sucked away the salty taste of sweat and blood along with a three-inch sliver of hickory that was dead and mounted to a shovel before I was born.

"Sigue cavando," said the one close to me. He wasn't laughing.

The other two digging men bent their backs to the task slowly. Not hurrying was resistance. It was a way of stealing a moment to rest and maybe looking around for some chance to run.

They didn't get the chance.

Again, I stuck the point of my shovel in the bottom of my grave. It penetrated no more than a couple of inches into the hard ground. I released the handle to pull another splinter. The old shovel fell over. I picked it up and angrily thrust the point down once more. The result was the same. Taking my despair, anger, and pain out on the old tool, I jammed it down again and again, shouting, "Kiss my ass, you dull-pointed son of a bitch." After that I kicked it, sending up a shower of dirt. The shovel accepted things much better than I did. It flopped up and settled again, pointing with my blood at a point someplace between Venus and the horizon.

Everyone was looking at me, even the other diggers.

"You too!" I screamed at them collectively, diggers and killers alike. I stepped out of my shallow hole.

The laughing one kept his weapon pointed at the other two men, who had stopped their digging. It was the one close to me, the serious one, who sighted my chest. He didn't say anything. He didn't have to. We both understood.

I understood one more thing, though. If he was willing to dig the hole, I would already be dead.

One backward step, and I turned away from him. One more step, and I was on the edge of the old Chevy's low beams.

The bore of the .40 was still warm from killing the crying man when it pressed up against the base of my skull.

"Your shovel is waiting, my friend," the serious man said. His voice was honey and gravel. "Come on. Let's make a rough job quick. Then you can rest."

Moving slowly, I opened my fly. There was a long moment where I had the worst case of bashful bladder in history before the water flowed.

Everything seems louder in proximity to death. My piss running into the dust of Mexico sounded like a horse filling a dry bucket. Behind me the killers laughed. Their surprised mirth made a noise like the scattering of birds off a fresh carcass. I must have looked pathetic or foolish or both being willing to get my brains blown out just to avoid messing my grave.

As soon as the muzzle of the .40 lifted from my head, I turned.

The moment he understood I was still pissing, my killer backed away in an awkward dance. He pointed his weapon to the ground. His eyes followed my water as he tried to avoid getting pissed on. He failed. When the stream of my urine crawled up his legs, he jumped higher. His laughing buddy cackled like an old crone. I let go of my meager weapon, put up both hands and pushed.

I hadn't planned anything beyond the last act of defiance. When I pushed, it wasn't very hard. I simply wanted him on the ground and feeling what he dished out before I died. It felt good. It felt even better when he kept stumbling back, his gun arching up and firing into the sky. As soon as the weapon flashed, the other guy swallowed his laughter in a panic and shot the men in front of him. The other two gravediggers fell like their strings had been cut by God as the ragged end of my shovel handle burst through the chest of the man I'd pissed on.

People who never experience real violence often wonder what goes through your head when things get hot and the cold night is streaked with the flame of tiny, metal-jacketed comets. If you're lucky and prepared by experience, nothing goes through your mind. You just react. You move.

That's what I did.

The serious one was dead. The other two diggers were dead. Laughing boy was pointing his weapon at me, and I ducked to the side, closing on him. He missed, and then his revolver clicked on a spent cartridge. He had used five on the guys in the grave and his last one missing me.

I passed again through my own grave and out the other side to pick up another shovel. This one had been dropped by one of the men just killed. I swear, when I picked it up, the heat of his fingers was still on the handle.

Laughing boy threw up his arms to defend his face as I raised my shovel. He needn't have bothered. I swung low, aiming the edge of the shovel blade at his kneecap. His screams were as loud as the gunshots had been. A second later everything went quiet. At least he had stopped laughing.

As I stood there leaning on the shovel, he started talking. First, he said, "Please." Then he said the worse thing he could have: "Longview." My name. Longview Moody—it's a stupid name given by a foolish man. Hearing it come from the mouth of the laughing guy only made me despise it more.

"Longview," he said again, his hands up in supplication.

"What?" I asked, not sure if I was asking what he wanted or just asking for clarification. I had been turned over to these guys with barely a word. It was possible that they had been told who I was, but why? I was meat to them—just meat to be disposed of.

He pointed vaguely at his crotch and said, "Badge." With two fingers, he reached into his pocket.

I nodded, smiling down. What did I care? Mexican cops are literally a dime a dozen on the border. The seriously bent ones go for the bushel price. I let him reach for the badge, thinking about the letdown he would feel when I showed just how little it mattered to me. Probably as little as it had mattered to him until he needed to hide behind it. People like me—bad guys, that is—are like the straights in this world. We like our cops to be on the up. Hell, no one likes a hypocrite, and there's no greater hypocrisy than a crooked cop.

Laughing guy got the badge out of his pocket and held it up. It was a gold shield with a blue "US" standing out in the middle like a flat punchline. Around the center it read, Drug Enforcement Agency—Special Agent. DEA—he was holding up a DEA badge.

I turned my head and spit into the dirt waiting for the cosmic other shoe to drop. My breath felt bad in my chest, and my gut was roiling. What should I do? What did I want to do? This was a man who would have killed me and never stopped laughing. I could have left him to die in the desert, but I'm not that cruel.

I'm much worse.

I lifted the shovel again and broke his other leg. When he reached for the dropped revolver, even though it was empty, I crushed his fingers under my boot heel and kicked the weapon away. He wallowed in the dirt like a fish hoping the next flop would take him to the water. His efforts dropped him into the middle grave along with one of the men he'd killed.

There wouldn't be any more laughter out of him. Somehow his screams were more fitting to the night. They fit my mood a lot better, I can tell you that. He rolled over onto his belly and tried to claw his way back up from the shallow grave. The dirt he pulled down got into his mouth, but he kept screaming. It fell into his face and hair, coating him with the dust I figured he would soon return to.

I stepped into the grave and stuck a hand into his back pocket. There was a lump there I thought might be the car keys. It was a handful of loose bullets. I threw them all away into the darkness, except one. I retrieved the revolver and his badge. The badge went into my pocket, and after I dumped the spent casings, the one remaining bullet went into the cylinder.

That was when I noticed that the laughing guy had stopped screaming and was watching me from his grave.

"You can't do this," he said. His voice was as weak as his supposition. He knew full well I could do it.

"I've done all I'm going to do." I held up the revolver and showed it to him. "The rest is up to you." With that, I dropped the gun.

"I can't."

"Sure, you can," I told him. "If you want it bad enough."

"Have pity."

I gave him a good hard look and even thought about it for a moment, a moment longer than it deserved. I said, "Nope."

He kept begging. I ignored him while I kicked around the dirt looking for the .40 that had been pressed up against my head. It was in the hole that was supposed to have been my grave. I rifled the pockets of the man with my shovel handle through his chest. He had a spare magazine but no keys. I wasted a couple of minutes looking for them before it dawned on me to check the Chevy. There they were, dangling from the ignition with a few other unknowns and a little plastic Jesus. The car started right up. Thank you, Jesus.

When I backed away and headed down the trail that led who-knew-where, I saw the laughing guy crawling out of the grave. He was reaching hard for the gun I'd left in the dirt. I wondered if he heard the same yowling coyote I did.

The body dump was deep in the desert. After twenty minutes on the same rutted dirt track, I was wondering if I had enough gas to get back to the States. That led me to a question. Was that where I wanted to go? I'd been making a cash drop in Juarez when I had been grabbed. A lot of people don't know that cash can be harder to move than drugs. It was my specialty. I started off stealing it and ended up moving it. Turned out there was a lot better money to be made in protecting cash than taking it. I say better, not more. Truth is that most guys who rob spend a percentage of their lives in jails and prison. A hundred grand would be a huge score for the average career criminal. And it sounds like a lot of money until you consider the costs. If he's under the thumb of a family business, he'll piece off a big chunk. There are taxes even on crime. Lawyers take a bite too. Then there's the real price—prison. Say you don't use a gun and get only fifteen; you do ten for your hundred grand. Working as a straight in any cubical hell gives a better return. Of course, if criminals were smart enough to run their own lives, lawyers would starve.

As I drove faster than a sane man would on what was more of a trail than a road, I tried to work out why I had ended up where I had. I'd showed up at the right time and place. My count had been perfect. My trail had been clean. Everything should have been fine. Still, someone had been pissed off.

I never saw who had hit me. It had been a hard lick upside the back of my head with the butt of a pistol that had brought me down. My head had been filled with stars, and sound seemed like it was coming through a thick wall for a long time. I don't think I ever went out. Not that it matters. One instant after the fireworks went off in my skull, I had hit the floor. Before I had settled fully, my hands were being tied behind me. After that, I had squirmed for a while on a carpet that smelled of old dog before my head had been bagged. Hands had gripped my ankles. I had been dragged across carpet before being hefted up by two men. They had taken me out and tossed me into the back floorboard of the car. I think the other guys were already in the trunk, so I can't complain about the transportation accommodations.

Replaying it in my mind did nothing to help me understand why. It did no better with the where. In the car, little had been said, and my head had been bagged. That had made time hard to figure. I could have been about any place within a couple of hundred miles of Juarez where I had made my drop.

Something moved in the bouncing headlights ahead of the Chevy. Black over black, they scattered like dark angels escaping a wound in the earth. Birds. They were dining on the carcass of an armadillo. I steered carefully, straddling the dead animal. In the mirror, I watched fluttering black shapes settle behind the car.

I wondered about Matias. He was my contact. For almost three years I had carried cash from various places in the States to Matias in one of three Mexican cities, either Juarez, Nogales, or Mexicali. I would make the drop and then got my pay for the run and a new burner phone. Matias would call the burner when he had a pickup. Until that call, I wouldn't know where I was picking up or which of my three drops I was heading to. It was a good system. It had been until I was coldcocked and driven out to the desert to die.

That night things had been wrong from the moment I had arrived at the drop house. Always before, Matias had been there with a grin and a beer. He was a rough son of a bitch who would gut a cheat without a thought. Other than that, he was a great guy. I never cheated or stole from my count. He treated me like a pal.

But a thin man in a suit and a room full of darkness and thugs had replaced Matias, his grin, and his beer. Matias had never needed much extra muscle. He was a hands-on manager. He didn't go much for the lights-off theatrics either. This other guy was obviously more of a background kind of man. He was tall and lean with a sharp-edged aspect of face and demeanor that chilled the room. Not that I had been able to see him clearly. When he had come between me and a backlighted window, I could see a long nose and hard lines.

The thin man had reached through the stripe of light coming through the window to take the cash from me. His hands were as much claws as hands. His nails were long and yellowed on thin fingers. On the skin that covered the talons were tattoos—skulls. Six fingers, four on one hand, two on the other, had the ink. They were startling because they weren't simple death heads but intricate, Día de los Muertos–style skulls. Each one was different. All were colorful, whimsical, and a bit terrifying. It was impossible to see them as anything but beautiful notches in a gun butt.

He had taken the cash, hefting it in his hand as though he could tell just by weight the value of what he held. After a moment of consideration, he had tossed the package onto a coffee table in front of an old couch. There is something about money. Even the most jaded treat it either with awe or calculated dismissal. Rarely is a bundle amounting to at least a million dollars treated casually—unless a paltry million is meaningless in your view. He dropped it as if it was nothing onto a table already stacked with plastic-wrapped bricks of cocaine and grass.

That was when I had known Matias was dead.

Knowledge can be a terrible thing. Until that moment, I could *believe*. It didn't matter what—I could believe anything I wanted. Once I knew, belief was gone. All the doors that lead to all the different hallways through which belief could go slammed shut. Only one door remained.

The man had said, "Hacerle desaparecer." Make him disappear.

That door had opened with the burst of fireworks in my head.

The track I drove finally opened and smoothed. It brought me up the back side of a trash dump stacked with tires, old refrigerators, and piles of garbage that were being picked over by coyotes and rats big enough not to be frightened by them. Eyes glowed back, red and green, as my headlights passed over them. On the other side of the pit, I came to an intersection. It was another unmarked oil-pan hazard. I stopped and idled as I tried to choose a direction.

Choosing was the excuse. I was coming down off the adrenaline high and crashing hard. Suddenly I was cold and sweating. My hands were shaking, and my stomach felt like it was full of snakes. At times like that, it's natural to ask yourself, How has my life ended up here? Natural but foolish, at least for me. I knew. I think most of us do, but I had no doubts.

A pair of green eyes watched the car. They remained at the edge of the road, on the far end of the headlights' reach. I turned up the heater. As I did, I noticed the pile of belongings in the passenger-side floorboard. There were four wallets, some loose cash, bits of paper, and a pocketknife. I grabbed my wallet and checked the others for money. A few bucks—not what I'd signed on for.

The .40 was still sitting on the seat where I'd thrown it with the spare clip. I decided to check it out. The loaded clip dropped out smoothly, and the slide racked back to eject the chambered round easily. It was a cared-for weapon, clean and oiled. I would have thought about keeping it long term if it wasn't a pimp's gun. Mexicans liked that kind of crap—nickel plating, fake-pearl grips. This one had all that and a few extras: seven notches filed into the metal of the handle running up the back edge. There was no chance they were scratches either. They were filed and finished smooth, spaced evenly. The notches had been put there intentionally by the same man who had kept the weapon clean. It gave me a little satisfaction knowing that man had died from a rusted and poorly maintained gardening tool. I counted both clips and reseated the round that had been chambered. Three cartridges were missing: one had killed the crying man, and two had been spent into the sky.

When I had everything back together, I looked up for the first time in a while. There were more eyes watching. The animals were closer as well. I could see them, dark-gray ghosts against a background of velvet black. They were circling in, getting braver as I sat motionless. If it weren't for them, I might have shut off the engine and waited for daylight. Instead, I pressed the gas and twisted the wheel right. In another few minutes I was rewarded with a streak of light crossing in the distance. Headlights on a real road. I hit the asphalt and took another right.

It wasn't long before I came out on Highway 2 near a town called Barreales. From there it was about twenty-five miles to Juarez, the nearest border crossing. I wanted nothing more than to be back on the US side of the border, but...

As I drove, and as my mind pushed aside the effects of the terror and anger, I began to think of other reasons to stop in Juarez.

The sky was still nighttime dark and frosted with stars as I approached the city limits. When I parked, the sun was just pinking the eastern horizon. I needed to be fast.

The drop house was six doors down from my parking spot. I hugged the darkest parts of the street in a stiff-legged lope to cover the remaining distance. I was counting on arrogance—theirs, not mine. A house like that one, filled with cash and drugs, would be surrounded by security cameras or armed guards in the States. In a poor Mexican neighborhood, cartel houses count on word-of-mouth security. Everyone for blocks knows what goes on behind the peeling blue paint and barred windows. The police know. Even the reporters know. Everyone knows. They know just as well what happens to anyone who talks about it. You don't even have to talk. Just look at the house the wrong way, and a poster goes up with your name on it and the word "Missing." You disappear. And if you're ever found, it's because your body is a message. Sometimes your body is one message, your head another, so on and so on.

The point is, no one messes with a cartel house because you'd have to be crazy to do it—more than crazy. Even the maddest of us have some sense of self-preservation. I wasn't crazy. But I was dead once that bag had gone over my head. Let me tell you, an escape from the grave is an experience that colors your outlook. After that, most people run off to blue skies, rainbows, and boat drinks. I wasn't most people, though, and I was pissed. An angry dead man is not an enemy to have.

I reached the door without raising an alarm. That was, I expected, where sanity would end. Everything else—well, that was up in the air until I went through the door. I acted without hesitation.

There was no kicking in of the door, no bursting in guns a-blazin'. I tried the knob. The door opened easily if not quietly. It squeaked. After it came to a halt, half-open, I waited. No one shouted or came to check on the sound. I crept in. An almost-shadow moved on the door as I passed. I looked back to the eastern sky. It was beginning to brighten from soft pink to a burning red.

The dark room was littered with bottles and men. I didn't see the thin man with the skulls on his fingers. I imagined him someplace close because the bundle of cash I had delivered the night—a lifetime—before was sitting beside the couch. Also on the couch, framed in the faint glow from the open door, was a man I'd never seen before sleeping with a shotgun cradled in his arms. He was a Mexican cliché, wearing stiff jeans and boots with long pointed toes. Around his waist was a tooled belt with a huge rodeo-style belt buckle in silver and gold. Over the top part of his face was a straw cowboy hat. In his open mouth was a gold tooth. I wanted to shoot him just because he made the other Mexicans look bad.

I restrained myself and went for the bundle of money. If life was like the movies, he would have woken and the sliding click-clack of the shotgun chambering a round would have warned me. Life isn't a movie. I'm always reminded of that by my own failures to be the hero or get the girl. Guys like him, cartel soldiers guarding a twelve-pound block of hundred-dollar bills, don't sleep with uncharged weapons. It was the sudden silence when he stopped mouth breathing that was my warning. I no longer had to restrain myself. He raised the shotgun. Or he tried without getting it very far. I had been keeping the .40 on him as I approached the money. My shot went right through the hat still covering his face.

Drunken, surprised men scrambled, as well as they could, to their feet, reaching for weapons. Again, I didn't hesitate. From the dead man on the couch, I turned and fired at the other men. My only chance was to kill faster than they could come to their senses. First, I shot the man on the chair, one to his heart before he even got to his feet, and then I started in on the men wallowing on the dog-stink carpet. Three of them. Three shots. The muzzle flash and reports of the .40 in the dark room were a raging thunderstorm of high-velocity metal.

I was wrong. There were four men on the floor. I had missed one passed out behind the chair. He got a shot off that touched the hairs on my ear as it passed. I turned, dropping and firing, using three bullets to bring him down. When I hit the floor, I stayed there. Men were shouting as they poured out of the bedrooms, angry ants after the nest is kicked. They ran shooting wildly. It was all cover fire; they weren't aiming, only hoping to keep heads down until they could find a target. My head was already down.

I dropped the .40 and grabbed the shotgun, pointing it down the hall and keeping it low. Two rounds of double-aught buckshot ripped the left foot off the first man and then raked away his face when he fell. The men who came after were taken out at the shins and knees. I finished them as they clutched at missing limbs.

When I rose again, I had the .40 back in my hand and ready. The last man was waiting. As soon as I showed against the brightening sky at the doorway, he started emptying his weapon. It was one of those giant .50 hand cannons with seven in the mag and one in the chamber. Those rounds would go through an engine block, or in this case a cinder block wall, and keep killing for a week. But unless your name was Schwarzenegger, they never hit the person you were aiming at. It was too heavy and too slow and kicked like Newton's third law on steroids. I let him shoot his wad and put one of mine through his eyebrow.

Subtlety is not in the cartel playbook. When the house was silent, I was certain it was empty of life other than mine. Still I checked. One by one, I quickly cleared the rooms. The next thing I did was check each body to make sure that they were dead. Then I had some fun. Grabbing up a discarded shirt, I used it to keep my prints off the guns as I fired every one I could find into the walls, ceiling, floor, and bodies. When I was satisfied with that bit of red herring, I pulled the DEA badge from my pocket and dropped it. I took the cash and a bundle of grass.

The rising sun was giving as much light as color by the time I exited the house. It was a sliver of red on a leaden horizon projecting orange on the underside of scattered clouds. My shadow was coming into the world, darkening with new reality as I walked.

I didn't see anyone watching me, no faces at windows or curiosity seekers on the porches. That didn't mean no one was there. Life was lived carefully in Juarez, or it wasn't lived very long.

TWO

Getting out of the house wasn't enough. I had to get out of the country and fast. The car I'd driven into Mexico was gone. I still had the Chevy. The problem was that it wasn't fitted with the compartments my car had been. Those weren't perfect for heading into the States, but they would have been better than nothing. My usual trips were south carrying cash. I didn't move drugs and rarely went armed. I got almost no attention going either way. Driving the Chevy, a vehicle with Mexican tags and a ragged-looking Anglo at the wheel, I would get a look. If I had the cash in the car, I'd get a long, hard look in a small room with too much light and too little air. That was why I had grabbed the grass.

At an all-night stop, I bought a gas station sandwich, some water, and a jar of pickles. Walking back to the car, I lifted the spray bottle of window cleaner that hung by the pumps. It took less than a minute to eat the sandwich. Then I got to work.

First, I emptied the window cleaner from the spray bottle and refilled it halfway with water. After that, I opened the package of dried and compacted weed. Tearing off two big clumps, I crushed them on the concrete to release the oils. That was something I had learned from cooking shows. The ground-down pile I scooped into the spray bottle. My weed-water mix got a good shake, and then I washed my hands in the pickle juice. I was still hungry enough to eat one of the dills before I got back into the Chevy.

The sun was up. Another day had begun for me and a couple thousand day laborers and domestics getting into line to cross the border into Texas. I didn't go straight in. I drove around slowly, and every car I passed that was going toward the border, I sprayed with the marijuana-infused water. When the traffic got to its thickest, I finally eased in with the flow. After a half hour or so, the Chevy was about a dozen cars from the checkpoint, and traffic was dead. Dogs were alerting on cars I'd sprayed. Those were pulled to the side and getting a good going-over.

A lot of people were out of their vehicles and milling around with street vendors and panhandlers. No one paid attention as I strolled out into the stalled traffic, giving everything around me a good but surreptitious spray. Lines started moving again. I screwed the nozzle off and dumped the bottle in the back of a truck.

Dogs were going crazy signaling at sprayed cars. Border Patrol agents had almost twenty cars pulled aside getting hard searches. It had to be frustrating. At least I hoped so.

The truck I'd tossed the bottle into provoked a huge response. It was big enough to hide a huge cache of drugs. It helped that the angry landscape workers were putting up just enough of a fight to make the edgy agents downright certain of their guilt.

When things are like that, the gringo heading home gets the once-over. Thankfully they didn't even bother to look under the seats once the dog sniffed the car and my pickle-scented hands and then lost interest.

* * * *

"What's the problem now?" It was my half-brother asking. He was older than me by a year, and we had different mothers. The man who named me Longview had named his first son Paris.

Our father's name was Buick. Names were apparently a familial curse.

Both Paris and I took after Buick and had an uncanny resemblance for half-brothers. Paris was a bit trimmer and well kempt. His hair was darker and shorter. Mine was sun bleached and hanging past my collar.

Paris had the home, the mostly full-time dad, and the Tindall name. The only thing I got from Buick was a face I had to share.

The old man was a bastard in so many ways. That's ignoring the fact that I was the literal bastard of the family. My mother moved us to the east side of Trinity Bay outside of Houston to be closer to Buick. He showed his appreciation by keeping us housed and a little food on the table. Dependency was a trap that my mother either didn't understand or didn't choose to challenge. Poverty can be like a toilet: smooth walls and a strong current pulling you down. That's where we were, in the middle of the swirl, while Buick watched us go around. We were not the dirty secret you would think. That's to say we weren't secret at all.

Buick Tindall was a Texas Ranger. Paris Tindall was a Texas Ranger. Longview Moody was a career criminal with a history of violence. Sometimes I can almost see a pattern in my life. There is one definite pattern. When I get in trouble, I call the one cop I know I can trust.

"I was set up," I told him, passing the phone to the other ear. My right one still had the creepy feeling of that bullet whizzing by and tickling the short hairs.

"Where are you?" he asked. Paris didn't sound happy to hear from me. I couldn't blame him.

"I'm at a motel in El Paso. I need to sleep before heading home."

"I don't know how much help I can be this time. There are some things going on. I've got a new job."

"A new job? What?" That was hard to believe. Paris loved being a Ranger, and as much as I hated to admit it, he was one of the good ones. In our family, the apples fell far from the tree and then rolled down hill.

"I'm going to be the new chief of police in Lansdale."

"The hell you say."

Lansdale, Texas, was a dead end on a road no one traveled, tucked into a bend in the border. Remember that movie *Lonesome Dove*? The town of Lonesome Dove was what Lansdale aspired to become when it had been founded by the grace of a horse dying and stranding its rider in 1897. It had grown but not well; a bigger hell is not necessarily a better hell. "Why?"

"Things," he answered. Paris was always good with words. "What about you? Need money?" There was the reason I could always forgive him. My brother never liked the way I lived. In fact, he could be outright judgmental and harsh about it. But that never stopped him from offering help.

"No. I need to tell you—"

"I have to go," he said. "Meet me at your place."

He hung up.

"Damn it," I said into the dead phone. Then: "Screw it." I went to sleep.

My dreams were of the underground. Darkness both surrounded and filled me. The organic taste of rot filled my mouth. It wasn't like the desert soil, dry dust. What fell into my mouth as I tried to scream was moist and rich. It was the soil of a forest floor, old leaves, and chewing worms. Then came the lightning. It came not in bolts but in sprays of light. Gunshot bursts of electricity expelled in barking thunderclaps. Some were small. Or they were distant; I wasn't sure. The sound came instantly in either case. Some of the flashing bursts were larger, concussive blasts of light and pressure like a shotgun in a coffin.

I wished I had a coffin.

When I woke, the sun was almost gone from the sky, replaced by thunderheads and a sweeping storm. Lightning fingers pointed south, accusing and betraying me at the same time. I tried calling Paris again. It went to voice mail. There was no point in leaving a message.

Before getting back onto the road, I showered again. It was the second time I had washed off the feeling of the grave since coming to this little motel. I left the key on the sweat-soaked bed and then walked out into the rain. A third wash.

* * * *

"What are you escaping from, prison?" the cashier asked.

I looked around to see if she was talking to someone else. She wasn't. "What do you mean?" I tried not to sound too concerned.

I had gone straight to a truck stop from the motel. It was a big one with showers and stacks of trucker caps. This one sold boots and had a rack of jeans. I picked up clean pants; a fresh shirt, the kind with pearl-snap buttons; and a burner phone.

The woman whose name tag read Rochelle pointed at what I'd laid on the counter. Looking at my little pile of purchases, I supposed it couldn't have looked more suspicious if I'd added a bottle of whiskey and a new pistol.

"Oh," I said, laughing a little I-just-got-it laugh. "Yeah, I am in a way." Then I leaned over the counter toward her, just enough to look down her cleavage and smell the powder she used on her skin. "My wife kicked me out."

She flushed a little red. I wasn't sure if it was because of what I'd said or what she imagined I was thinking. She was pretty, and it made me wish. I wished I wasn't headed home right away, and I wished I hadn't had the night just past.

"That's a shame," she said, and she meant it. "That's sixty-four eighty-seven. Where will you be landing?"

It was a casual question. I read more into it than was there probably because I was feeling like an untied string. "You know, Rochelle...you smell prettier than a Sunday morning." I looked at her face again. "I won't be landing for a while, but I'll think of you while I fly." I pulled two hundreds from the roll I was carrying. "You keep this and have a little fun tonight. Maybe you'll think of me."

I changed in the shower room. When I left wearing my new things, Rochelle blew me a kiss. I felt almost human. Only almost. I was about an hour outside of El Paso when I started crying. I don't like it, but it happens after a fight. It happened in the army, and it happens now. Don't mistake it for weakness. It's not even guilt. I don't know what it is other than stress, but it's part of my routine. How sad is it that I have a routine for dealing with death and killing?

Once that was over and the new phone was charged, I pulled over and set it up, and then I called Paris again.

"What?" he asked, sounding even more rushed and annoyed than before when he knew who was calling.

"It's me," I said.

"I thought you were going to your place."

"I am," I told him, in my best explaining-calmly voice. "I was in El Paso, remember?"

"What were you doing there?"

"You don't want to know."

"I don't want to know in an official capacity?" he asked.

I hated the smug sound of righteousness that crept into his voice. It wasn't a surprise. He and I had stopped surprising each other a long time ago. As a matter of fact, it was probably the predictability of each of us for the other that was the hardest part of our relationship.

"You don't want to know in any capacity," I said. "And before you ask again, I don't need money."

"I'm glad to hear it." There was an edge of disbelief in his voice.

I wondered if Paris liked being the guy who kicked his brother a few bucks when I got into trouble. I didn't ask about it. Instead I asked, "What's going on with the official thing? Why are you taking this job?"

"There are some things I need to do. I was just bailing water as a Ranger. Maybe down in Lansdale I can pull some people to shore."

"What people?"

He didn't answer, and the cheap phone creeped with static when there was no sound coming in.

"Paris?"

"What are you running from this time?" He always had a way of cutting right through to it.

That time it was my turn to hold back an answer.

"You can stop," he said. "Running. Everything."

"And do what?"

"Come help me."

"I can't be a cop. Forget the joke of the situation. I have a record."

"People with parking tickets have records. You're a felon with a jacket."

"Is that how cops talk?" I passed a slow-going SUV and stayed in the left lane to go by a couple of semis.

"You're a big-stripe con with a stretch in Angola. That could help me."

"I'm glad it helps you."

"It can help you too," he said. "In the long run."

"The longest." I think I did a good job putting bitterness into my voice.

"I talked to Daddy the other day," he said. The change and the subject both brought me up short. I cut the wheel quickly and crossed into the right-hand lane just ahead of a truck. No horn, but I could see him flipping me off in the mirror.

Funny thing about us southern boys. We may get to be ninety, but we'll still refer to our fathers as Daddy. When we're not calling them sons of bitches.

"You're not going to even ask about him?" he had the balls to ask me.

I ignored his question and the judgment in it. Instead I told him, "I killed about a dozen men in Old Mex last night." It was a blunt and shocking statement. I knew that. I knew also that he would have to deal with the image and the knowledge of the kind of man I'd become. I didn't care. It was self-serving to impose the reality of my life on him with the unmistakable accusation that if our daddy had been a father to me, I might be where he was. I still didn't care. But I said, "Sorry."

"So am I," he said. I could tell he meant it. "Do you want to talk—"

"No."

"Got it."

"Are you all right?"

That question was not what I expected. I had to think about it.

"You still there?" he asked after a long moment of noisy silence. Then: "Are you doing okay?" His voice was different that time. The question was different too. "Are you all right" meant "Did you get hurt?" But "Are you okay" meant something else.

"I don't know," I said, and I didn't know the truth of that until I said it.

"Do you need me to—"

"No," I said again quickly. Then: "So tell me about this thing in Lansdale. How I can help?"

"Do you want to?"

"I don't know. How can I? You won't tell me what's going on."

"I can't."

"Jesus Christ," I said, letting my annoyance show. "I just told you about—"

"Long," he said, speaking with quiet emphasis. "You didn't tell me anything. You said something, and you said I didn't want to know. Maybe I do; maybe I don't. But this—this thing I have going on. I don't know—I don't *know*. So I can't tell. It's important, though."

That was my brother. Things to him were important. He had a conscience and a sense of responsibility, and he kept them close. People like me, we can lay such things aside. It made him someone I could trust and need. I've never felt like he needed me before.

"Is there money in it?" I asked.

"Doubt it," he answered right away.

"You're hiding something,"

"Could be."

"How is it a guy like me can help a guy like you? And mind you I'm asking how, not what."

"Let's just say I have a lot of latitude."

"I don't buy it," I said, thinking things over. "Towns like that want a button-down chief who shows up to breakfast with the Rotarians and the Lion's Club. A city council doesn't give latitude."

"I wasn't hired by the city council. I've been brought on by the Justice Department."

"You're going in as a fed? That means someone is bad. And that means attention. You don't want me there."

"You can help."

"How?"

"I can't say right now."

"Can't?" I asked, making sure he knew I didn't believe him.

"I don't want to. There are things about this you can help me with."

"Things about being a fed—pretending to be a chief of police—that your brother with a record can help you with. Sounds like you're already in trouble."

"Maybe."

"You're just walking in and taking over?"

"More or less."

"Good luck with that."

"We can talk about it when you get here," he said. "When will that be?"

I could picture him looking at his watch. He was a grown man, a cop, and he still wore a Star Trek watch.

"I don't know," I answered. "At least another eight or nine hours if I drive straight through. I doubt I can do that."

"Tired?"

"Exhausted."

"It's not just fatigue," he said. I knew what he was doing—trying to get me to tell him more about the night before.

"You're right," I said. "It's not." I left it at that, and he was quiet on the other end.

When he finally did speak, he surprised me again. "Secrets aren't good things to have, little brother."

"Go peddle your papers someplace else, John Smith," I said.

"We'll talk when you get here." He said that like he meant it. I began to think that I never really knew what our conversation had been about. "I'll be waiting."

"Okay."

"It'll be good to see you," he said. And, again, it sounded like he meant it, and that was weird. He broke the connection before I could say anything more.

I dropped the phone and pressed the gas at the same time.

It had been a strange talk. I thought about it and decided both of the calls had been strange. I hadn't picked up on the vibe of the first one because I had been tired and feeling dragged through the mud. Vibe was the thing all right. All the words had worked. They just hadn't felt correct. Paris and I had always talked and cursed and laughed openly without being open. It was a guy thing. It was a half-brother thing too. But it wasn't good for actual communication. Reading between lines becomes part of some relationships. For some reason, though, Paris seemed like he was writing his lines in a different language.

Nothing I could do about it from the highway. I turned on the radio and tuned out my thoughts.

After four more hours, I was weaving and barely keeping my eyes open. I pulled off into a rest area and tried to sleep in the car. It worked for a while. Eventually the noise got to be too much. Rain had moved north, and the sky opened just as the sun slunk down into night. A bunch of bikers pulled into the stop to wind their engines up and shout at each other.

After another hour of driving, I faded out again. I pulled off into the gravel lot of a cinder block bar. The building was long and low, dark as hell, but glowing with the same neon-red beer-sign light I expect to spend my eternity in. There were a couple of military guys in uniform eating burgers at the bar. I took a table and joined them in choosing the big burger. Some guys when they get out crave reconnection with the military. Some of us don't.

I had been good at soldiering. Truth be told, I was an idiot to have gotten out, but the grass s always greener anyplace but Afghanistan. At least the parts I was in. I was only out a year when I ended up in Angola prison for two. It was like the army was a vacation from the life I had been forging since I began setting the world on fire at thirteen. The army was where I got my high school degree and where I read books without pictures for the first time. It was also where I learned to kill. I guess it wasn't that different from the life I ended up with.

One of the women working tables dropped a few coins in the jukebox and then punched buttons. Even before she walked away, there was a hiss and a pop of contact. The jukebox had actual records, 45-rpm memories of a lost world. I finished my burger, sopping up ketchup and grease with my last fries while listening to Conway Twitty sing "I See the Want to in Your Eyes." Even though I was exhausted and had a long way left to drive, I ordered a beer. The next song was another old one called "Country Bumpkin." Before it was over, I had gone through half the beer, and I was crying again. I put my face behind my hand and leaned my elbow on the table. There wasn't a lot of point in trying to be silent. I wasn't the first one to cry over his beer in that joint. I tried not to blubber, at least. Things got worse when B. J. Thomas started singing "(Hey Won't You Play) Another Somebody Done Somebody Wrong Song." I ended up the only customer in the place. The waitresses gave me a wide berth and sad eyes. I couldn't get out of there until the jukebox started playing "Convoy." I was glad I still had a lot of road to go.

It was in that sparkling, clear dead zone of darkness and starlight between nighttime and morning that I approached home. Grave-digging time: I'll always think of it that way. I pulled off the highway and cruised, looking for just the right spot. I found it not far from the mobile home park where home was waiting.

First I stopped at a liquor store and bought two six-packs of beer, cheap stuff. Along with that I got a disposable lighter and a red tote with a huge beer brand printed on it. I put the cash and gun in the bag. Next, I stopped at a gas station, bought a gas can, and filled it.

With all my purchases, I drove to an industrial area I had picked out earlier. I parked in the shadows about fifty feet from a bunch of kids. They were hanging out, breaking bottles, and smoking by the dock doors. The kids watched me hard as I got out of the car. I walked away with my big red bag, leaving the car door open and the engine running. The beer, the gas, and the lighter were on the seat. I figured about dawn, the Chevy would be burning down to its tires someplace far from my trailer.

"Paris," I said as I opened the door. I didn't shout, but I wasn't quiet. I assumed he was sleeping, but you don't walk in on an armed man without announcing yourself. All the lights were off. I wanted nothing more than to go straight to my bedroom and collapse on the bed. The only thing that stopped me was the thought of dropping on top of Paris. Since he hadn't answered me, I assumed he wasn't on the couch.

I flipped the switch, and the overhead light sparked. Of the two bulbs, one came on. It flickered three times before it held. The shade was broken. The entire fixture was dangling from wires. Only after the flickering stopped did I have the sense in my head to look down. Paris was on the floor, his hand inches from the toe of my boot.

He was dead. There was no hope, no crouching to touch his neck in search of a pulse. There was too much blood for that.

THREE

When I had released the Chevy to its fate, I had held back two things: the cash and the .40. At that moment, it was the gun I was grateful for. I pulled it from the tote bag and stalked through the dark trailer. It was wasted effort. I was alone with the body of my half-brother.

Nothing had been taken. Aside from the damage to the light and carpet, nothing was disturbed. The violence had been about killing.

Someone had stormed through the door in a surprise blitz. They had taken Paris down, made sure he was down forever, and then left. It had probably taken less than a minute. I didn't know for certain, but guessed that the thin man with cartoon skulls on his fingers wanted his money back.

I thought about timing. The last time I had talked with Paris was about ten hours before. Cartel killers could have easily beaten me here. They didn't even have to drive from El Paso. It would have taken a phone call to hire out a local gang. Just as likely, they already had people in Houston who could have set up at my trailer and waited for me to come home.

My head had been spinning from gulping breaths since I'd seen Paris on the floor. I was in danger of hyperventilating. It took a moment of struggle to get control of my breathing and stop my brain from reeling.

Paris.

I'd never wanted to talk to him so badly.

There was no time to think about what I wanted. No time for grief. There was a question hanging over me: Would they come back? If you didn't know us and just showed up to kill the average-sized guy with reddish-brown hair who lived in this trailer, you might think you'd done your job. If you had seen me before, though, you might have realized your mistake and waited outside for your real target to come home.

I turned around and slammed the door closed and then locked it. I knelt beside Paris. He was wearing jeans but no shirt. That means he had had no badge on when they came through the door. His pockets were empty. Had they checked his ID and taken it?

I had to know before I walked out.

My bedroom was a mess. No surprise there. It had been that way before I left. Beside the bed was a clean area on the nightstand. Paris had put the beer cans in the trash and had his phone plugged in and charging. His wallet was under the phone. Had anyone looked, they wouldn't have put it neatly under the phone. I opened it. Tucked inside was another flip-out case holding his Texas Ranger shield and Department of Public Safety ID. There was an open and unaddressed manila envelope in the nightstand drawer. I took a quick look and saw papers labeled "US Department of Justice." Paris's pistol was in the drawer. It was a World War II vintage Colt 1911 .45 in a formed and fitted leather belt-clip holster. It had been a gift from Buick.

Paris was not the target. I was. I couldn't help him anymore. Maybe I could use his death to keep myself alive. I hated myself for the thought. Not enough to keep from covering up the truth.

I dumped the paper from the envelope and dropped in his phone, the charger, and his wallet. I clipped the .45 to my belt. Back in the living room, I stashed the package in the tote. Once again, I rifled through Paris's pockets. This time I was searching for his keys. I found them and tucked the ring away in my jeans.

The next thing I did was much harder. I lifted Paris's body at the shoulders and took him down the hall with his feet dragging trails of blood on the low carpet. It wasn't a have-to thing. I just didn't want to leave him lying on the dirty floor. There were so many things about what had happened that I didn't want. I had to do the one little thing I could.

I placed Paris in my bed and covered him. I was gentle as I could be. I removed my own wallet and tucked it into his pocket. It was a poor ruse, but it wasn't about forever. It was about weeks at best. My new snap-button shirt was bloody and ruined. I pulled it off and took a fresh one from the closet. That was the extent of my packing. I had enough cash to dress myself for a thousand years. I didn't think I'd need that long.

I put a candle on the bedside table. It was one of those scented things a woman had left in the wasted hope of clearing the man funk from a cheap rented trailer. The candle lasted longer than she had. I lit it and left it there beside Paris.

"Goodbye," I said to him as I paused at the door.

I pulled aside the kitchen stove, wrenching it until the flex line pulled from the iron gas pipe. It was just a crack, not a gaping tear. I thought for a moment about working it to a faster flow, but I didn't have much more in me. Besides, if they were coming back for me, they would have shown up by then. Even though it was a small leak, I could smell the propane already. At least I could smell the stuff they put into it to stink like that. Propane was heavier than air. I couldn't see it, but I could imagine it spilling out onto the floor and filling the trailer like a flood. By the time it got up to the candle, there would be a hell of a lot of gas.

I got in Paris's truck and ran without a plan. When it was impossible for me to drive farther, I stopped at a motel. It was the kind of place that was popular on the state highways before the interstates bypassed everything. The Texas Lodge Motel was a strip of a building divided into ten rooms. Off to the side there was a cluster of four separate cabins. The sun was well up past morning, but the red neon was still lit showing off the word "Vacancy."

They took cash and didn't ask questions. I asked for the cabin farthest from everything. The only other car in the lot was a beaten-down minivan with fake wood peeling away from the side. In the window of the van was a sign that read, "The Sweet By and By Gospel Music Hour." I wasn't in the mood for music.

* * * *

After sleeping the day away, I got up. Sleep hadn't done much to drive off the fatigue. I ate from a vending machine. Then I tried to watch TV. I fell back to sleep watching a *Law and Order* rerun. About four in the morning, I woke again. There was another *Law and Order* playing.

Old TV wasn't holding my attention, and I couldn't sleep anymore. I pulled out Paris's .45. It was clean and oiled and needed no attention. I set it aside, and then I pulled his phone from the tote bag. It had been plugged in and charging when I'd taken it from the bedroom, but I'd shut it off before tucking it away. I'd been afraid of someone tracking it as much as I had been of it ringing. What would I say to whoever called?

I hit the power button, and the phone chimed as it booted. The screen showed a password security screen. Stymied. There was no telling what his password would be. And the phone was the kind that only gave a few chances to get it right before locking up terminally.

It was a puzzle and a distraction. I sat on the floor with the phone and thought about Paris. He wouldn't have made a password out of a bad association. That meant that I got to sit and think about Paris and all the things I knew were both good and important to him. Those happy thoughts were like a small gift.

My first try unlocked his phone. NCC-1701 was the designation code for the Starship *Enterprise*. It turned out that Paris was not as deep or complex as I was trying to give him credit for.

I kind of wanted to feel a little embarrassed of him, but that was overpowered by an odd sense of pride that I knew him as well as I did. I missed him.

In the smallest hours of the morning, I explored my brother's life through his phone. It was an intrusion, a complete violation that I did without hesitation. Information was like insulation. The plan was to keep Paris between me and the killers looking for me. Maybe I could wrap myself up in that a little tighter. I had no doubt that someone would figure out the body in the trailer wasn't me. If Paris was alive and going about his business, it would take longer for anyone to get a hook on the ruse.

I flipped through the text messages. What I dreaded most was finding a woman he was involved with. The last thing I needed was to be getting romantic calls. There were none. Not just no romantic texts—no texts at all. Paris had cleaned the log, and nothing had come in since then. I checked the calls. That was a different story. Maybe he wasn't a texter. I thought about it and realized that I'd never gotten one from him. Then again, I'd never sent him one either. My own log would be just as barren. It wasn't as weird as I had thought at first.

The call logs went back a couple of weeks. Most of the contacts were incoming calls from M. Janssen JD. He had called nine times since I'd turned the phone off and put it in my tote. That was too many calls for casual interest. M. Janssen had a reason to expect Paris to pick up. There were calls from someone named Heck too—quite a few. That was the number Paris called most.

I called voice mail to dig a little deeper. Nothing. I looked at the log again. Since I'd had the phone, there had been eleven calls, nine from M. Janssen and two from Heck. No messages. Whatever it was Paris felt he couldn't tell me, I was sure these two were involved. That meant the JD after the name M. Janssen was for Justice Department.

The phone rang, and I about browned my shorts.

The display read M. Janssen JD. Of course it did. There was no picture to go with the name. It rang again, and I couldn't help looking at the phone like it was about to summon a demon rather than a voice.

It rang a third time, and I had to tell myself that this was part of my plan.

Halfway through the fourth ring, I pressed the answer icon.

"Where the hell have you been?" a man asked. I could only assume it was the M. Janssen listed. But I didn't know that, did I? Then he asked, "And what the mother fuck are you doing in Oklahoma?" I was right about the phone being tracked.

"Who's this?" I asked.

"Milo Janssen—who the fuck do you think it is?"

"You woke me up," I lied, trying to put the sound of sleep in my voice. "I couldn't read the thing."

"Who says you have time for sleep? You're supposed to be on your way to Lansdale."

"I am," I said. "I just got caught up in things."

"Yeah," he said, and I could hear the gears shifting. "I heard about your half-brother. That was fucked up."

"What did you hear?"

"What do you think—I don't keep track? Anything that involves you comes up on the radar. And if your brother's trailer makes a fireball bigger than the dawn, I will definitely know."

"You're keeping tabs on my family?"

"Not really," he said.

I could hear the shrug without seeing him. There was something else. When I saw him, I was picturing a black man. Something about his voice. Sometimes you can't educate the street out. Some guys never want to.

"Longview Moody is something else though," Milo went on. "He worked for a bunch of bad people having a big break-up. I had to keep an eye on him."

"And?"

"*And* I looked into it. By that I mean I looked into what the locals were doing and who they were looking at."

"Yeah," I agreed. "Find anything?"

"He ran in rough crowds. You know that."

"So, no connection to anything..."

"Getting a little on edge?"

"Maybe," I answered, truthfully. "Maybe we should meet and talk before I roll into town."

"If I ever need to come meet you face to face, it means things are completely gone to hell, and you don't want to meet me then. I'm like the comic book guy: you wouldn't like me when I'm angry."

"What makes you think I like you now?" I asked, trying hard to keep the relief out of my voice. No face to face meant he didn't know Paris that well. It made things easier. I wasn't going to push.

"What makes you think I give a greasy crap? To answer your question, though, and my first question when I heard as well—no. We haven't found any connection to your brother's death and your work in Lansdale. In fact, I got the feeling that the local boys might be letting this one slide as just another death from drink and MHRD if I hadn't done my look-see."

"MHRD?"

"Mobile home–related death."

"I see," I said.

"It's a redneck thing," he said.

"No doubt about that."

"You been in touch with your dad?"

That question put my hackles up for more than one reason. I was about to spit out something angry when I remembered that this guy thought he was talking to Paris.

"No," I said, forcing calm. "I've stayed dark. Just in case."

"He's doing the ID."

"What?"

"Your father. He'll do the ID of the body with the locals."

I thought about that. Thought hard. I had to wonder, if he knew it was Paris, would he wish it was me? Then what if he figured it out? "I thought the fire might have made that impossible."

"DNA. He's not going in to look at—that. You're right, the fire was…well, there won't be a visual ID from what I understand. Your father is giving his DNA to make a comparison."

That was something I'd never imagined.

"Where have you been?" Milo asked.

"I made myself scarce. Like I said, just in case."

"Okay. I can deal with that, but you need to keep in touch a little better. I can't be losing track of you. These are bad people."

"Which ones?" I asked, casting a line.

"All of them," he answered, ignoring my fishing. "When can you hit town?"

"A couple of days at least. I—"

"Two days." He jumped in and cut me off. "You got two days, and I want you to skip putting the bro in the ground."

"Why?"

"Do you know why he's dead?"

"No."

"Right. But you have suspicions it wasn't a natural thing, or you wouldn't have hit the road, right?"

I didn't answer. I didn't like that Milo was sharper than his name would suggest. Who'd ever heard of a black guy named Milo, anyway?

"So," he went on, "because of that, I don't want you around to attract any attention. Any attention at all. No dirt by association."

"That's—"

"That's the way it is, my man. Fucked up and spit out, but there's nothing to it but to do it."

I wanted to argue, but it made things a lot easier not to. Not that there would be much of anyone at my funeral. It was possible that someone could spot the difference between me and Paris. My mother and Paris's were both gone. Never thought that would be an asset. There was Buick, but I had a feeling the old man would be afraid someone might ask him to kick in.

"Whatever," I said.

"Yeah, whatever," Milo echoed.

"We should go over things again," I said, looking for more info.

"Why?"

I couldn't think of a reason. I didn't know enough to come up with anything. Milo saved me again with his assumptions and trying to be supportive.

"I know the feeling," he said. "I used to get the same thing before an op in Iraq. But we've talked it out. It's good. All you have to do is be a cop. Don't worry about infiltration. They *will* come to you."

"Thanks," I said. "Clear as mud. Who'd I screw to get this dropped in my life?"

He laughed. He was supposed to. It was a casual, meaningless comment. I needed to learn to keep my mouth shut.

"That's funny coming from you," Milo said. His laughter didn't sound easy then. There was a certain edge to it that made my hair stand on end. "You know exactly who you fucked and how," he said. "And you're lucky this office isn't the Texas Rangers."

"I don't feel lucky."

"That's a true thing there. Get some sleep—it's what? Four forty-five there?"

"Yeah."

"And keep in touch." He ended the call.

After that I was in no mood to try for sleep. But I had a plan.

Showered, dressed, and packed, an hour later I stepped out into the fresh morning. The few belongings I had went into the truck.

I drove away from the rising sun toward the next little bump of a town. It didn't have much, but it had a Western Union and a Waffle House. I figured I'd take advantage of both.

It wasn't that I was all that hungry. It was more about killing time and the idea that I would get on the road and not stop for food for a long time. My long run into nowhere had dumped me out somewhere north of Durant, Oklahoma. I needed to be at Lansdale along the Rio Grande in two days. That was only about seven hundred, miles but I needed to do it without going through Dallas or any other large city. I wanted to skip the interstate as well. Paris knew a lot of people in law enforcement, and law enforcement knew me. That meant the smaller state highways and towns. Probably not much more in distance, but it added hours to the drive. Time to think. Too much? Too little? I guessed I'd be seeing.

Lansdale sat right on the border at a wide part of the river, way down in the wastelands between El Paso and Laredo. It was also right on the edge of the Big Bend National Park, seven hundred thousand acres of Wild West Texas. Getting there was nothing compared to the big question. Why the hell was I putting myself through it? The world always seemed to come back to those why questions. I needed to get my head around what. What would I find when I got there? And what the hell did I think I would do about it?

Waffle House stretched out into a couple of hours with steak and eggs and endless coffee. When the clock ticked over to eight, I paid my check and went out to the truck. Paris's phone was much better than the burners I was always using. It had directions and

Internet access. I used both while I sat at breakfast. I'd gotten the name and number of a funeral home in Houston. That was the call I was waiting to make. Most businesses opened at nine. They listed their hours beginning at eight. Nature of the beast, I thought. People who need to make arrangements feel like they need to get it done quickly. They wake up early if they've slept at all and make a call they'd hoped to never make.

The phone was answered on the third ring. I told the professionally sympathetic man who I needed arrangements for. After the basics, I asked about costs. He tried to upsell me a bit, not too hard. I asked for the middle of everything but went a couple of notches better on the stone. I asked if it could be changed later if it came to it. He assumed at first that I was asking about adding a name later. A wife. When I explained that I was asking about an actual change, there was a long silence. It couldn't have been a common question.

"The thing is," I told him, "I'm doing this without my family getting involved. We don't always agree."

"Say no more," he told me, and his speech sounded like a literal light coming on. "I can commission a shallow engraving on a smooth field. If things change...well, then we can have the granite blasted out to a rough panel and reengraved."

"It sounds like you're the man with the plan."

"Solving delicate problems is my livelihood," he said.

I didn't doubt it.

After solving delicate problems, I went to the Western Union office and sent the funeral home $9,300. I had been careful to keep the cost under $10,000. Banks and money-transferring businesses had to report cash transactions that size to the feds.

Being rich was expensive. I'd spent more money since taking that bundle of hundreds than I'd ever spent in such a short time. The bundle looked untouched. In the truck, I thumbed through it and made a rough count.

Each currency strap of $100 bills totaled $10,000. There had originally been ten of those in each stack. $100,000. There were five stacks in a row. $500,000. And there were three rows. $1.5 million. I guess that's why the bundle hadn't dwindled. It was harder to spend $1.5 million on underwear and funerals than I would have thought.

Procrastination—even necessary procrastination—can only carry you so far. Before setting out, I did some more shopping. At a gun store, I bought two boxes of cartridges, one each for the .40 and for Paris's .45. I also picked up two spare clips for each. A cleaning kit rounded out the purchases. I thought for a moment that the guy behind the counter was going to ask some questions. It was just my nerves. Gun people in Texas knew when to keep their mouths shut.

Next I stopped off for gas and an oil check and to top off the tire pressure. The truck had one of those spares that cranked up and down on a cable. I let it down and pretended to put air in the spare. While I was under the truck bed, I tucked the .40 and the bulk of the cash, both wrapped in trash bags, into the wheel's interior space. I ratcheted it up tight. The .45 I kept in the cab with me. After all, I was no longer Longview Moody, convicted felon. As of that point, I was Paris Tindall, former Ranger and now chief of police for Lansdale, Texas.

The drive started in green farmland north of Lake Texoma, a giant reservoir of water fed by the Red River. The air was clear, and the day was hot without brutality. I headed west and then south on county roads and turned on the radio. Willie Nelson.

I had a thought and pulled out Paris's phone. I'm not much of a technical person, but there is one thing everyone who has a reasonable fear of being tracked knows. If your phone can tell you where you are, it can tell someone else. There was no telling how deep Milo Janssen was into the phone. I suspected that he'd supplied it to Paris. But however deep it was, I didn't want him dogging my every step. There was something else I knew. Turning it off didn't always do what you expected.

It wasn't easy to do while driving. If I'd had sense, I would have pulled over. I didn't. Steering with my knees and elbows, I managed to get the back off the phone and remove the SIM card.

After the phone was truly dead, I relaxed and hit the gas. The green rolled by and slowly burnished into dry brown.

FOUR

Driving at night would have been a good idea. I didn't figure that out until I'd been driving in the glare and heat of the west Texas sun for too many hours. By then the daylight was fading into a smudge of color on a darkening horizon. I was hungry again and thinking about a little sleep.

That wasn't my usual routine. For all my adult life, I had been a drive-till-you-can't kind of guy. Then I would get a few winks in a truck stop or rest area. Movement always felt like accomplishment.

Not this trip.

The farther I went, the more I felt like I was pushing against hard winds. There were no gusts out there running against the road. I knew that. They were inside me. Blowing against my mind. It was a strange sensation. Usually I went where those winds blew. Fighting them was entirely new to me.

I rose in the morning later than I had expected and put off driving. When I did go, the sun was still in the east but high. It chased me like a cat worrying a mouse. From high in the morning sky, it arced overhead, herding me with the kind of harsh light I'd spent most of my life avoiding. Every mile of that drive felt like scrutiny, the kind that burned away all the ideas you had about yourself and left you bare to your own eyes. I've never met the man who could well stand what he'd see in that light.

Maybe Paris.

Maybe that was why I was driving so slowly and felt so exposed. Once I had made the decision to become my half-brother, I'd never once asked myself, could I live up to it—to him? Even if I laid aside the pitiful self-doubt in that question, I had to admit I knew nothing about being a cop. What was I doing? I had more money than a man like me had ever dreamed of walking away with. No one was looking for me. I had a good truck, and I was just a few hours from Mexico. Why take the harder road?

I squinted into the glare as the sun passed in front of me, lightly, like paws of a cat hemming me in. The only real choice felt like the one that led into the teeth. At the next gas station, I stopped for a fill-up and a pair of cop-style reflector sun glasses.

Lansdale had changed since I had been through it last. The biggest change was the people. The town was larger than I remembered. Town limit signs were pushed out at least a half mile. Much of the space that had been taken over was filled with new trailer park developments. The squat and featureless cracker boxes were lined up like teeth in in a rich kid's mouth, straight lines and perfectly aligned. Some of them, those on the outskirts, seemed to have been placed with less care, as if the town no longer had the time for good orthodontics.

I cruised in on the main road from the east and past the same old motel I had been at before. Even it had a new coat of paint.

I made a pass down Main Street just to look around. The oldest part was still lined with the vintage stone buildings. All of them had Mason's seal cornerstones dated at the turn of the last century. Beyond that stone core, in each direction, were new frame and stucco or metal-skin buildings touting mostly one-dollar products or payday loans. Continuing to the west, where I recalled the town ending in a blunt cut of asphalt and a sign at the edge of the dirt reading City Maintenance Ends, there was more and newer town. To the north was a residential development with nice homes. Surprisingly, given the water situation in the area, some of the homes had lush green lawns. To the south, closer to the river, were a couple of fast food places mixed in with a taxidermy shop, a used-car lot, and two places piled with junk that bore signs reading Antiques. It all looked like a normal growing town until I got to the new and improved City Limits sign.

There the real changes started. Roads were new blacktop rolling into hills that had been turned artificially green and verdant. A golf course was the last thing I would have imagined taking root in this land. Beyond the course was another new road. It was guarded by twin stone posts. One was hollow and housed an attendant. The other was solid mounting for a twenty-foot-long iron gate topped with spear points. Those points looked a little sharper than necessary for decoration. On the guard post was a polished plaque that read, in fancy black script, Gun Hills Hunting Lodge and Private Club. The only thing that struck me as stranger than all that was the weirdness a bit farther down the road and closer to the river. Buildings were being constructed. Most of the work though was being done behind tarps. I couldn't see much. I could see enough to know it wasn't everyday construction. Thick foundations were being poured into dense nests of reinforcing bar. There were a lot of commercial trucks parked around the site. Most trades were represented, but there seemed to be more electrical and information-system contractors than anything.

In the mess only one business looked to be finished and open. It was a bank, a big one. I knew that only by the fact that it looked like every other bank in the country. It had no signs up, not even a Grand Opening banner, but it was the one building that looked complete with cars parked out front.

Adjacent to the big-dollar construction site was a low-dollar, lower-rent-looking bar. It was the kind of place with lots of neon out front. It had a broad gravel lot with ample parking for bikes and big rigs. Out back were parked several small trailers. I had no doubt that when the sun went down, there would be little light back there but lots of activity. The trailers were cribs for the working girls.

Someone had thousands of acres of nothing to put the First National Bank of the Middle of Nowhere in, and they chose the spot next to a whorehouse.

There was a boom going on, and all of it seemed to be happening beyond the city limits sign. Booms don't come without something exploding. In this part of the country, that means oil. I hadn't seen anything that said oil. I hadn't seen anything that could keep me from bed any longer either. I circled the truck back around into town. When I got to the Desert Drop Inn, I wondered how it was still the only place to get a room with all the construction. Then I parked and didn't care.

The fresh paint was a combination of stark, glossy white and bright-green trim. It had an old-fashioned feel that matched the semicircular two-story building and the kidney-shaped pool in the center. I half expected the other cars in the lot to have fins on them once I got out of the truck. Not that there were many cars in the lot.

The woman at the desk was named Lenore. The name fit in an odd way. She had raven-dark hair and skin that mixed the shades of many races into an entirely new tone of soft darkness. As if beauty weren't enough, she was decorated with ink and silver jewelry. Her right arm was a colorful swirl of flames and tiny bats rising on the light into tattered skies sparking with stars. It was an intricate and hypnotic tableau. At her wrist, under the dangling silver bracelets, was a circling of bright, grinning skulls and flowers. Their stylized Day of the Dead look reminded me of the fingers of the thin man who had sent me into the desert.

I signed, remembering at the last moment that I was Paris Tindall, not Longview Moody.

"Sleep well, Chief," Lenore said, handing over the key.

Her eyes were a hazel that leaned toward green and gold. I dropped my gaze to keep myself from giving an invitation I could not have lived up to. When I did, I noticed another bit of her ink. There was a colorful flower disappearing into the top of her shirt.

When I looked back up, Lenore's smile had changed. It was even better. She turned around. I wasn't sure if her hair moved like that naturally or if she worked at it. I let my gaze sweep over her. The sweeping was interrupted by the dainty .25 pistol holstered at the small of her back. After that I noticed that the tattooed pin-striping wound through with more skulls and flowers behind the weapon.

"You always go packing?" I asked her.

"I don't always have the chief watching my—back." She didn't turn to look at me until she said the word "back." She looked and wiggled at the same time.

It was a nice view, but something else caught my attention. That had been the second time she'd called me chief. The first time I had heard the word but not the meaning.

"You know who I am?"

"Of course. I've been expecting you."

"Why?"

"Only two places around here to get a room. Desert Drop or the hunting club. You haven't been invited up there yet, have you?"

"Gun Hills?"

"Been doing your homework?" She asked the question with less wiggle but something more in her eyes as she stepped up closer.

"And did anyone tell you to give them a call when I checked in," I asked.

She smiled. Her face lit with it. The bright-green-gold and polished wood of her eyes promised a knowing of secrets.

Lenore's was an Eve-offering-the-apple smile. "You want me to wait?"

"Depends."

"On what?"

"On what they'll want when they get here."

She nodded, leaned forward, and said in a breathy whisper, "Talk."

I looked her over again. Early thirties, slim but wonderfully hippy. Her shirt was tight against a belly that was flat but soft. Lenore was a lot more woman than girl. She was used to being looked at too. I lifted my attention back to her eyes and said, "I've had enough talk. If anyone is coming to shoot me, call them, and get it over with. Otherwise, give me a couple of hours."

She laughed and then said, "You got it, Chief."

The first thing I did after opening the room door was put the bedspread over the window. Adding it to the curtains tamped down the light, making the small room cave-like. Second, I turned the air conditioner to max.

I wish I could say I slept easily and dreamed of Lenore. It didn't happen. I did fall asleep quickly, but my dreams were a chaos of black impressions that left me on edge and sweating. Sweat turned cold quickly in the dark room.

When the knock came, I was still sitting in my underwear on wet sheets. It had taken longer than I'd thought. What little light leaked around the combination curtain and bedspread over the window was red. It was evening.

Time to put my pants on. That was my sole concession to decorum. I added the .45 belt-clip holster, but I doubted that it qualified as clothing. I just knew that without it I would have felt naked.

There was no knowing who was at the door, just as I'd had no doubt that someone would show up. My guess had been that it would be cops, one or a delegation of them, wanting to know where they stood. If the Justice Department was picking their new chief, the rest of the cops had to be nervous. Then there was that other side of the dropped coin. It could be the feds themselves, a handler, here to lay the law on me.

Leaving the lights and my shirt off—I didn't want to appear overly friendly no matter who was knocking—I opened the door and stepped back.

Hot air dug claws into the ceiling and pulled itself in, chasing the chill out along the floor. Light shifted only in shade, not volume. Through the doorframe was a darkening sky bruised red and purple. Long streaks of clouds pointed west, their leading edges painted by the sinking sun. They looked like rockets blazing with the heat of friction as they left the earth.

Then there were the men.

The fat one was standing at the door. He had knocked. The other one stood back. He sheltered his face under a straw hat and leaned with one foot on the railing. The aspect of his body and posture kept his back slightly to the setting sun and his head turned. He appeared to be looking at something other than my door. That didn't change the fact that I could feel his eyes staring in my direction. I took a small pleasure in the fact that he could see me no better than I could see him.

"Chief Tindall," the fat man said. His voice had a well-buttered cheerfulness.

"Yeah," I said. "I'm not set for visitors."

"Oh, we understand," he said. "We understand. But it's just me, Bascom Wood, from the city council. We met last month."

I stared at him a moment, thinking it was all over. I was thinking I should put my shirt on and get in the truck.

Then he asked, "Remember?"

I nodded. "Yes."

"Good. Good." He grinned and then pointed at my head. "You let your hair grow. You'll want to take care of that."

I reached up to run my hand over my ragged cut. Paris always had short hair. My mind worked over a couple of lies to tell. I was on vacation—or—things were busy. I hadn't had time—

"In fact—" Councilman Wood seemed to be thinking very hard about something.

"Is there something I can do for you?" All I could do was to try to distract him off of me and back to what they came for. "It's been a long day. I'm tired."

"I wanted to welcome Chief Paris Tindall personally."

There was something about the way he said the title and name all together. Or I thought there was something about it.

"Good. Good." Wood tried to steal a glance backward at the man on the railing. "Very good. I'll give you a day or two before I come see you at the station. I imagine a man wants to get to know his troops one on one without the bosses looking over their shoulder."

"Bosses?"

"Well, uh, well I know there are some...*special circumstances*, but the chief still reports to the city council."

"I don't rate a visit from the mayor?"

Even in the low light, I could see Bascom's jowls droop. His eyes shifted nervously. "I regret that we still have not filled that position. Since the passing of Mayor Bell...uh..." He wrung his hands and glanced side to side, trying to see without moving his head. The councilman looked like a politician forced to listen to a racist joke without knowing who was around. "City operations remain with the council until...uh...until such time as new elections can be arranged." He nodded, seemingly happy with the explanation, and then said again, "Yes. Arranged."

"Is that what you're here to tell me?"

"What?" He stepped back from the threshold like I'd been the one to knock on his door, and holding up copies of *The*

Watchtower too. "Not at all. Not at all. This is just a welcome visit."

He seemed to have a habit of repeating himself when he got nervous. He was definitely a politician because he was literally double-speaking. It helped me to understand something though. It wasn't to him I was speaking.

"Who's that with you?" I asked.

The man in the background chose that moment to put a cigar in his mouth. He lit it with an old-fashioned lighter, the kind that had a big flickering flame and closed with a resolute metal snap. After that snap, the yellow glow that lit the lower part of the man's face was gone. I saw only his chin and mouth. That, along with the snakeskin boots under a cream-colored western suit and sky-blue silk shirt, was enough to tell me of his Mexican heritage. He exhaled a thick cloud of cigar smoke before walking to the balcony stairs. Behind him lingered the smoke and scent of the San Andrés black leaf.

Mr. Bascom Wood watched him go and then turned back to me. He was Mexican or at least Hispanic, not a recent immigrant. His English was Texas, through and through. Other than heritage he shared the appreciation of western wear if not the actual sense of style with his compadre. His suit was denim, his boots scuffed, functional leather. He wore no hat. My guess was because of a pride in his Vitalis-slicked hair. He probably had the same pride in his drooping mustache.

"Pardon my friend, Chief Tindal. Relations with law enforcement have been strained here in Lansdale with all the growth." Bascom used both hands to gesture vaguely outward at the word "growth." I counted five gold rings on his piggy fingers. Three were on one hand, two on the other.

"I'm not here to make things difficult," I said. I didn't altogether know why I was there. It was a sure thought, though, that not making things difficult was high on Bascom Wood's list.

I was right. He smiled broadly and relaxed, and then he said, "Good. Good. Everyone will be glad to hear it." He continued to stare at me.

"Is there something else?"

"It's not just the hair, you know." Wood pointed a fat finger at my chest. "You lost weight too."

My spine stiffened.

"And your voice—"

"It hasn't been a good time for me," I cut in, trying to sound bothered and not desperate. "We've had a death in the family."

He nodded and then said, "I had heard that. I'm sorry."

I believed the first part. Not the second.

"Chief." Again, he put a little spin on the word. "I can't wait for you to get started."

"Then maybe I should get some sleep."

"Oh yes. Of course. Of course. If you need anything—anything at all—don't hesitate to call on me, my friend."

"Sleep," I said. "I need sleep." I closed the door before he could say anything more. I wasn't always intentionally rude. The fact that he'd met Paris concerned me. I didn't want to encourage contact. One other thing concerned me: the snappy dresser behind Bascom. I knew when someone was trying to put me off balance. I didn't rattle that easy.

Sleep. I'd said that was what I wanted. No chance. I was completely awake, and the edgy feeling would make sure I stayed that way. Maybe it was time to check in.

I slipped the SIM back into the phone and let it power up while I hit the bathroom. Before I had flushed, it was ringing. Milo.

"You killed the phone," he said.

"Hello to you too."

"Screw hello. I want you to keep in contact. I want you to roll over and kiss me good night before you close your eyes and smile at my pretty face in the morning. Do you get me?"

I killed the phone again and let it sit while I dressed in a new snap-front shirt. Western plaid—I was stylin'. I tucked the tail and rolled the sleeves. Seeing the bare skin of my arms made me glad I always waited to sober up after deciding to get tattoos. Sober, I had no desire. The one I had was high up on my shoulder, covered even by short sleeves. It read "Airborne."

I had planned on powering up the phone again and seeing what Milo had to say. When my boots were on, I realized I was hungry. The phone stayed on the stand as I went looking for a meal.

The hunt turned out to be doubly productive. Right next to a local taqueria was a barber shop. The barber was sweeping up and ready to close his doors until I told him who I was. He gestured to his chair with a smile so forced I thought his face would break. It didn't ease up when I told him what I wanted. My hair was well over my ears and shaggy. In five minutes, it was buzzed to a barely there flattop. I paid in cash and tipped well enough to have a new friend. He smiled warmly when I handed over the money. Before I went out the door, he said something to me in Spanish. I can get along with most exchanges but can't say my vocabulary was as deep as it should have been. Most of my conversations were either threats or drug related.

When I shook my head in incomprehension, the barber cupped his hands in front of him and then gestured for me to do the same. As I stood with my hands in front of me, he retrieved a bottle from the shelf behind his chair. He held it up to show off the fancy writing on the label. It looked like a bottle of Jack but smelled like wildflowers, sandalwood, and cedar. He poured a healthy puddle in my hands and then mimed putting it on his face.

I splashed it on and stroked it down my neck. He handed me a towel for my hands. I went out smelling like I'd just spent a month in a secluded north woods whorehouse. It grew on me. The smell disappeared as soon as I stepped into the joint next door. It was replaced by the glorious scent of grilling meat and corn frying in hot oil. Then there was the beer. It must have been soaking into the planks of heartwood pine flooring for generations. The old wood was black as cast iron and worn into depressed trails around the bar and kitchen. As I stood there taking in the atmosphere that already felt like home, someone called, "Chief."

Lenore had her hand up at a back table. "Chief Paris," she said again, waving me over. She was alone with a beer and a pile of chips in front of her. Everything about the little scene was shining. Her smile. The glistening glass of beer. Even the chips had a glossy coating of oil. It was like having died and finding myself in Tex-Mex Valhalla.

"End of your shift?" I asked when I stepped to the table.

Lenore kicked a chair out. In one smooth motion, she pointed to it and then lifted her hand to wave in the air. "You a beer-drinking man? Join me?"

"Oh, my God. My momma said there'd be girls like you."

She kept waving her hand, but the rest of her stopped everything to look and smile at me. It was a nice smile.

"You mean temptation?"

"I mean the kind of girl I'd want to marry."

Even the hand stopped moving for an instant before she burst into a kind of seated-dancing gyration. The laugh that accompanied her wiggle was a funny, weird guffaw that still managed to be girlish. Sexy as hell.

"I'll take that as a yes," she said and then waved with new force. "Ernesto! Un cervesa por favor." Her Spanish was as elegant as mine. There was something else, though, a different kind of accent that I couldn't place. When she brought her hand down, she held it in front of my face and waggled her fingers. "For future reference, I like emerald cut. Nothing too big but very shiny."

"Yellow gold or white?"

"Look at my skin." She ran a finger up her left arm and back down. Her skin was dark. Part of the color came from her ancestors and part from the sun. It was impossible to say how much from which.

I must have looked confused.

"White gold or platinum." She said it like I was missing something obvious. I liked the way she looked at me even when her look said I was a little slow. "It would stand out on my skin."

"I'll keep that in mind."

"And tell your mama."

"I would if she was still around." I thought of my mother, Dotty. For a second I thought I had made a mistake before I realized Paris's mother was gone as well.

Ernesto sat a beer down in front of me and asked if I wanted a menu.

"I'm starving," I said and then looked at Lenore and asked, "What's good?"

Without a hesitation or worrying about what I liked, she told Ernesto to bring me an enchilada platter. Then she told him, "Grande." As soon as he left, she said, "I am sorry."

"About what?"

"Your mother."

"It was a long time ago."

"It bothers you. I can tell."

I shrugged and then dipped a chip into salsa and ate it. There was almost no flavor. There was instead a flowing current of pain that split at the back of my throat. Some of it rose, like a hot gas, into my sinuses. Some fell slowly, like thick clots of blood and acid. A bit lingered at the back of my throat. What reached my gut bloomed into a churning heat. My eyes watered, and I coughed hard.

Lenore pushed my beer forward, into my hand. I was gulping it down as she said, "Habanero dip. I should have warned you."

As I was chugging and coughing, two people stepped up beside the table. Lenore said to them, "Have you met the new chief?"

I raised my head with the glass still pressed to my lips. Then I raised my free hand in greeting. Nearest me, grinning at my distress, was a woman in uniform. She was almost as tall as me. She was wearing boots that pushed her up past six feet. Like Lenore, she was womanly—not girlish at all, with hips and bust—but this one had muscles too. Even with the definition in her arms, she still managed to make the khaki shirt and badge look feminine. MMA champion feminine, but still...

As I set the empty glass down, I turned to the other person, a man, also in uniform. He wasn't grinning. I couldn't tell what his expression was because it fell as soon as I looked at him straight on. It not only fell; it broke when it hit the floor. He struggled to put it back together. What he constructed was something hard and angry. Something about me surprised and pissed him off. He was Hispanic, shorter than the woman, a lot smaller than me, slim but cut, and gym-built hard.

Before I found my voice, he turned and walked out without looking back or answering the female officer's calls.

"I'm sorry," she said. "He's been a bit moody lately."

"Because of me?" I managed to ask.

"Some, I think." She examined me without the smile then. It was an honest look that said I wasn't what she expected, but judgment would come later. "Some romantic problems too, I think." She turned to look at Lenore when she said that, and I was grateful that Ernesto chose that moment to place a fresh beer in front of me.

"Habanero dip," Lenore said to the other woman as though that explained every shortcoming I could ever have.

The officer nodded. I took the chance to look her over her again while my mouth was engaged. She was a blond-haired, blue-eyed Nordic beauty who looked like she could lift a truck. Her name tag read Gutiérrez.

When I sat my glass down, she put out a hand. "Officer Bronwyn Gutiérrez."

"Really?" I asked, taking her hand. Score one for tact. "I mean…" I shrugged and said again, "*Really?*"

She smiled, a practiced and familiar kind of smile that, I was sure, she saved just for this conversation. "Mother was a USC English major. Dad was a labor organizer and lawyer."

"And you're a cop."

"And I'm a cop."

"Which way do you lean, Officer Gutiérrez? Literature or labor organizing?"

"I lean more to nine-millimeter, sir."

Lenore grinned at me and then looked away with the expression behind her beer glass. She was saying, "You're on your own."

"Well…" I started but stopped. I didn't have any idea what to say.

"I notice you're more of that old-school kind of cop," Gutiérrez said.

It was an opening. I thought, only for a second, that I could say, "I'm no cop," and walk away. But there was beer, food, and pretty women with interesting edges to them. I wasn't going anywhere yet.

"What makes me so old school?"

"The forty-five behind your back."

"You like the forty-five?"

She shook her head. "The nine-mil is all business. That big thing is all carnage and anger."

"My father gave me my weapon when I became a cop."

"Oh, I—"

"That pretty much describes him too. Carnage and anger. I'd say you have a lot of your mother in you after all."

She smiled again. A little relief was showing. She was a hard person not to like.

"What's that smell?" Gutiérrez asked.

Lenore took her face from behind her hand long enough to say, "He got a haircut. Next door."

"Ohhhh, I see."

Ernesto placed a heaping plate of enchiladas in front of me and another plate with tacos for Lenore.

"Join us, Bron?" Lenore asked.

"Can't," Gutiérrez answered. She canted her head in the direction of the door. "Work and Hector call."

"I guess I'll see you tomorrow," I told her.

"We'll be on at three," she said and then left.

"That could have gone worse," I said to Lenore, who was already biting into a taco she'd slathered in the habanero sauce.

FIVE

enore was as easy to talk to as she was to look at. We spent
another half hour talking and laughing in between eating
the amazing food. There was a small awkward moment when I
was thinking about asking her back to the motel room and she
looked like she was thinking of saying yes if I did. I didn't. There
were too many questions and way too many secrets to make that
a good idea. Yet I think she knew I was interested. She looked
back and caught me staring at her ass as she went to the door.

I paid the bill even though she'd offered it as a welcome dinner. Despite my roving eyes, I can be a gentleman. For once in
my life, I was a rich gentleman. After paying, I lingered at the
bar. More beer was a temptation. Getting drunk felt almost like
a necessity. I hadn't in quite a while, and I'd had more than my
fair share of excuses. There were plenty of excuses not to as well.
Most of all I didn't because it was not what Paris would have
done. I was Paris, and I wanted the masquerade to keep me safe.
There was something more. Something I would not have imagined when he was alive. I couldn't have thought it about myself
when I was walking around as Longview. I didn't want to shame
him—me—us. Whatever we were. Paris was the better part,
and I didn't want it tarnished by the weakness and failings of
Longview.

All that feeling was a long way of thinking that brought me
around to ordering an iced tea at the bar. No sugar, slice of lime.
That was the way Paris liked it and how I had it. Drinking—life

in general—seemed simpler when I was Longview. I don't mean the people-trying-to-kill-me, digging-my-own-grave moments. I had led a dangerous life, but even so, those kinds of experiences were not how I lived day to day. Who could? Thinking was the issue. Since I had run from the trailer with my brother's identity in my pocket, I had spent a hell of a lot of time thinking. Longview reacted. Things happened around me. I moved from one situation to another. Rarely did I examine the paths I was on or look beyond the cash I was earning. Paris was thinking about everything and worrying about it all. I can't claim that I was thinking like Paris, simply that being him required a lot more thought and effort than I was used to.

That's what my brain was gnawing at when someone sat two stools down from me at the bar. He was a hard man with a big, soft belly, Mexican, with pointy-toe boots and a hand-tooled leather belt buckled with a rodeo trophy. He was an echo of the man I had killed on the couch. Like me, he was wearing the western uniform of a plaid pearl-snap shirt. His was short sleeved and tight around meaty biceps that were colored by swirls and arcs of tattoo ink. The main design on the arm closest to me was another colorful display of reverence for the dead. It featured a skeletal cowboy with two guns and a broad sombrero. When he turned to wave at Ernesto, I saw that the other arm carried a female skeleton. She was wearing a black dress and veil. Man and woman, lovingly detailed in death.

Once the man had gotten Ernesto's attention he said, without turning to look at me, "What are you looking at?" It was a challenge.

"Ink," I said without looking away. I knew how things worked when someone tried to take your measure in a bar. Normal guys, the ones who listened to their mothers about manners, the ones who never had to fight, would excuse themselves or try to explain. In a testosterone pissing contest, backing down invited more trouble. Anything less than standing up and giving back was backing down.

Ernesto set the bottle in front of the man and then went back to the far end of the bar.

"You looking at the ink, but you thinking about something else. That right? This that kind of bar?"

"No, sir. If you're looking for a date, I think you're in the wrong place."

Ernesto snickered and then turned his back to wipe down a bit of bar that was clean to begin with.

"What you saying, man?"

It was a good feeling. Taunting and posturing were the kind of thing Longview excelled at. There was a fight waiting to happen, and I was looking forward to it. The harm I might do to that guy or to myself was like a cork that perfectly fit the hole through which my life was draining. There was a moment where I needed the violence. In that moment was illuminated the faces of the men I'd killed in the drop house. Flashes of gunfire and the rush of justified rage. The funny thing was, I started looking for other faces—anyone who would not look back at me with anger or disappointment. There were more holes draining my life than plugs to fill them.

"Forget about it," I said to the man. Then I lifted my tea in salute. "No harm, no foul."

"The fuck is that supposed to mean?"

I turned away from him to take a long drink of my tea. It was cold. The glass was dripping wet. The feel of it in my hand helped me to ignore the desire that my fingers seemed to have to curl around the grip of the .45. Lime in the tea added a bright tang that cut away the vague feeling of hot blood I had in my mouth. When I set the glass back on the bar, I said, "It means I'm not letting you get to me tonight. It means your manners don't control my actions. You good with that, compadre?"

He was leaning on his left elbow the side closer to me. With his right hand, he took a swig of beer. It was quick and loud. There was no savoring to it. The action was a placeholder, something to let him think about what to do next or what to say.

When he sat the bottle down, it clunked loudly on the varnished wood.

Maybe to be helpful—maybe because I'm more of an asshole that I like to admit—I slid a coaster across the bar and in front of him.

He stared at the offering as if I'd pushed a naked picture of his mother under his nose. "Well, maybe you already got to me. *Compadre.*"

"Can't see how," I said, swirling the tea and ice. Both hands itched for something. I wrapped them around the glass, wetting the palms and fingers in the condensation, and then rubbed the moisture in. "I don't even know you, do I?"

That was the first time it hit me. It could be the *other* me he had something against. Paris.

He took another quick swig of beer that he swallowed behind clenched teeth and open lips. I was gratified to see when he set the bottle down that time, it was on the coaster. Then he lifted his left hand with the back presented to me.

"See this?"

It was hard to miss. I was amazed I hadn't noticed before. The ring finger of the hand was gone, the nub covered with a dirty bandage stained through with cream yellow and rust red. The other fingers were dark and shot through with coarse black hairs that matched the grime under the nails. On his middle finger was a bit of color. Upside down but still grinning at me was an intricately tattooed skull in bright white with pink and turquoise. This was the second time I had seen a Día de los Muertos skull tattooed on a man's fingers. There was still no doubt about the meaning.

It caught me off guard, but I wasn't going to share that information. "See what?" I asked. "The nub or the Mexican Hello Kitty?"

"You got a big mouth."

"I've heard that before."

He put the hand down on the bar and took another quick drink of beer before he said, "Día de los Muertos. You know what that means?"

"Day of the Dead," I said. "But I don't think you're talking about a fiesta day."

"I'm talking about accounts. You know what I mean? Compadre? I'm talking about bones and doing what you say you will do. I'm talking about mi lugar en la familia. Mi lugar en la mesa. My place in the *family*. My place at the *table*. You get me? Usted cucaracha blanca." After he called me a white cockroach, he took another drink of beer keeping his gaze locked to my eyes. His stare never wavered. Swallowing and then gasping loudly, he put the bottle back on its coaster and leaned in. "I'm talking about respect, motherfucker."

He put his wounded hand on the edge of the bar to push himself back as he stood. At the same time, he reached around behind his back with his right. There was nothing subtle about his actions and no surprise. As soon as the remaining fingers of his left hand wrapped around the bar sill, I raised my glass. I brought the thick bottom down like a hammer on his bloody stump.

Forgetting the gun at his back, he clutched the hand; its bandage was already seeping fresh blood. He tried to say something. I couldn't understand a word through the screaming. I dropped my glass on the bar and stood, extending my right leg behind him at the same time. Then I put my left hand at his throat and pushed, twisting and leveraging my body with all my strength. He hit the old beer-soaked floor with a loud thump.

I thought he would stay down for a few seconds at least. My new friend was tougher than that. He rolled over to get his hand on the pistol in his belt. Unfortunately for him he had a choice as he went left. He could either roll onto his wounded hand or extend it away from his body.

"Don't do it," I yelled as his right hand reached for the weapon.

He didn't listen.

The impact of my glass on his stump had been a kiss compared with the feeling of my heel stomping on it. Bones broke. I could feel the snapping through my boot. Fresh blood flowed out from under my foot to soak with the beer into the floor. For a moment, I thought there were sirens from approaching police cars. It was more screaming. I had to give him credit for stones if not brains. He reached again with his right hand, trying to get the pistol at his back. That time I didn't stomp. My foot was already there, and I simply ground it down, adding more weight and pressure with each inch his other hand moved closer to the gun. There's no telling if he passed out or gave up first. My bet is on passed out. He was too stupid to give up.

For several seconds, I watched him. My boot remained pressed down hard on his bleeding hand until I was sure he wasn't faking. Even then I didn't lift my weight off him until I had taken the weapon from his belt. It was an ancient .32 automatic with broken grips wrapped in tape—a drop piece, a gun you can use and then leave at the scene, disposable and untraceable.

"Call 911," I said to Ernesto. When he stayed where he was, staring over the bar at the man bleeding on his floor, I said, "Ernesto. Llama a la policía." He nodded and went to the phone at the other end of the bar.

I dropped the magazine from the pistol and jacked the round from the chamber. It was a small gun. The man's finger would barely fit through the trigger guard. He probably planned on using it as a finisher rather than the main event. Everything about his attitude said he was wanting to get his hands on me and give a little hurt. Of course, it was possible it wasn't me or Paris he was after. Anyone who showed up to take the job of chief in Lansdale could have been the target. It was a reasonable thought. Almost comforting. I tossed it away when I looked at the hand again. There was something personal there. He had showed me the tattoo and the missing finger like I had had something to do with it.

Lights, circling red and blue, spun across the front windows. Officer Gutiérrez came through the door. She looked ready for about anything except seeing me standing over an unconscious man with his weapon dangling from where I gripped the trigger guard.

"What happened?" she asked, resettling her own pistol into the holster.

"I started the job a little early," I told her. "Take this guy in. We'll want to talk to him once he's able." I hoped that sounded like something a chief of police would say.

"Uh…take *him* in?"

"You see anyone else that looks like a bad guy?"

"Yeah, he's a bad guy all right, but we don't get to touch him."

"What are you talking about? He just tried to touch the hell out of me."

"He works for the bank."

"I don't care if he bakes the best cookies in town. He needs to be arrested for assault and weapons charges unless he has a permit for this piece of junk." I raised the gun to show her.

Gutiérrez leaned in close and lowered her voice. "It's the whole thing with the DEA. The bank being built outside of town and the people doing it are under DEA protection and jurisdiction. Don't you know all about it? I thought you were brought in by the Justice Department."

"I thought that was a secret," I said, without whispering. The truth was that I had assumed without thinking it through. I had never asked. The real truth was I didn't know what the hell I was doing or why. I was foundering in dark waters looking for shore or a rope and wondering how I got here.

"Please," she said. "There are no secrets here. At least none that are kept very long. Everyone knows you're a Texas Ranger and a DOJ insert."

"What else do they know?"

"They know you were about the last choice. They know after Chief Wilcox was killed, the next guy lasted about a month. And they know your arm was twisted to get you here. What was it?" She looked at me then, from boots to hat. Her blue eyes held a knowledge that withered and diminished me.

"What?"

"What do they have on you?"

"Your guess is as good as mine."

"I bet it is."

I stepped back from the man on the floor, feeling suddenly exhausted and a bit scared by the size of the boots I had stepped into.

"I'll call the DEA guy. He'll come take him." Gutiérrez nodded down at the floor. "You want to give me the gun?"

"No," I said, but the thought behind the word was, Fuck it. "I'll keep the gun. You take him. Cuff him and read his rights as soon as he's awake."

"It won't work."

"What won't?" I asked, stepping over the body to the right side. "Arresting him?" With the toe of my boot, I kicked his right hand away from his body. It was extended and palm down just like his broken left. "Or sending a message not to screw with the new chief?" Bones snapped loudly as I stomped my heel into the back of the hand. A forward lean put the weight of my body on the ball of my food, and his fingers broke like corn popping in a hot pan.

"Oh, my God." Her eyes, blue and deep, went wide in astonishment. They seemed to have lost all their sense of knowledge.

"The message is, point a gun at me once, and you never will again."

Gutiérrez had more questions. She had a lot more judgment too. I didn't feel like talking either. I got out of there. The manly scent put on me by the barber had mellowed. It blended with the smell of night air, moist from the river; dry earth from the desert; mesquite; and cactus flower. I drove with my windows open, taking the wind in my face and into my lungs.

Twenty minutes of wandering had brought me to no greater clarity. I took a dirt road to the top of a hill and stopped. Above me the stars sprayed across black nothing. I looked into the nothing. Out there was darkness beyond the absence of light. It was the kind of void that rejected vision, color, even warmth. Looking up, between the stars, was like looking at the darkness within a grave.

It wasn't until then that I understood I hadn't escaped that night digging in the dirt of old Mexico. Once you set foot into your own grave, you can never leave it completely behind. Maybe that's why I hadn't run off yet, why I hadn't taken the money and bought a life someplace else. Every direction I turned—any turn we all make—the darkness remained ahead.

When I got back into the truck, I was thinking about Lenore.

There was no plan, just hope, when I pulled into my parking spot at the Desert Drop Inn. I'd decided to splash a little water on my face and brush my teeth before going to the office to see if I could track her down. If my attention hadn't been focused on the neon-lit office when I stepped into the darkness at the bottom of the stairs, I might have realized sooner that something was wrong. It shouldn't have been dark.

On each end of the motel, a staircase landed at the entrance to a little cove. The cement cave held ice, candy, and soda machines. Even if the overhead light was off, both the vending machines had lighted fronts. Like I said, it shouldn't have been dark, but I was looking for the wrong thing.

My foot was on the first step when something hard slammed into the back of my extended thigh. It was like being beaten with an electric eel. My leg gave way, dropping my knee onto the concrete step. I was under attack. A second blow, aimed at my kidneys, struck. Had it landed correctly, I probably would have been wadded up on the floor pissing blood on myself. Because I was already falling, the aim of the blow was off, and it struck the gun in my belt before glancing into my back. I rolled away from the attacker, putting my left side and arm between me and his club as I reached back for my weapon with my right. That was the first time I saw him. He was smaller than me but stocky, solid looking in outline, which was all I could see.

Expecting another swinging blow, I tensed my arm and hunched my shoulder, tucking my chin. Just as I got my weapon clear of the holster, he struck. The impact didn't come at my side or my head like I had expected. He hit me with a jab, tight as a knot and hard as regret, right into my gut. A baton punch. My attacker had a handled baton. Once you've been hit with one, you never forget the feeling. He had swung it against my leg and back, but he had tucked the long end and punched with butt of the short end. He was a cop.

The air rushed out of my body, and a dam of pain kept it from returning. I was in danger of blacking out. If that happened, I was at his mercy, and that was the one thing that I had not found to be in great supply lately.

"Who are you?" the attacker asked. "Who are you really?"

The pistol in my hand seemed to weigh a hundred pounds, and my hand felt like it was as many miles away, working by remote control. I managed to lift the .45 but had little hope of getting the gun in front of me and aimed. No hope at all, once I saw the motion of his arm raising the baton to strike at my wrist.

Before he could disarm me, I fired twice into the soda machine. It spit and then started pouring. My gut relaxed, and I gasped in a rasping lungful of air.

When gasping finally turned to breathing, I was alone. I stayed that way too. It took five more minutes for me to make it up to my room, and in that time, no one showed up. No curious onlookers. Most telling, no cops.

SIX

"What the hell do you mean, you let him go?" I asked DEA Agent Darian Stackhouse without shouting at him. I was practicing restraint, and it was mostly working.

I had arrived at the Lansdale Police Department at the crack of eight forty, not being sure what time chiefs of police reported to work and not caring. I was limping, my knee swollen from the impact with the stairs, my back bent to favor one side, and my gut bruised by the baton blows.

When I got in, the first thing waiting was Stackhouse, there to read me the rules of cooperation between the various agencies involved in what he called "critical relations."

"Why weren't you briefed on this?" he shot back without quite yelling as well.

"Good question," I said. "It wouldn't have made a difference. He pulled a weapon on a police officer." I was exaggerating a little but not enough to bother me. "Maybe you grant immunity for that when it's you. When it's me, he's lucky to be alive."

"Oh, knock off all the cowboy crap. You overreacted to a misunderstanding. You have no jurisdiction. The man was never in your custody, and he never will be."

"How's his shooting hand?"

"Broken to shit. How'd that happen, and why didn't you take him to the hospital?"

"Who knows?" I shrugged. I had dropped my voice to a normal level. Raising it hurt my stomach muscles. "And how could we have taken him to a hospital? He was never in our custody. In fact, I've never seen the man. Until I see him again, that is."

Stackhouse didn't say anything to that. He looked at me like I was a dangerous animal that had just started talking to him through the bars of the zoo. DEA Agent Stackhouse was a black man. Former military—I could tell from how he stood and moved. He wore a loose-fitting suit jacket, the summer-weight kind in khaki, and it looked like a safari jacket. Even at that and without a tie, he still looked restricted.

I sat down at my new desk. Stackhouse smiled and took a breath. He sat as well, spreading his hands as he did in a placating gesture. "Look," he said. Then he thought about what he wanted to say next. "We're all on the same team, aren't we? I mean, we want to keep things safe and stop the bad guys."

"I don't think so." I wasn't smiling. "Not if we're playing by different rules. Seems to me you're working closer to the bad guys than to the good ones."

"You don't understand all that's going on."

I smiled. I'd always hated to be told I didn't understand when it was used in place of an explanation. I leaned back and put my boots up on my bare desk and put my hands forward in the same kind of placating spread he had used.

"I don't like the DEA," I told him.

His smile dropped away.

"As a matter of fact, I'm not fond of any of the three-letter agencies. I think you all like fighting the war more than you like solving problems, and I think you all believe rules are what you enforce more than what you follow." I smiled again, big and friendly. "Does that make things clear?"

"As a mountain spring when the snow is melting." Pretty words and a hateful look.

"Tell me about the bank."

"As far as I know, the bank is a private venture to which the DEA has no ties and no information. I do notice that it is outside of Lansdale city limits. That makes it no more a concern of yours than it is of mine. Does that make things clear?"

"As the Rio Grande after a hard rain," I said.

"I guess we understand each other." Stackhouse ignored my sarcasm.

"I guess we do."

"What do we plan to do about it?"

"I'm not much at making plans," I said, pointing a finger around the office. "That's how I ended up here."

"You don't seem to understand the nature—the scope—of the conflict we are engaged in."

"Your war on drugs." It was an obvious statement on an obvious thing, tossed off without thought. As soon as I said it, it had a deeper meaning—a deeper connection than I had bothered to make before. I started listening harder to what he was saying.

"War," he said, leaning forward in his chair and giving me a "leadership" look in the eyes. Definitely military. "On drugs, with drugs, financed by drugs—an entire criminal system on our border. It has claws in the Mexican government. I'm talking about an unstable nation ruled by violent criminals—revolution. We can't keep the lawnmower wets out. You think we can manage a million refugees and the crime families mixed in? War there—is war here. That can't happen."

"You believe all that?" I asked him, holding the eye contact. "What have you done to stop it? Corruption in Mexico is an old story. How many cops and politicians do you own?"

"Fuck you."

"You don't want to stop anything. You want it unstable in just the right way. Teetering on the edge."

"You're not much of a cop, are you?"

"High praise, I'm saying."

"What about your brother?"

"What do you—"

"He was part of the problem too, wasn't he? Running cash across the border."

"Yeah? What would you know about it?"

"I know he ran afoul of some people. He was working for the Guzeman DTO. They got taken over by the real bad folks—La Familia de los Muerto. Longview Moody ended up in the desert one night."

"Longview was found dead in his trailer after a fire."

"Yes, he was. That's a strange thing. I understood he was dead and buried in the Mexican desert; then he pops up at home and dead of a house fire."

"Not all that strange, maybe. Information is a used car. You get what you pay for."

"Maybe. But I heard something else. I heard you were at his trailer that night."

"Sounds to me like you hear a lot of shit, Stackhouse. I hear things too."

"Um-hum, I bet you do."

"I hear there's a house full of dead cartel boys in Juarez, and it was a DEA agent that did the deed."

"You stow that. You lock it tight. Lives are at stake."

I thought it was interesting that he said "stow that." I'd heard army grunts say the same thing, but not often. It pegged Stackhouse in my mind as navy or marines. SEAL? He was definitely an ops kind of guy.

"Who are you losing control of, Stackhouse? Your guys or your *other* guys? Anyone unaccounted for?"

Stackhouse stared at me like I had just produced a wand and made the desk dance. It didn't last long, though. He shut his mouth and stood. His shoulders were square and his back straight. He wanted to come across the office and kick the life out of me. I had to admire his restraint.

"Listen here," he said. Even his voice was tense. "I don't know what kind of game you think you're playing, but it's dangerous."

"You put yourself on the side of a man who wanted to kill me. There's no game."

He went out. I stayed behind my desk for a few moments, savoring the silence. I'd never had a desk, let alone an office. It was a weird and strangely inspiring feeling. I felt like I imagined Paris had felt all his life.

There was a knock on the door. The savoring was over.

It was Gutiérrez. "They were right," she said instead of a greeting.

"Who? And about what?"

"Everyone on the force that you haven't bothered to meet yet. They said you look like crap in a cheap basket." The insult in the words wasn't supported by her tone or her expression. Gutiérrez had a losing coach's idea of motivation.

"They said that? Are you quoting?"

"Are you not even going to take the job seriously?"

"I don't know. Is this department in the habit of turning dangerous people loose?"

"Yes, we are. I told you the DEA was involved, and they've been running things around here for the last couple of years."

"And now I'm here."

"And now you're here, and no one has an idea what's going on. Even you, I'm thinking."

I nodded just to seem like I was listening. I probably looked more like I was agreeing. Once I realized that, I stood and picked up the one thing that had been on my desk when I came in: a gold badge that read Chief of Police—City of Lansdale. I pinned the badge on my shirt and went out to the department common room.

"Listen up, everyone," I said. All noise and voices stopped. That was a little intimidating. "I'm Long—" I stopped. A flush of heat rushed up my neck into my face, followed by a twinge of nausea. There were so many ways to fail that I was stunned to have made it as far as I had. "My name is Paris Tindall. Chief Tindall now. I guess everyone knows that I got this job because of unusual circumstances. I haven't been here long, but I'm beginning to think this whole town is an example of unusual circumstances. I imagine that you're like me and want things to get back to something like they once were. I don't understand everything. I do understand that."

I looked around, and everyone was watching but giving nothing back. They didn't know me. They sure didn't trust me. Gutiérrez had the only friendly face in the room. When I looked at her, she nodded slightly. Encouragement but not bold.

"What changes right now"—I went on trying to make eye contact with each person—"is this idea that some people are somehow off limits."

There was a harrumph from a fat man behind a desk in the far corner. It was the kind of sound intended to be derisive but deniable—a chickenshit sound.

"What's your name?" I asked when I turned to look at him.

There are two ways guys like that respond when you call them out for acting like the jerks they are. Either they backtrack hard and fast, or they pretend none of it has real meaning. That guy went the no-big-deal route.

He leaned back in his chair and pulled his seersucker jacket around his belly. It didn't close. "Mark Walker," he said. "Detective Walker." He shrugged hard as though he'd made some kind of point and then stretched out his hammy arms. There were no shirt cuffs under the jacket sleeves. Short-sleeve shirt, seersucker suit: it made me wonder if his tie was a clip-on. Walker brushed his chubby fingers over the top of his head, straightening the comb-over that covered about as well as his jacket. "And I'm the entire detective staff, by the way."

That drew another huff of sound from across the room. That one came from the small black woman in uniform at the dispatch console. It was aimed at Walker and not me. I let it go.

"What's the deal?" I asked Detective Walker. "You don't like what I said, or you don't believe what I said?"

"Hey, you're the boss," he said, holding up his hands like they were a kind of denial in themselves. I noticed the expansion band of his cheap watch was stretched to the limit and digging into his wrist. "I didn't say anything."

Like I said, chickenshit.

"All I'm saying"—I picked up my thought—"if you have a reason to make an arrest, bring them in. No matter who they are. If someone is in our custody, they remain there until *I* say so."

Gutiérrez cleared her throat, and it wasn't very subtle.

"What?" I asked.

"Or the judge…"

I waved my hand at her like I had it covered. "You all know your jobs. All I'm saying is that if it's legal, and it's right, do it. Anything that strikes you as the wrong thing, bring it to me, and we'll figure it out together."

The whole room kept looking at me. I couldn't help thinking that I'd given something away or made a complete fool of myself.

"So…uh…any questions?"

Walker grunted again. I didn't even look.

"Good," I said. Then I returned to the safety of my barren office and closed the door.

Before I sat, I pulled the phone and SIM from my pockets and put them together. It wasn't three minutes before it rang.

"Milo! My man!" I answered, keeping things cheerful.

"What the fuck? What the holy fuck do you think you're doing?"

"Colorful," I said. "That how you greet old friends?"

"We're not friends. My friends aren't braindead rednecks thinking the world is their own private Wild West."

"What am I doing here?"

He stopped ranting, and the line went silent for a lot longer than was comfortable.

"Milo, what am I doing here?" I asked again.

"What do you mean? You brought it to us. Or have you forgotten?"

"No, but—" I had been afraid of asking because I was sure he had already covered everything with Paris. This was worse. I tried another way of going at it. "Things are muddy here. A lot is happening in this town, and I need to know if we're doing the same jobs. You and me."

"What's going on?"

"You first. Give me some clarity. Help me think things through."

"You told me your *friend*, your—contact there, was concerned about the death of the former chief. When the city council hired the replacement, and he was killed, it was hard to ignore."

Two words stood out there. Milo put a weird emphasis on "friend." And "concerned" seemed way too small an idea when you talk about two cops being killed.

"Yeah," I said. "Have you thought about my brother's death?"

"Okay, yes, I get it. And you're right: your brother was murdered. There was an impact on the skull above the right eye. It could have been a gun butt. His throat was slit. Someone making sure but doing it quiet. The fire was probably to cover things up. He was dead before the fire. There is no doubt about that. But he had his own issues. There was nothing specific to tie his death to what you were looking at. If someone is killing top cops at Lansdale, you would be the target, not Longview Moody."

It's probably a selfish and self-absorbed admission, but until that moment, I had never considered the idea that Paris had been killed because of who he was, not who I was.

"Look," Milo said. "I know this work is not your kind of thing, but cop murder and cartel activity puts that whole town at risk. Keep your eyes open and your shit tight. You dig what I'm sayin'?"

"See, that's the thing. I do, and I don't."

There was a sigh on the other end of the phone that said a lot about what Milo thought about me. None of it was good.

There were a lot more questions I wanted to ask. I didn't. I was trapped between my lie and a hard place. I couldn't get the information I needed from him without telling why I didn't know the things I should. I changed directions. "Tell me about the DEA."

"DEA?" He echoed the initials slowly, putting extra meaning into each letter. "Why?" His question was like a warning, a sign in small lettering standing in the middle of a big space that read "Minefield." By the time you could read it, you'd be in the middle.

I backed out. "Never mind," I said. "This part of the border is crawling with them."

"Stay away, and don't involve them," Milo told me. "The last thing I need is a pissing match between us and them. You just concentrate on finding out why cops keep getting killed."

I got off the phone after that. Then I spent a chunk of time hiding in my office trying to figure out how to do a job I had no business doing. I was saved, or at least distracted, by a knock on the door.

"Come on in," I called, assuming it would be one of the cops. It was Bascom Wood, the fat man from the night before.

"Chief Tindall." He came in and pushed the door closed with his back. "I told you I would come visit."

"You told me you would give me a day or two."

He pursed his lips and seemed to consider what I'd said. "I needed to talk to you." One of his chubby ringed fingers flicked out toward an empty chair. Without waiting, he claimed it. "We need to talk." It sounded like a line from a movie.

"What about?"

"You know." The statement was without subtlety or added meaning. Bascom Wood was certain.

So was I. "What do you want?"

"To know who I'm speaking with first."

I didn't trust him. How could I? But he knew. "Chief Paris Tindall," I said. "You confirmed that last night. To your friend."

"Maybe a mistake. One I can correct in the light of day."

"Look, Bascom." When I said his name, I saw his nose crinkle. "Councilman," I corrected.

He liked that better. "You cut your hair. It makes a difference. You look even more like him." Councilman Wood was less agitated than he had been the night before.

"Whatever mistake you think you made—there's no reason to correct it until you know you have to. Is there?"

"*Chief Tindall.*" He said the title and name in that same movie-drama kind of way. Either he was accusing me or accommodating me. "Would you be a member of the Drug Enforcement Agency?"

I snorted a little in surprise and distaste. "No."

"You sound like you mean it."

"DEA Agent Stackhouse left here not long ago."

"And?"

"And he wasn't happy. Neither was I. They let go a man who tried to kill me."

"I heard he had a brother."

I didn't say anything. I kept my gaze set to his and didn't blink.

Councilman Wood did. "But you're a cop." He said it as a statement. It was a question.

"You think they would have dumped me in here if I wasn't?"

"FBI?"

I didn't answer.

"ATF?" He wiped beads of sweat from under his nose with a ringless finger. "CIA?"

"The CIA is not a law enforcement agency, Councilman Wood."

Bascom Wood nodded knowingly. He looked like a poker player who had caught someone in a bluff. "No. But things are past that here, aren't they? Laws. Enforcement. Maybe even sides."

"Tell me about the man you were with last night."

"You will be hearing from Simon without me getting in the middle."

"I have questions."

"I'm sure you do, Chief. I'm sure you do." Mr. Wood stood and rubbed under his nose again. "I don't know if we can work together."

"What's that mean?"

"Lansdale isn't a town. It's a small boat. And everyone has their own paddle in the water."

"That doesn't help me understand anything."

"Until I know we're paddling the same direction…"

"What direction?"

His eyes brightened with decision. He opened the door and spoke loudly. "Chief Tindall."

Faces in the front office turned to look.

"I'm glad we got to talk again," the councilman went on. "I'm looking forward to working with you." He extended a hand but didn't come forward.

I came around the desk to stand with him in the open door. We shook. His grip was clammy but firm.

"Since we can't judge each other by who we are," he whispered, "we'll have to judge by what the other does." He let go of my hand and grinned as he turned to go through the door. "Let me know if there is anything I can do for you." Bascom Wood waved at officers and citizens as he sauntered to the exit.

Two of the cops he waved at were on the way out the door themselves. Gutiérrez and her partner, Hector, nodded at the big man as he left. She turned to look at me. He, deliberately, looked at the floor when I caught his eye. Hector didn't want to look at me, and I figured the reason had to be the new shiner around his eye. Two and two got together with some other things kicking around my head, and it added up.

"Chief," Gutiérrez said, stepping back from the exit. "Getting a lot of work done this morning?" The sarcasm was friendly but I ignored it.

"What are you two up to?" I asked, looking straight at Hector.

After an uncomfortable moment of silence while she waited for her partner to answer, Gutiérrez finally said, "We're going out to a domestic. A frequent flyer."

"You stay and cover for me. I'll go with Officer…"

Hector squared his shoulders and the line of his mouth. He looked straight into my eyes and held his gaze. It was not a friendly look. "Alazraqui," he said. The tone of his voice perfectly matched his eyes. He offered his hand.

I kept my stare on his eyes and my hands at my side.

"Hector Alazraqui," he finished, letting his hand drop.

Gutiérrez watched what passed between us, and again, when things seemed too silent for her, she interjected. "Most of us just call him Heck."

I nodded. "I thought they might." His continued look at me was a dare, an argument he'd started without me that he was dying to continue to my face. It would be continued, I decided, but later. "You drive."

The cruiser and its air conditioner locked out the dry heat and gritty wind of the day. It did the same for the sound of the road, leaving us too close for anyone's comfort, two antagonistic peas in a cold and quiet pod. I looked out the window and let the atmosphere do the work. It wasn't that I wanted him to talk. I wanted him ready to talk. I think it would have worked too if the town was larger. As it was, we went out, curving around the Desert Drop and up a hill. Behind the yucca and mesquite was an area that had recently been bulldozed flat and planted with cheap trailers. It was the largest expanse of mobile homes I had ever seen in my life. The other developments I'd seen around town had been planted with at least a small bit of care. This one looked like a war cemetery laid out in a rush to cover over the leaving behind. Between the prefab bits of heaven, there were no plants of any kind. The mobile homes, none of them skirted and many still resting on tires, looked just as lifeless as the community they occupied.

"What's this?" I asked. Hector jumped. Even to me, my voice sounded loud after the silence of the drive. "'Possum walk over your grave?" I asked.

His answer to that was a renewal of the earlier hard looks. When he turned back to the road, he said, "Tin City."

"Tin? Like sheet metal?"

"Yep. Developers putting in all the big stuff out closer to the National Park bought this land for nothing. They put in trailers and rent them to their own workers. It sucks their earnings back into their boss's pockets and keeps them close enough to work but far enough away not to spoil the view."

He pulled up in front of a trailer. It was one of a hundred clones parked in rows.

"You sound like you don't approve," I said.

"Do you?" He asked, looking at me again. The look answered his own question. He assumed I would approve of the modern-day model of the company store. "Whatever." He pushed the shifter into park and opened the door. When he stepped out, heat rushed into the car.

"Hang on," I said to Hector's back as he walked to the trailer's steps. He didn't turn or respond at all. He was already knocking by the time I had closed the car door. When I reached the bottom of the steps, he was passing through the screen door. He let it slam closed behind him, the aluminum smacking and then rattling loudly.

I didn't knock. I pulled the still-vibrating screen door open and stepped in. The only one in the room who looked at me was the slight, dark woman with bruises old and new on her face. She wasn't pretty, but it was a hard thing to look good after a beating and harder still after a lifetime of them. Her face was a map of choices in men that showed only one ending. The man, her partner, was sitting in a reclining chair that was more rip than vinyl. His face was in his hands, and he was staring at Hector's boots.

"You know how it is," he said. "I didn't mean nothin'. It was just an accident."

"The neighbors heard the accident going on for twenty minutes," Hector told him.

"It's between us. Ain't nobody's business but ours—me and Becky—and you don't hear us complaining or making a fuss, do you?" He lifted his face from his hands to look at Becky.

Hector turned to her and said, "This will keep happening until you choose to make a change. You can get counseling." He held out a small card.

Becky shook her head.

"Will you press charges this time?"

Again, Becky shook her head; then she looked at me. Having a stranger witness this ritual seemed to be the worst part of it for her.

"You a new cop?" the guy in the chair asked.

"This is the new chief," Hector said without turning to either him or me. Becky looked around at the mess surrounding us. She was more embarrassed to have someone she considered important see her house than to see the state she was in.

"Wouldn't it be usual to get them apart and talk to them separately?" I asked Hector. "Maybe putting her on the spot in front of the bastard who treats her like a punching bag is not the best way to offer help."

"The fuck?" Becky's husband glared at me and started to rise on shaky legs. "You can't—"

"I can." I pushed him back, and he collapsed back into the chair. When he did, I caught the strong odor of booze. If it came from his huffing breath or from the stained batting of his seat, I couldn't tell.

"All we can do is talk," Hector said. "And offer help. She doesn't want help. I've offered till I was blue. And I've been here eight times in less than two months."

"Is that true?" I asked Becky. "You don't want help? Or are you just afraid that this is what you get in life? He's the best you deserve?"

Hector looked at me with a kind of horrified rage. I was doing the wrong things the wrong way. He was wondering just how bad I would make things. Becky looked at me too. There was something different in her eyes. It might not have been actual hope, but it was something that said she didn't deserve her life.

"Hang on…" Hector groped for what to call me. He knew I wasn't Paris. "Chief," he finally said. It looked like the word had a sour-milk taste in his mouth. "I don't know how you think…" He stopped and thought about what he was saying. He looked at the man and the woman listening in and pulled himself back from what he wanted to say. Instead, more calmly, he said, "This isn't how we do it. I hope you know it. I hope you know how wrong what you're thinking about can be."

I smiled at him. At his understanding. I grinned, in fact, and then I turned to the man on the recliner. "Take her outside and talk about options, Officer Alza..." It was my turn to stumble over his name. "Alza..."

"Alazraqui," he finished for me.

"Easy for you to say." I was only half joking. The man in the chair looked like he was going to laugh, but the warning in my look stopped that.

"But—" Hector started.

"Don't worry about it," I told him. "Things are going to work out here." I had never stopped looking at the man, who was now cringing back into his chair a little.

"Come outside with me, Mrs. Padilla." Hector took her arm and urged her toward the door.

"What's going to happen?" she asked.

"Nothing," he answered, but there was a lot of doubt in his voice. "They're just going to talk." They went out the door, and Hector had the sense to pull the main door shut. I heard the screen slap and rattle again in its frame.

"Gonna do the tough-guy bit, huh?" the guy in the chair asked. There was a false sound to his bravado. The smug tone, however, seemed genuine and completely natural to him. "I know you can't touch me."

"You sound sure of yourself."

"'Course I am. You want to scare someone, you don't send the chief of police."

"Why's that?"

"Chiefs always have something to lose. They like the rules. You want someone scared, you send one of the Indians."

"What's your name?"

"Padilla, Rand Padilla."

"Has that happened to you, Mr. Padilla?"

"What?"

"Has anyone come around trying to scare you? Anyone from the Lansdale Police Department?"

He grinned like he understood something and scooched forward in the chair. "Maybe," he said. "Maybe that boy out there and his big grain-fed bitch got a little pushy. That what's going on? The new guy comin' in like Santa Claus making his list?"

"Okay, they got tough with you. What happened?"

"You know what happened. I work for the Machados, and the Machados own this town."

"So Alazraqui and Gutiérrez backed down?"

"Who?"

I jerked my thumb over my shoulder in the direction of the closed door. "My boy and the big blonde."

"Yeah."

"That make you feel like a big man?"

"Screw you. I don't have to be big. I just gotta do my job, and you gotta do yours."

"Well, see, we have two problems here."

"Whatchu mean?"

"I mean I'm not who you think I am. And I don't work for anyone but me."

He looked at me for a long moment, like he was translating Latin in his head and coming up with something that still made no sense.

"Come outside with me," I said, pointing again at the door.

Padilla must have come to some conclusion that I didn't catch. He reared back in the recliner and kicked out with his foot right at my crotch. Two things about that made me happy. He missed his target, jamming his heel into my hip. Assault against a police officer was the excuse I had been hoping for since I had laid eyes on his wife.

The kick hurt. It turned me to the left as I buckled forward and almost went to the floor. Padilla rolled out of his chair, landing on all fours. He started off crawling and then scrambled up to his feet as he went for the hallway. I had no idea what he had back there to run for, and I didn't want to find out. I caught my fall on the arm of the chair and made it my weapon. The vinyl ripped but held enough for me to turn the chair over on Padilla's flailing feet.

He struggled for a moment, like an animal that couldn't understand the trap it was in. When he stopped flailing and turned to see what was going on, I hit him. It wasn't fair, and it wasn't gentle, but trapped animals are the most dangerous ones. Besides, if there was one lesson my father left me with, it was to never give someone an even break. They might use it to kill you.

My downward punch to the jaw bounced him off the floor. It didn't take him out. Another one like that would probably break my fingers. Instead of throwing another punch, I dropped a knee on him, right in the ribs, just under the shoulder blade. I knew without asking it hurt. He reached, trying to get any kind of grip he could on me. It couldn't have been easier than that. I took him by the wrist and twisted—hard. At the same time, I stood, pulling him after me. He had the choice of coming along or letting his arm slip the socket. He stood.

"Okay," he said, raising his free hand.

I twisted a little more.

"Okay, okay, okay!" He was shouting by then.

"How many times did your wife ask you to stop?"

"I'm sorry." He whined the apology.

"I know." I pushed his head into the cheap trailer paneling. It went through the wall and out the one behind it. He was lucky his head missed the stud.

Through the paneling, I could hear him. I wasn't sure if he was sobbing or puking. Either way I was glad I couldn't see it.

"That your truck outside?" I asked him.

"Yeah," he answered. The words were soft and thick, sounding a lot farther away than they were.

"You're going to get in it and go."

"Where?" He shouted the question, holding on to his last bit of defiance.

"I don't care. You're just not welcome here anymore."

"I got a job."

"They'll get by without you. And Mrs. Padilla will be better off."

"You can't separate a man from his wife."

"I can. You've figured that much out, haven't you? The only question is, do I separate you by miles or by six feet of dirt?"

"Fuck you!" was his shouted answer.

God, you gotta love a spirited debate. I responded with the toe of my boot in his ass. Then I made my point three more times until he started blubbering again. "You going quiet?" I asked.

I took his quiet shaking as a nod and pulled his head from the wall. He dropped to the floor.

"Keys?" I asked.

Padilla pointed to a little plaque on the wall by the door. It read, "God protect us as we travel, by air or land or sea. Keep us safe and guide us, wherever we may be." Below the prayer were three hooks, one holding a set of keys.

"You believe in God?" I asked him.

"Of course I believe in God."

"Then you better believe the ass kicking you got today was nothing. I catch you around here again, and you'll be answering to him damn quick."

"What about you?" he asked, sounding like a child, full of spite and blame for everyone but himself.

"Me?"

"You're gonna answer someday."

"I'm good with that. Get your keys."

SEVEN

Outside his trailer, trudging through blowing dirt, Rand Padilla didn't look at his wife as he got into his truck and started the engine. He looked at me long enough to flip the finger as he stood on the gas. Dirt and gravel showered behind him as he hit the road.

A real cop probably would not have let a man who'd been drinking on the road. That, along with a lot of other real-cop stuff, was clear on Hector's face as I approached the car.

"That's—"

I cut him off. "I don't care to hear it. Mrs. Padilla," I said, nodding to her. "Your husband has decided to take a little time for himself. I understand this may put you into some difficulty. If you need anything, anything at all, just call me at the station."

"If he's not here to work, I'm not sure I can keep living in the trailer." She looked at the cheap, rolling tin house like it was a mobile palace.

"Just call. I'll make sure you're not left out of doors."

She didn't say anything, at least not in words, but I knew a thank-you when I got one. She went back into the trailer. Hector and I got back into the cruiser. "Go to the road. Turn right," I told him.

To the right was a copse of trees I had spotted from the barren land of the trailer park. There were mesquite and oak and one big cottonwood that littered the ground with peeling bark and dropped branches. We parked under the spreading limbs in a bit of pressed dirt that showed signs of a million high school hang-out parties.

I stepped out of the car as soon as it was stopped and went around to sit on the hood. Through the green there was a view of the river bottom and the town. Wind moved the branches, and the world felt cooler. It was a live sort of cool, shade and breeze, natural compared to the sealed-in cold of air-conditioning.

Hector shut off the engine. I felt it die under my ass. Even though the vibrations were gone, the heat remained, and the metal immediately began ticking and refitting itself as it cooled.

"Why are we here?" Hector asked as soon as he opened the car door.

"You tell me." I brushed at a fly that started circling my face.

"How should I know?"

It was a fair question. I didn't answer it. I swatted again at the pest; then I nodded. I wasn't sure if I was nodding in response to Hector or the questions in my head. Either way a nod was as good as a wink to a blind man, and we were just a couple of guys feeling around the dark.

The car door closed behind me. Hector came around the fender, giving the car—and me—a wide berth. He stopped, out of reach, with his hands on his hips. The snap closure on his patent leather holster was open.

"I thought you might want to finish the talk we started last night." As I spoke, I kept my gaze cast out through the green frame of trees and over the town. It was like looking at a painting.

"Who are you?"

I turned to Hector, and looking at him was more like looking through the wrong end of binoculars, oddly distant and distorted. "Who am I not?"

He set a foot behind him as if my question was a physical blow that pushed him off balance. Or maybe he was just adjusting his stance to pull a weapon on me. "What's that mean?"

"You know what it means. Last night you asked me who I was. That means you knew at first glance I wasn't someone else."

"Paris."

"Yep. How'd you know? Or better yet, how'd you know him?"

"You're not a cop at all, are you?" He asked the question like it was a condemnation. Everything not cop was less than cop.

I looked back at the town, and wind moved the trees again. Heat rising from the asphalt and buildings made the air ripple.

"You're going to tell me what's going on and what happened to Paris." It was a threat, spoken with a soft, even voice.

When I turned from the view to look at him again, Hector's hand was on the butt of his pistol. His gaze was focused on me but not on me—more like it was centered on something about two inches behind my eyes. I wondered what, or who, he was seeing.

"You're his contact." I said it like a matter of fact. It seemed obvious to me.

To Hector it seemed like something else. His face fell, literally. The tension was jerked out of the muscles, and the look of righteous anger transformed in the fall to an expression of stunned hurt.

"*Contact?*" He tried to put a sneer into the word, but all the power was artificial. It was vocal paint on rotten walls. The word itself had kicked him in the gut. "Is that what he said? I'm a contact?" The questions fell without his even trying to support them.

"No. I mean, he didn't say anything about it…about you. It was my assumption."

"Assumption?" He tightened his fingers around the butt of the gun and squared his shoulders, forcing some steel back into his spine. "Assumption?" he asked again. The question was for him, not me. I was sure he was stoking his own fires. "What gives you the right to assume? You come here—wearing a badge you don't deserve and a…a…*stolen* face. It's not his. I'm not even sure if it's yours. You have his face worn like a mask. And it doesn't fit because you can't be him. His bones…his center is different—better. You can't live up."

Hector pulled his weapon. That was the first indication I had of danger. I had once again completely misunderstood something, and—as always, it seemed—my mistakes were aiming guns at me with homicide in their hearts.

I stood from the hood of the car and put my hands up in front of my body. My palms were turned to Hector, their emptiness on display. Without turning my head or eyes, I searched the periphery of my vision for anything to help my situation, a distraction or a witness. As I looked, Hector eased forward, leading with the barrel of his gun.

When it drifted upward to my chest and centered on my heart, I said, "I didn't take anything from Paris. He was my brother."

Once again, my words hit Hector with a violence beyond my hands or gun.

"*Was?*" he asked.

Small words always seem to hit the hardest.

"He's dead," I told him. "Killed." I said that like it was a distinction with real meaning.

Hector had tears in his eyes.

"What was he to you?" I don't learn easy.

His weapon came back up. "What the fuck do you think he was to me? How can you tell me like that?" he asked. When he spoke again, his voice took on the trembling of his gun hand. "How much hate do you have in your heart?"

"I don't hate anyone here."

"Liar!"

"I'm just telling you. He was my brother—what're you blubbering about?"

It was a stupid question. I may as well have kicked Hector in the heart because the shock that showed on his face was the kind of understanding that comes in charged bolts of electricity. I think I understood the same moment he did.

"He never told his own brother." That said it all—for him and for me and for Paris laid out on a slab so far away.

"You and Paris?" My question faded, unspoken but still loud.

"Yes."

"I never knew."

"That's obvious." Hector holstered his weapon and turned his gaze both downward and inward. "The world is full of obvious things, I guess."

"Obvious or oblivious. How could he hide being gay?"

"Why did he feel like he had to?" Hector's question cut right to it.

"Who knows about you?"

"What? That I'm gay?" He stood straight and presented himself as if on inspection. "That I'm—maricón?"

I nodded, ashamed of the motion. Still, I asked, "Who knows?"

"My family. My friends. The people who know me."

"Work?"

"That's different. Being a cop is—"

"I didn't know my brother like I should have. That's obvious. I haven't…ever. But I do know that being a cop was who he was, not just something he did. It's more than different. And he didn't have much of a family or people who knew him. Except maybe you."

"I thought he was ashamed of me."

I shook my head as I settled back onto the hood of the cruiser with my gaze turned down, looking into the dust. Hector's boots were leaving deep sole prints as he wandered. He seemed calm now, but the prints were a map of despair.

"I don't think so." I said it to him, but I was still looking at his prints in the dirt. "Between the two of us, I'd say I was the one he would be ashamed of."

Hector stopped his aimless walking. "He never told me he had a brother," he said before sitting beside me on the car.

"That doesn't surprise me."

"What now?" he asked.

"It's a hell of a question," I answered. "Are you sure you want to ask it?"

"What else have I got?"

I shrugged. "His funeral."

"What?"

"You asked me what was next. You'll want to go to his funeral."

"When?"

There was a moment of panic as I realized I didn't know. I had made arrangements with the funeral home to pick up the body and hold a service. I'd never planned on being there. I didn't even know if the DNA test that Milo had told me about was done. How long did those take? And what the hell would it show?"

"I don't know," I told Hector.

"You don't know? How complicated can it be? It's a funeral—oh."

"What?"

"You mean it's me you don't know about. You think I'll make some kind of scene."

"No. It's about me." I looked at Hector and made sure he was looking at me. "They think it's me that's dead. Paris was in my trailer. I thought someone was trying to finish a job they had started on me. When I took his place, it was just to get a little distance. But come to find out, he was involved with something that might have come looking for him too." I spread my hands like a magician's reveal. "So that's it. I don't know if I was the target or if he was. If I go to the funeral, there's no telling who might show up and spot the switch. Buick, our father, certainly would."

"How did you think you were going to get away with this?"

"I didn't. I just thought it would get me away long enough to think."

"Why didn't you go into Mexico?"

"Some problems don't care about borders."

"Can I ask you one question though?"

"Only one? I guess you deserve that."

"Why is your father named after a car?"

"Not just a car," I told him. "'Buick is an entire luxury line from General Motors,' is the way he always answered."

We almost laughed.

"Hell, I don't know," I said, and it was the truth. "He just is, and that sums up his whole life. A car, a machine, something dead and rusting in a junkyard. Never a man. Never just a human being."

"Wow."

"What?"

"They say gay men have daddy issues."

I shrugged. "We are what we are."

"You got that right." He stared at me. I could see thoughts traveling across his dark eyes like visible telegraphic pulses of energy. "I want to go."

"I know."

"Well?"

"Let's see what we can work out. In the meantime…"

"I'm not going back to work," Hector said, and he meant it.

"How about a beer?"

"God, yes."

EIGHT

I gave Hector some cash and sent him for beer. Once he was gone, I pulled my phone and called the funeral home. As I talked, I paced under the shade, kicking up rocks and crushed cans. When the call was over, I stood staring out over the town and enjoying the feel of breezes on my sweating skin.

Hector returned. Standing by the open door of the cruiser, he called ten-seven into dispatch. Shorthand, I assumed, for off the clock and out of reach. I reminded myself to see if those cop codes were on the Internet. It seemed like a handy thing for a police chief to know. Even though I had confided in him, I didn't want to reveal the true depths of my ignorance to Hector unless I had to.

The dispatcher's voice was replaced by another. "Heck? Are you...okay?" Gutiérrez sounded concerned.

I took the mic and answered. "He can't talk right now." I grinned at him and let the statement sit there a moment before I keyed the mic again. "And when I arrive in the morning, I would like the vacation schedule and a copy of Officer Alazraqui's accumulated time on my desk." For good measure I said, "We're out," before shutting off the radio.

"She's going to think you're firing me or killing me," Hector said as he fired up the cruiser.

"Sometimes it's good for people to worry."

"I think she figured out that we had a run-in last night. Between my eye and how you looked—" He shrugged. "She's a good cop."

"I hope so."

Hector took the mic back and offered beer in return. "Which would you like?" he asked, holding sixes of Lone Star and Victoria out in different hands.

"I'm not picky."

"That's not something to brag about."

"Don't I know it," I said, popping open one of the Mexican beers. Hector had Lone Star. "I called the funeral home," I said. "His body hasn't been released yet."

He opened his beer and stared at the opening a moment before drinking. After draining half the can, he looked at it a little longer before asking, "How do you feel about..."

"What?" I watched Hector tilt up his can and take another long drink. "Him being dead? Me being alive?"

He shook his head with the can still at his lips. When he lowered the beer from his mouth, he used the back of his hand to wipe away a drip. Then he said, "No. How do you feel about who he was?"

I must have looked oblivious because he had to spell it out.

"With me." Hector lifted a finger from the can and pointed it at his own chest.

"Who am I to judge anyone for anything?"

"There's no need to judge. But you gotta feel something, right? I mean, you didn't know. He wasn't the person you thought he was. Paris was someone important to you. You have to feel something."

"Do you think people can change?"

Hector opened his second beer. It spit when the top popped, and he had to hold it out over the dirt to dribble foam before he could take the first drink. As he watched the froth bubble up and fall, he seemed to be thinking. "People are who they are, I believe."

I nodded.

"But what they know and what they believe changes. Maybe they aren't different, but they *do* different. Does that make sense?"

"Maybe," I conceded.

"I don't know," Hector said. "I hope it's a way people can change. If not, this world is fucked."

I opened a fresh can, and we clinked our beers together. "I've seen some things," I said. "And I've learned some things. There is a lot to not like about the man I was before…"

"Before what?"

"Before Paris died." I raised my can and used it to make a circle in the air that included nothing and everything. "Before all of this."

"What do we do now?" he asked.

I heard him take a swallow from his can. "Hell if I know." My answer was aimed at the dirt. "I still don't know which of us someone wanted dead. It looks like we were both good targets for someone. Something is going on here in Lansdale too."

"You have to ask yourself if the answers are worth what you have to pay."

"Ain't that the truth?" I lifted my head and can to take a long drink. "But I have the feeling that being here—being Paris—may be the only thing keeping me alive."

We kept talking and drinking until the beer was down to the last two and the sun was down to a muted yellow spreading out from the Big Bend National Park. Golden hour in Texas.

Driving back was out of the question. I might have tried it, but Hector had better sense than me. Besides I was still new at the responsible life. He put in a radio call to Gutiérrez, who came with another officer to pick us up.

I don't know how it got divvied, but the other officer drove Hector in car number four. Bronwyn Gutiérrez drove me back to the motel in her cruiser.

"My truck's at the station," I told her.

"It'll keep until tomorrow."

It was best that I didn't drive since I was drunk enough that it never occurred to me I should be concerned about the $1.5 million under the spare tire of that truck.

She hardly said anything the whole drive over. It was a surprise when she parked and asked me, "Is this the kind of cop you are, Chief Tindall?"

I thought it over long enough that she shut off the engine while she waited. "Pretty much," I answered.

"Just like your father."

"What?"

"You're just like your father. Lazy and drunk."

"I'm not nearly as mean as he is. Buick would have probably punched you already."

"Why haven't you?"

"Give me time." It was supposed to be a joke. I don't think it came out that way. "How do you know Buick, anyway?"

"Mostly by very sad reputation. And he was here in Lansdale about nine months ago."

"Why was he here?"

"He was helping the old chief, Wilcox. Something about grants."

That made sense. Buick had a lot of experience as a Ranger working with other departments. Years ago, he got off the road and into the homeland security business. He knew everything there was to know about squeezing blood out of paperwork. Better than that, he knew all the people he needed to know.

"You ran a check on me, didn't you?"

"I did that the moment your name came in from the DOJ. What didn't come up was how they bent your arm to take the job."

"They didn't. I asked for it."

"Really?"

"Apparently."

She shook her head, and a strand of blond hair fell from her tight braid. It was an end-of-the-day look. "I don't get it."

"Sometimes you find yourself between a fire and an open window."

"Whatever." She dismissed my explanation. "If you jumped, you better be able to fly. I don't see that anyone is waiting to catch you."

"Why, Officer Bronwyn Gutiérrez—I didn't know you cared."

"I don't. I'm just afraid you're going to get someone killed."

"Like the last two people who took this job?"

"Not like them. They had the good grace to die alone. I'm afraid you'll take someone with you."

My head was a bit off balance. It wasn't drunk spinning, more like the feeling of standing in a boat when a surprise wave comes through. I hadn't eaten, and I didn't want to have this conversation. It didn't seem to matter; everyone else wanted to talk.

Outside the car something moved. I didn't see it. My eyes simply caught the motion and the color pink at the edge of the still-burning headlights.

"Turn off your lights," I told Gutiérrez.

"Why?"

"I need to see something."

"Won't you see better with the lights on?"

"Just turn them off."

She did, but gave me the kind of look women reserve for drunks and fools.

I focused my attention—and slightly swimming vision—on the dark concrete cavern at the end of the motel row. Where last night Hector had jumped me, something was again moving. The new darkness brought it forward. It was a man.

"What are you looking for—"

I held up a hand to quiet her, keeping my gaze on the figure in the shadows. "I think someone is watching us," I told Gutiérrez, using my still-raised hand to point.

At that instant, fresh light—a pair of dim and yellowed headlights—swept the length of the motel. Along with the light came the noise of tires crunching on gravel and brakes squealing to a stop. The same man who had visited me at my room with Bascom Wood was momentarily caught in the headlights.

"There." I pointed again.

But Gutiérrez had turned away to watch the passing car. "What?"

I'd only seen a glimpse of the man. It was enough. He'd been wearing a black suit this time with a summer-weight straw hat. It could have been anyone if not for the pink silk shirt and pointy-toed boots long enough to curl at the tips. When the light had run over him, he'd frozen, but once it had past, he was gone. He had become one of the shadows.

I pushed open the car door and stepped out into the heat and hanging gravel dust. Gutiérrez came out of the car as well. When she stepped around the open door, I noticed her hand on the butt of her service weapon. She was reacting to my tension more than suspicions of her own.

I felt better having her there.

She turned to look at the quiet parking lot and scan the empty highway out front. I followed her eyes in darting glances, keeping my attention on the shadows in the cove. Putting my hand on my own pistol, I took a step toward the dark recesses of the concessions nook. As soon as I stepped from gravel to concrete, the overhead lights came on quickly, followed by the illuminated fronts of the soda and candy machines.

Lenore was standing alone among the machines, wiping her hands on a rag and looking me in the eyes. "Someone keeps shooting my soda machine," she said. "You wouldn't know anything about that, would you?"

"Where'd your friend go?" I asked.

"Which friend is that?" Her eyes were hard to read, but the motion of her hands in the dirty cloth seemed angry.

"The one that was back there with you," I said.

"No one back here but this chicken, Chief."

Maybe I was wrong. Anger and fear can often look the same. "Do you need help?" I hoped the question carried more than a casual offer. If someone else was listening, if she was in danger, I didn't want to make things worse. I hoped she understood.

"Aren't you the gentleman?" She grinned at me in a way that made me feel that she had not quite decided yet if she was insulting me. Lenore tossed the rag on top of the soda machine and sauntered out onto the sidewalk.

Women have a way of wrapping your hopes in tangles tighter than Christmas lights and then ignoring them completely.

She nodded at Gutiérrez, who had moved back to the open door of her cruiser. "Bron."

"Lenore." Gutiérrez nodded back.

I watched Lenore walk away, heading for the office door.

Gutiérrez watched me. "I don't like what you're thinking."

"What am I thinking?"

"It's not a good idea."

"Why?"

"You want details? I don't have them. But she knows all the wrong people, and she knows them too well."

I thought of the conversation I'd had with Lenore about visitors. "You think she's dangerous?"

"Hell yes. I just don't know how."

Staring down the row of motel doors, I saw a small light bloom in the office window. A printed glass saint's candle sat on the sill.

"I'm going to bed," I said.

"Alone," Gutiérrez stressed.

"Alone," I agreed. But I kept my eye on the office as I climbed the stairs, hoping the door would open. It didn't.

I entered my dark room and got an instant sense of claustrophobia. The air conditioner was off. The room was hot and stale. More than that, it felt unwelcoming. It was probably my imagination or the situation I'd found myself in, but the little room felt like a trap waiting to spring shut.

I flicked the light switch and then moved quickly away from the door. I left it open, but didn't want to be standing framed like a target. After I checked behind the bed and in the bath, I closed the outer door. The little safety flip latch was missing. I couldn't recall for sure if it had been there before, but the screw holes where it was supposed to be mounted were there.

I crossed the room and opened my side of adjoining doors. Then I knocked on the far side door. Not too loudly. Not quietly either. I gave five seconds to hear something and then hit it with my shoulder. The exterior door was metal clad. Those inner doors were cheap manufactured wood with vinyl coating. It only took the one lunge to break the latch from the door.

That room was dark with no air-conditioning as well. I left it that way.

In my registered room, I did the old movie trick of putting pillows under my blankets. I turned the air conditioner up full and turned out the lights.

I put myself to bed in the adjoining room, stripping down to my underwear and keeping my .45 right beside me.

There was no drifting off. I fell into slumber like a sinner into hell. My dreams were dark and frightening but unable to shake me from a sleep that would have looked like death to anyone watching. I know because I didn't move. When the door to the other room was kicked open, I woke in the same facedown, back-aching sprawl into which I'd settled.

There was no jumping up and catching the intruder. I rolled away from the door between the rooms and dropped behind my bed. At the same time as my body hit the floor, three quick shots barked out. The shooter ran. That was when I got to my feet and charged out to the balcony. Someone was running hard down the far stairs. There was a truck idling in the lot with its lights off. I didn't have a line on the runner, but I put two in the truck's hood as he jumped in the open passenger door.

Before I turned away, I caught a bit of bright color from below. The single candle on the ledge of the office had turned into a little shrine. Lenore had added more candles, a statue, and a bunch of flowers.

Returning to my secondary room, I emptied the phone and SIM from my pants pocket. Before I put them together, I changed my mind. I didn't feel like talking. I left the pieces on the bed. Still dressed only in my undershorts, I stood at the balcony railing and looked at the sky. To the west were darkness and starlight. To the east was a growing glow of pink and gold at the horizon.

I kept an eye out on the highway in both directions. No lights. No sirens. I'm not sure I'd ever felt as alone in my life.

There was no point in trying to go back to sleep. I pushed chairs against each exterior door. After that I pulled the plastic bag from the wastebasket and tied the .45 into it. My pistol stayed with me in the shower.

Cleaned and shaved, I dressed in my last clean clothes—khaki pants, and a white cotton shirt. I added my badge before walking out the door.

It wasn't until I was on the balcony staring down at the parking lot that I recalled leaving my truck at the station and why. Paris's phone was back together in my pocket. I pulled it and then realized I didn't know the number for the police department.

"Screw it," I told myself before dialing 911.

The woman at the desk didn't seem impressed with my need to be picked up. I thought about apologizing but not long. I told her to send one of the daytime officers out and said it like I owned the place. At least I was learning to sound like a cop.

A black woman officer arrived to pick me up. She was short and small. Her face was stone, and there was no doubting I was the reason. We rode in silence.

I spent that day making enemies. It seems to be about my best talent. I didn't tell anyone what I was looking for or why. I started blindly digging into file cabinets. I wasn't exactly sure what I expected to find, but Gutiérrez had mentioned my father and grants. Buick was an old hand at sniffing out federal money. I didn't know a lot about grants myself, but I did know they left paperwork behind.

I ignored everyone else in the office as I savaged the files. If they thought their new chief was crazy, they didn't say it. I doubted they would. Everyone in the department knew I was a DOJ insert. They did give me some hard looks though.

After I'd been at it for a couple of hours, Detective Walker showed up. He was wearing a different seersucker suit. It fit him about as well as the last one.

"You wanna tell me what you're looking for?" He asked the question like a man who had the right to know. Then he pulled back slightly. "Maybe I can help. Or set you off in the right direction."

"I'm sure you have plenty of your own work to do," I answered, without looking away from my pile of files. "No need to worry about mine."

"Someone's gonna have to clean up that mess."

"You volunteering?"

"I'm just sayin'—"

"Well, don't."

Walker puffed up and rocked on the balls of his feet. "Your daddy said you were a straight-arrow cop."

I'd had him pegged right from the start. Walker was the kind of man who liked to speak at angles instead of head-on. He liked to have deniability. He called me a straight arrow without quite suggesting it was an insult. It was interesting that he brought my father into it.

"You know Buick?"

"Met him a few times. We had drinks. He's a good cop."

I heard two things in that last statement. Walker admired Buick. And I wasn't his idea of a good cop. I didn't care about either one. The two of them were the same model of man, like they had rolled off the same southern-cop assembly line. The difference was that my father, for all his faults, was good at his work. Buick didn't mind corruption, but he hated incompetence and weaseling. I doubted he would have much good to say about Walker.

"During your advanced firearms training?" I asked.

He stopped rocking, and the smug look dropped off his face. "What?"

"Advanced firearms training." The blank look on his face told me all I needed to know. I dug a little deeper though. "The military urban-combat training for close-quarters automatic weapons use."

"I haven't had that."

"How can that be?" I tried to sound surprised. "Buick was here working up grants for the department, wasn't he?"

Walker shrugged. It was an uncomfortable motion. "I guess. Something like that." He looked away like someone who was about to suddenly remember something important he had to do.

"That's usually one of the first things he puts in for."

"I wouldn't know anything about that."

"What would you know about?"

"Huh?"

"What would you know about? What grants? What training development."

"I don't know," he said, already backing away. "I think all of that worked through the DEA."

"Why the DEA? These are development grants for local police."

"How would I know? Anyway, you can't work down here at the border and not work with the DEA. It's just the way it is."

"Yeah." I looked around the office before leaning in to Walker. "Tell you the truth? That's something bothering me."

He moved back, trying to create more distance. "What?"

"I've been asking everyone, so don't feel picked on."

"Asking what?"

"About the relationship between this police force and the DEA. I think we're getting the splintered end of that stick. You have any ideas how we can change that?"

"No, I don't." His answer was quick and terminal. "I've got work to take care of."

"Don't let me stop you."

He didn't.

I left the mess of files for someone else to put away. I'd found nothing about grants or federal funds in the paperwork. After talking with Walker, I was certain that I wouldn't either. He was on the phone as I went back to my office.

My phone buzzed a couple of minutes after I shut the door. Darian Stackhouse was calling.

"Chief," he said.

"Darian," I responded. It was a discourtesy. I wanted to see what it would bring up.

There was a pause from his end. I could almost hear him mentally cursing me. Then he said, "We got going on the wrong path the other day."

He was taking pains to keep things civil. That was interesting.

"I wanted to reach out. To see if there is anything my team can do to help you out."

Walker was definitely a pipeline to them. I'd lied to him when I said I was asking everyone about the DEA. Who else, I wondered.

"I can't imagine what that would be," I said, as if I hadn't a care in the world. "If there is anything you think I should know…" Tossing the conversational potato over to him did a couple of things. It made him wonder if I was ignorant or cagy. It also put him in the position of having to volunteer information if he wanted to lead me to where he wanted.

"I'm glad to hear it," he responded, just as grandly. "Let me know if there's anything at all we can do." We were both playing the same game.

"You wouldn't know anything about a shooting at the Desert Drop Inn last night?" I asked.

"Isn't that where you're staying?"

"Yep."

"No. I don't."

I believed him. He sounded like it was something he wanted to know about.

"Anyone hurt?"

"Nope. Someone's truck got shot up though."

"Well—it's a dangerous world."

"It sure is."

It had been another short, violent night. I was exhausted. I left as Hector and Gutiérrez were coming on. We exchanged looks and waves but no words as I drove away. My first stop was a hardware store. I bought some tools and some lumber. On the way back to the motel, I picked up a pizza.

The remainder of the afternoon was spent nailing boards to the floor in both rooms and putting 2x4 braces at the doors. I also nailed boards over the windows. I kept them covering the curtains so they couldn't be seen from outside. They wouldn't stop someone who was serious about getting in, but it would make it impossible for them to sneak up on me.

While I worked and chewed pizza, I planned what to do next. I decided to head out to where the bank was being built and poke around. If that didn't provoke anyone, it would be off to that fancy gun club. I was ready to start throwing mud around and seeing where it stuck.

I ran one more errand. I went to the store and purchased new jeans and white shirts. If I was going to shake things up, I wanted to look good. Around eight o'clock, I fell asleep in front of the TV.

Because of my plans for the day, and because no one shot at me in the middle of the night, I was already up and dressed when a furious pounding started on my door. It was the city councilman, Bascom Wood.

I opened the door, and he said, "They took my son."

NINE

"Who took your son?" I asked Councilman Wood even as I pulled him by the sleeve into my motel room.

"They did." His statement sounded imploring. Then he said again, "*They* did," as if the new emphasis answered everything.

"Stop." I said it as much for me as him. Bascom was worked up and worried about his kid. I was completely in the dark. It was no time for pretending that I knew things I didn't. "Who took him, and how do you know?"

"The Machados. The Machados took him. It had to be. I did something wrong. I said the wrong thing. That's how they work. It's my fault, but Baron shouldn't have to pay."

"Baron?"

"He shouldn't have to pay." Bascom was close to tears.

"Is that your son's name?" I asked as calmly as I could. "Baron?"

"Yes."

It seemed to be working; he was breathing better and looking right at me.

"How do you know they took him?" I asked slowly. "Did you see it?"

"No. Baron was gone this morning."

"Just gone? No notes? Was there a break-in?"

"No. Nothing like that. He was gone. He was just gone. I went into his room, and he was gone."

"Your wife?"

Bascom shook his head and looked at the floor. "It's just us. My wife went away. It was a long time ago."

"Who are the Machados?"

His head popped back up. "The Machados—*the Machados*. The brothers. Eladio and Simon Machado—the reason behind everything that happens here. Baron would not have been harmed without them knowing. Without their approval."

"And what did you do to piss off the Machados?"

"It's because I talked to you."

"To me? You didn't say anything—"

"They don't know that."

"But they know you talked to me."

He tilted his head in a sorrowful gesture that wasn't quite a shrug. "I don't know what they know."

"That's why you came to talk to me. When you knew I wasn't Paris Tindall—you thought I could help you get out of your situation."

Bascom Wood stared at me. His eyes were desperately sad. He held his mouth in an angry line. The anger was at himself, though, not me.

"The Machados?" I asked him. "Did they murder the previous chiefs?"

His eyes blazed to match the angle of his mouth. That time the anger was all at me. "My son first."

"Come on." I pulled him out of the room and down the stairs. Once at my truck, I used Paris's cell to call 911.

The woman on the board asked, "Another ride, Chief?" She didn't bother to keep the annoyance out of her voice.

"No. I want you to get hold of officers Gutiérrez and Alazraqui. It's an emergency; get them in, and have them meet me at—hang on." I tossed the phone to Bascom and said, "Tell them where we're going."

"Where are we going?"

"Your home. We want to see where this started." I opened the door of my truck and pointed over to his car. "I'll follow you."

* * * *

Bascom Wood and his son lived in one of the 1950s ranch houses off the city center. It was red brick with white-painted trim and a deep porch. The first thing I noticed was how obsessively neat and manicured everything seemed for a man and son living without the moderating force of a woman. It was the kind of home you see in magazines at a doctor's office when there is nothing else to read.

One step into Baron's room, and I was convinced that he'd run away.

The bedroom was large and cozy. But it was perfect. And if there is anything in the world not perfect, it's a teenaged boy.

The twin bed was made with hospital corners showing. Sheets were bright white. The folded bedspread was printed with stars and galaxies. There were shelves with books lined up by size. Interspersed among the books were Star Wars action figures. The largest was a model of Boba Fett, the bounty hunter, and his ship. On the walls were two perfectly aligned posters from the latest movies. In the corner, hanging from fishing line over the desk, was a model of the *Millennium Falcon*.

Gutiérrez arrived first. She came in while I was still staring at the perfection of Baron's room.

"Back here," I yelled when I heard Bascom let her in the front door.

"What's going on?" she called back as she made her way down the hallway. "Wow," she said as soon as she stepped into the boy's room.

"This is Barron's room. He's Bascom's son, and he's missing."

"Missing?"

"Bascom thinks kidnapped," I explained.

"But you don't?"

"I don't."

"Why?"

"Baron is sixteen. Could you live like this at sixteen?"

"I see your point, but…"

"But what?"

"Is that enough?"

"I don't know," I said. "There might be other issues."

"What does that mean?"

"Things I feel more than I know."

"Oh…" The way she said it carried a great deal of judgment in such a small sound.

"Put it together with a room like this, and I see a lot of pressure on a kid."

"Maybe so, but you need to know that Councilman Wood is involved with some powerful people. He's deeply involved with the expansion of the city limits and all the new construction."

"He's involved with the Machado brothers."

"He told you that?"

"Yep."

"Then he's afraid."

"Very."

Gutiérrez shook her head and said, "But you don't think they took his son?"

"What's more likely? Those powerful people kidnapped the boy with no notification and no reason that Bascom understands. Or the kid's not getting along with Dad and just needed some space."

"In that case, why are we here?"

"A kid is missing. You don't ignore that."

Gutiérrez stared at me for a moment like I had grown a second head.

"And no matter how it turns out, it may be the excuse I need to kick some doors."

"I don't get you," she said. "For a moment, I think I do, and then…why are you here? The truth."

"I don't think this is a kidnapping, no matter what Bascom is into." I left her standing in the room.

Bascom was waiting in the hall. "Did you find anything? Clues?" he asked with tempered hope.

"One big one," I answered. "How about if we have some coffee?"

At the kitchen table, we sipped from cups in matching patterns. I noticed that there were no plastic cups or cartoon glasses that most people can't seem to avoid collecting.

"When was your last fight with Baron?" I asked.

"How do you know we fight?"

"Your house is like a temple. Sixteen-year-old boys don't like conforming to anything but their friends. You don't have a lot of rebellion room around here."

"His mother wasn't much of a housekeeper. It was an issue."

"I bet."

Hector came in, and I pointed down the hall to send him to Gutiérrez.

"I wanted Baron to have a good home. A place to always feel safe and welcome," Bascom said.

"Safe I can see. Did he feel especially welcome?"

"It's his home."

"What were the fights about?"

"Everything," he said. The truth of the word and the price of it were on Bascom's face. "His room. His clothes. Friends. He wants a car."

I suddenly regretted all of what I had put my mother through. "What about a girlfriend?"

"No." He shook his head sadly over his coffee cup. "Baron is awkward."

"Awkward? How?"

"He was always…you know…sensitive. I tried to get him to play football. He's big. He could do it."

"He didn't want that?"

"He tried out for the play. He's going to be Hugo in *Bye-Bye Birdie*. Crap like that scares normal girls away. They want a real man."

It could have been the sound of his voice. It might have been that I'd become more sensitive to certain things. Maybe I was already tuned to jump. But hearing Bascom say "real man" in that way made my skin crawl a little.

Gutiérrez appeared in the doorway behind Bascom. "What do you want to do?" she asked.

I knew that question. It was a handoff. I was the chief, and she was placing the burden firmly into my hands.

"Bascom," I said. Gutiérrez instantly frowned at me. A professional would have said "Mr. Wood." I got it but didn't backtrack. "What kind of phone did he have?"

Bascom shook his head.

"What does that mean?" I asked him. "If you don't know, find one of your bills. We can track the phone or at least get records to see if he was making plans with anyone."

He shook his head again. "You were right about fighting. We did all the time. Yesterday it was about his friends and how he acted."

"Acted?" Gutiérrez asked the question.

I was glad it wasn't just me.

"He's sixteen. His friends are geeks. And he thinks he's going to Hollywood to make movies. I wanted him to grow up."

"You wanted him to man up," I said.

"Yes."

Hector was standing behind Gutiérrez then. He was half a head shorter, or maybe that was because he was staring at the floor. I thought he was hearing something that he'd heard in one form or another all his life.

"What about the phone?" I prodded.

"I took it away." Bascom looked up at me. He blinked a couple of times and then turned to include Hector and Gutiérrez. "I thought it would help. Those phones—those kids—they spend all their time in another world. I thought I could toughen him up a little."

"Where is it?" Hector asked.

"In my closet," Bascom answered. "Locked in my gun case."

"Get it," I told him.

As soon as Bascom went from the kitchen, Gutiérrez said, "It won't help. We'll have to get records from the service provider."

"She's right," Hector agreed.

"Why?"

"The phone will be password protected," Hector explained like I was the slow pony in the race. "No sixteen-year-old boy is giving that to his father."

"Here is the phone," Bascom returned to the room and set the blank unit on the table along with an envelope. "And there is the bill. Do whatever you need to do."

I picked the phone up, and the screen lit with an input pad and a blank line labeled Password.

"Excuse me," Bascom murmured. He stepped back out.

Gutiérrez and Hector came in to get a closer look at the phone.

Bascom stopped at the threshold of the kitchen door and turned back. I gave what I hoped was a look of hope and encouragement. He opened his mouth as if about to say something. His eyes were glazed. His posture was slumped and beaten.

"We'll find—" I almost made a promise I didn't know if I could keep. "We'll do our best to find Baron, Mr. Wood."

He nodded, but there wasn't much meaning or energy behind it. "I know who has him," he said.

"I know you think you do. And we'll check it out. We won't leave anything undone until we find your son." I felt a little proud that I was doing the right thing, the cop thing. The fact that I was imitating TV shows didn't bother me.

"My son didn't run away." He nodded at the phone. "You think you'll find something in that?"

"There's a good chance." I pecked at the keypad.

"I'll leave you to it." Bascom nodded. With that he shuffled from view.

What I had typed on the password screen didn't work. I wondered how many chances you got before the phone locked up.

Hector asked me, "Who?" He tilted his head in the direction Bascom had gone.

"He told me the Machado brothers took his son." I fidgeted with the phone as I tried to work through connections in my head. "The guy we kicked out of his trailer mentioned the same name to me. I'm guessing the Machados are the jefés in town.

"This is not something we can get into," Gutiérrez said.

"More hands-off stuff?" I asked. I tapped at the phone's screen again. My first try was Skywalker. The second was DeathStar. I wasn't wrong. I was certain. But I wasn't right yet.

"Out of our jurisdiction. Machado is on the DTO radar. We need to let the feds handle it."

That stopped me. I turned my attention from the phone up to Gutiérrez. She was looking right back at me.

"DTO?" Hector asked.

"There's nothing to handle yet." I pecked the name Boba Fett into the password box. Then I held up the phone to show off the unlocked screen.

"You did it?" Hector sounded disbelieving.

"Tell you what," I said, speaking to Gutiérrez. "Why don't you head back into the office?"

"Why?"

"Just in case things get messy and we have to call on this Machado guy." I looked up and right into her eyes. I wasn't smiling. "Me and Hector will handle things with the kid. I'll call you if we need you." I don't think I could have been clearer.

She must have thought so too.

Gutiérrez straightened. She looked at Hector and then back at me. There were a hundred questions on her face, but she had the sense not to ask them. "Sure," she said. "Whatever you want."

Once we heard the screen door clap closed behind her, Hector asked me, "What was that about?"

"We need to have a talk about Officer Gutiérrez," I told him.

"Why?"

"She's DEA."

TEN

The kitchen was quiet. Neither Hector nor I were talking. He was thinking about Gutiérrez and reconsidering everything he knew about his department, I imagined. I was scrolling through text messages on Baron Wood's phone.

"How do you know?" Hector asked. "About Gutiérrez, I mean. How can you say she's in the DEA? She's been on the Lansdale force over a year."

"When did things start to go all Wild West around here?" I paused on a picture of a teenaged girl making a kissy face that had been sent to Baron. She was pretty. The pair of them had been sending each other a lot of texts and pictures.

"I don't believe it."

"Sure you do," I told him. "You're just not admitting it yet."

"How do you know?"

I held up the phone, showing Hector the picture of the girl. "Her name's Louisa Rey. Know her?"

He looked and took a good long time about it. "No. But that doesn't mean anything. The way people come in and out of those trailers, there could be a hundred kids."

I nodded and walked my fingers one by one through the text messages.

"Tell me about Gutiérrez," Hector said. "She said something that set it in your mind. I saw you looking at her."

I held up a text message. It read,

I'm going off leash. Picnic at the bend?

Louisa answered,

About time. I have wine and all day.

"What's the bend?" I asked.

"It's a long bend in the river where the kids go to hang out and party."

"Let's go."

We didn't get farther than the living room where I had assumed that Bascom Wood was waiting and worrying. He wasn't there. He wasn't anywhere in the house either. I checked each room as Hector looked outside.

"Car's gone," Hector shouted out as I stalked through the short hall.

I glanced in each room. I didn't do it thinking the councilman was hiding. It was a just-in-case exercise and a place-holding action.

"Where can we find these Machado guys?" I shouted the question from the bathroom.

"Probably up at Gun Hills," Hector called back from the front room. When I joined him, he added, "Wood can't be crazy enough to go up there."

"Why?"

"Eladio and Simon Machado, that Gun Hills lodge—all the people around it are cartel."

"Let's go."

"We can't go up there. It's out of city limits. That's county."

"Gutiérrez wants to leave it to feds. You want do drop it on the county sheriff. No wonder things are screwed in this town."

"We have to follow rules."

"I don't. Let's go."

The screen door slapped closed again as we left the perfect house behind.

"Call in," I told Hector once we were in my truck and on the way. "Send a car out to the bend looking for Baron and his girlfriend."

"How do you know?" Hector asked me again when dispatch had a car on the way. "About Gutiérrez and the DEA. You could be wrong."

"Yep," I agreed. "I could be. But she said something that put the stopper in it for me."

"What?"

"You know how people pick up language that lets you peg them. Like when someone says affirmative instead of yes, there's a good chance they're military. You hear a couple of hard guys talking about doing a bullet in the shoe—you know they're cons. Right?"

"Sure. I guess so."

"Gutiérrez said the Machados were on the DTO radar."

"Yeah. I didn't know what that meant."

"A few minutes ago, you said Eladio Machado and the people up at the lodge are cartel."

"What about it"

"People like you and me say 'cartel.' In the DEA they talk about drug-trafficking organizations. DTOs."

Hector nodded and looked like he was thinking it over. "Okay," he said. "It makes sense. But why is DEA putting someone on our force?"

"That's the big question, isn't it?"

I pulled up at the Gun Hills gate. "Which of the Machados is the big dog?"

"Simon is the dog. Eladio does the siccing," Hector answered.

There was one guy in the little shack. At each side of the road beyond the entrance, another man was standing. They were partially hidden under the shade of clustered pinons and oaks. None of the men looked happy to see us. The one closest to the road had a hand inside his jacket.

If I hadn't been dealing with guys like that every day for the last few years, I might have been intimidated. Pointing to the badge on my chest, I told the man in the shack, "Chief Tindall."

"We know who you are," the gatekeeper said. "What do you want?"

"I want to see Eladio Machado."

He sneered. "Who says he wants to see you?" Then he raised his head and shouted over to the two roadside guards, "¡Mira! Este cabrón Policia viene con su verga en la mano para ver a Machado." He said the asshole cop was here with his dick in his hand. They all laughed without mirth. The sound was hard and challenging.

"I imagine that's for him to say, don't you think?" I smiled to let him know I was just thinking of his best interests. Then I pushed the smile farther out on my face and asked, "¿O Usted tienes los bolas para deshacerse de mí? ¿Tal vez usted y sus amigos quieren seguir hablando de mi verga?" My Spanish sucks, but when I asked if he had the balls to get rid of me himself, he understood. Then when I said maybe the two of them would rather keep talking about my dick, he knew he was being insulted.

No one was laughing then. "Hey, cabrón—you know who you're talking to?"

"You're the help, amigo. Don't pretend Machado isn't holding your balls in his pocket."

Discipline in the lower ranks is a great thing. I could push their buttons all day long, and they couldn't do a thing on their own unless I tried to get past. Hector didn't look quite as confident. He was staring straight ahead. Either he was trying to show he wasn't connected to the ass at the wheel, or he was trying to appear unconcerned. What he managed was a creepy disassociation that only drew attention.

"¿Que pasa con tu punk?" the gatekeeper asked. What's with your punk?

"He's sick and pissed-off tired that you haven't picked up the phone and called your jefé." I pulled my phone and held it up for the guard to see. "Maybe I should call him myself. Think he'll be bothered?"

The gatekeeper backed down, slowly. The other two eased back from the road, returning to the shade. The phone conversation was quick and mostly one-sided. The gatekeeper said a cop wanted to come in; then he listened grimly, staring past me while keeping his eye on Hector. Then, with obvious disappointment, he said, "Go up to the main building. Someone will meet you."

I shot him a big screw-you grin.

He whipped his arm, pointing up the road, and shouted, "¡Vamonos! ¡Ahora mismo!"

We rolled past the gate with me still grinning. Then I turned and asked Hector, "What's going on with you?"

He shook his head. If the action was for clearing or meaning, I couldn't tell. Then he said, "Sometimes I think I was born in the wrong place. Maybe just the wrong culture."

"What are you getting at?"

"That macho crap. You sling it as easy and ready as they do. Paris fit in too. He could wear machismo like a disguise. No one ever thought he wasn't one of the guys."

"And you?"

Another headshake. That time I took it as clearing. Like shaking away the image on an Etch-a-Sketch. "I never fit in."

We pulled slowly into a long sweeping curve of impossibly smooth asphalt. It followed the landscaping around outcroppings of rock and groupings of mesquite and alligator junipers so we got a tour of the grounds before ever seeing the buildings. I had the feeling that Hector didn't want to continue that conversation. Just to change the subject, I asked, "So what do you know about these guys?"

"Drugs, guns, whores, and the worst kinds of violence you can imagine. These are the guys the other families are afraid of."

"Afraid? To me, fear never seemed to play a big part in these guys' lives."

"That's business. La Familia de los Muerto is almost like a religion. They worship murder. Everything else just pays the bills."

I took my foot off the gas and froze. We rolled into the last straight shot up the hill before the main building and crawled to a stop. Behind my rigid face, I cursed myself for an idiot and a fool. All around me were hints and connections that I hadn't had sense enough to catch. I had patted myself on the back hard enough for figuring out a kid's phone password. It had never occurred to me when Darian Stackhouse mentioned La Familia de los Muerto that they were here.

"Why'd you stop?"

"Because I'm an asshole," I replied. "I not only don't know what I've gotten into; I actually thought I was hiding."

"I don't understand."

"I don't either." I pressed the gas pedal, taking my time approaching the hacienda-style building. Three armed men waited at the door.

"You should wait here," I told Hector.

"That's not a good idea."

I shoved the lever over into park but left the engine idling.

The men watching us had automatic weapons. The guns were slung and hanging loose. There was nothing reassuring about their casual stances. They and their weapons were ready.

"Probably not," I said, without looking at Hector. "There's not a lot about this that's been a good idea."

"Yeah. But we're in it together now."

"No, we're not. Because you don't even know what you're in."

"Maybe you should tell me."

"Not the time." I pushed the door open. "Get behind the wheel. If someone comes and tells you to leave, don't argue, and don't ask questions."

"Why would that happen?"

"That's a question." I tried to look confident—like maybe I was joking. I don't think I pulled it off. "If I don't come out, you can keep my truck."

"You're freaking me out a little bit here."

I closed the door and spoke through the open window. "Might be good to be a bit on edge."

"You think it's that bad?"

"I don't know. Probably not. But—"

"What?"

"Nothing. This is my fuck-up. I'll do my best to keep you out of it."

Hector had more to say. I didn't give him the chance. When I started walking, the man beside the door opened it and then went through to wait on me. One of the men who still waited outside the door nodded and said, "Chief Tindall." He had a Texas accent, not Mexican. "I'm Joaquin. Please come inside."

I couldn't help thinking, "Hell has a doorman." But I went through. The gunman followed, and Joaquin came last.

We went down a long entryway that looked like it was made for a rustic Gatsby with a cowboy fixation. At the end was a pair of french doors. The leading man took up a station to the right. One of the men behind me took the left, and the one called Joaquin stayed at my back.

Someone stepped up behind the glass and opened the doors. It was the same man who had braced me at the bar. He had the kind of vicious smirk you see on mean kids caught torturing insects. His hands were still bandaged and swollen.

I don't know why, but I glanced at the door handles. They were levers, not knobs. It struck me as a bit funny. Lucky for him. Thinking of him trying to twist a regular doorknob made me feel a little better. No matter what happened to me, I'd always have the pleasure of knowing I messed this guy's life up.

"Voy a quitar esa sonrisa de tu cara y meterla en por el culo." He told me he was going to take the smile off my face and stick it in my ass. His voice was low and rough. It was a movie-villain kind of snarl.

That made me feel even better. If they knew who I was or had plans for me, there wouldn't be foreplay. That didn't mean that they wouldn't figure it out. For now, though, I was just another cop.

"Good luck with that," I said. Then I asked, "Dime, ¿cómo te limpias el culo con esas manos bonitas?" How do you clean your ass with those pretty hands?

"Chingar su madre." He pushed in close and held my eye, trying to make me back down. I'd never give him the satisfaction.

"Álvaro—" Joaquin warned him.

"Sí, Álvaro," I said, keeping my gaze locked with his. "Escúchalo." I told him to listen just as you would to an unruly child.

He broke first, glancing over my shoulder at Joaquin before telling me, "Your gun. Hand it over."

"No." Refusing wasn't something I thought through. If I had, I probably would have turned it over. Once I said it, though, I wasn't backtracking.

Álvaro held out a bandaged hand and waggled it at me. His fingers didn't move.

"No," I said again.

"You're not going in armed. Estúpido chingadera." He was right; I was a stupid fucker.

"I'm here in an official capacity. As a courtesy. Not on my knees asking for money. You can pass that along, and I can talk to the boss, or I'll be going. Either way, I won't be disarmed by you. Puta." I put as much of my own sneer as I could into the last word calling him a bitch.

Even with his broken hands, I think he was ready to throw a punch. It didn't get that far.

"Álvaro!" That time it was someone else shouting at him. I couldn't see the man, but the voice gave me a chill. "Envíalo en," it said: send him in. Sounds and voices connect with events in such a way that they can call back not just memory but all the feeling of a moment. The last time I had heard that voice, I had been certain I was going to die. It had said, "Hacerle desaparecer." Make him disappear. Then fireworks had gone off in my head, and I had woken in the back seat of a car on my way to dig my own grave.

I don't know how my face looked. Álvaro's face looked like that of a boy interrupted while torturing insects—concerned about being caught but hopeful to get back to his activity soon. He gestured with his mummy hands, indicating that I should go into the room.

Three steps inside and I was face to face with the same man who had sent me to die in the desert. I looked behind me to see if anyone was waiting to crack my skull and bag me up again. Álvaro remained by the door. That didn't calm my fear.

"You are the new sheriff," the thin man said.

My heart shuddered on the next beat. I had expected— I didn't know what I expected. Casual chat wasn't what I was afraid of; that was certain. I was relived he didn't offer a hand to shake. I doubted that I could have handled that.

"Chief," I said. The word was reaction more than response. There was a vapor lock in my brain, and I was grabbing at any clear thought.

He raised a questioning eyebrow.

"I'm the chief of police in Lansdale. Sheriff is an elected county position."

"But we are not in Lansdale."

That was true. And I'm sure it was something that should have made a difference to me. It didn't. But I didn't have an answer to the statement either. "You're Eladio Machado," I said instead.

He raised his head and looked down a bent nose at me like he was working on a memory. Eladio Machado was a skeleton of a man. Everything but that broken and badly set nose was emaciated looking. The eye sockets above his nose were hollow. The orbs themselves were dark—not just shaded. The darkness was within them. His sclera was shot through with red. His brown irises were more shadow floating on blood.

"Have we met?"

Every hair on my body stood in a creeping march from the bottom of my spine up the back of my neck. The sensation became a tingling like crawling ants in my scalp. "No," I lied.

Machado raised a bony finger and asked, "Are you sure?" When he ticked the air, his hand moved, but the ill-fitting suit he wore barely twitched. He was rattling in his own clothes. You look like someone…"

"I have—had—a brother who did business with families in Mexico."

"Of course," he said, nodding. His gaze didn't let me off the hook.

There was a liquid sloshing sound, and ice clacked in a glass. I turned.

We weren't alone. Sitting on a white leather couch was the same fancy-dressed man I had first seen with Bascom Wood. He was sipping from a highball glass and rattling it noisily. This time he was wearing a western suit in gray with a shirt and bandana in purple. His boots were lizard or snakeskin with long pointed toes. He was making a point of being noticed. At the same time, he refrained from noticing me or even Machado.

"You see," Eladio said. "I have a brother as well. Perhaps you have met Simon. He takes care of many family interests in the Lansdale community."

Simon continued to ignore me, and I decided to do the same. "Do you know Bascom Wood?" I asked Eladio. "He may be on his way here."

"Why would the councilman come here?"

"He seems to think that you have something to do with the disappearance of his son."

Eladio nodded again with his head up and looking down his nose. He didn't appear surprised at all.

"Are you here to investigate his claim?"

"I'm here hoping to keep him from kicking the wrong box of bees."

That time he lowered his face and looked at me straight on. The corner of his mouth curled up in a cruel smirk.

"I think the kid is playing hooky," I explained. "I don't want Wood to get hurt for his worry."

Ice rattled. No one said anything.

I turned to leave.

Before I made it to the door, Eladio said, "Chief."

Álvaro put his wrapped right hand up to my chest. I slapped it away.

He didn't scream. But he wanted to.

I turned around.

"I'm certain I remember your brother now."

I pushed past Álvaro, who was still clutching his hand under his arm. No one stopped me or said anything as I headed to the truck.

Hector was waiting behind the wheel with the engine still idling. Without quite running, I crossed in front and got into the passenger seat.

"Go," I told him.

"What happened?"

"Just go."

He dropped the truck into drive, and we looped around a fountain and headed back the way we had come.

We didn't talk as we cruised down the mirror-flat blacktop that carried us back to the gate. I didn't talk, anyway. And I didn't hear Hector if he did. I was rattled and scared and thinking that I was nowhere near as tough as I pretended to be.

When we reached the gate, it was standing open. The gate-keeper grinned and waved as we passed.

Where the club road gave way to county asphalt, there was a bump and change in quality of construction. From there it was just a few miles into town. Considering that Hector had picked up on my mood and pushed the truck well past the posted limit, it should have been a quick trip. It wasn't.

Behind us, a black SUV with government plates came up dangerously fast.

Hector tromped the gas, and the truck downshifted into a burst of new speed. It was wasted effort. Ahead of us, another SUV, this one not new or shiny and bearing no plates, pulled out, taking up the center of the road.

We were forced to a stop.

"Wait here," I told Hector.

"Again?"

I didn't answer. I got out of the truck and walked back to wait at the bumper. Darian Stackhouse got out of the rear SUV.

"Tindall," he hollered over as he slammed the driver's side door. As he approached, he said, "You're a major pain in my ass."

"Try to imagine the disappointment I feel knowing that."

"Tell me what the hell you were doing up at the club."

I put my elbows up on the bed of the truck and leaned on them like I might if I was puzzling through a big question. "I want to know the truth about what you have going on here. What are you hiding?"

"I'm not hiding shit. You know what I am? I'm a lid on a pot. I'm trying to keep everything inside and cooking just right. You get me? The stew or the soup or whatever is inside the pot is hot and almost boiling. I'm there to keep it from boiling over or cooking too slow."

"You're a lid?"

"I'm a fucking lid. And you're one more flame under the pot I just don't need."

"How about if you try being a cop?"

He squared his shoulders. I noticed his fists were clenched. "If you had a goddamned clue, you would shut your mouth," he finally said.

"I can testify."

"Testify to fucking what?" He took a step away from me. "Are you going to drag your half-brother into this? Because Longview Moody was a piece of work himself. I can toss out anything you got from him."

"I can testify to direct knowledge of Simon Machado ordering murder."

"We're the DEA."

"I can take you to four bodies. Two were murdered by the Machados. Two were men who worked for them. One of the men working for the family carried a DEA shield."

"That's exactly the kind of crap I'm holding inside the pot."

"And I can give inside knowledge about the organization, especially the flow of cash across the border."

"Longview again?" Stackhouse walked back like he could distance himself from what I was saying. Standing directly behind the truck, he looked it over like he'd never seen a Ford before. "Your brother was as worthless as the people he served. The only service he ever did the world was getting himself killed."

I stretched my arms, leaning back from the top rail of the truck bed. "Are you protecting the people who killed my brother?"

Stackhouse placed his hand on the weapon at his hip.

There was a slight change in the idle of the truck. I didn't hear it. I could only feel it through my hands resting on the metal box of the bed. Hector was watching everything through the rearview mirrors. I was sure he couldn't hear us, but he knew something was going on.

"Whatever you have in that pot is going to burn," I said. "And it's going to take the whole house with it. I'll make sure of it."

"You're not going to make sure of shit." Stackhouse pulled his weapon and brought it to bear on me. "Some things are bigger—more important than your bastard brother."

The idle of the truck changed again as Hector popped the gear selector from neutral to reverse. Stackhouse was struck above the knee by the bumper, and the top of the tailgate hit under his left arm. He went down hard. His automatic cartwheeled in a high arc before bouncing to a grinding stop on the road.

As if the next moment had been choreographed, all the doors of the waiting SUVs opened to spill more men with guns. They aimed at me, but I was already standing over Stackhouse with my .45 angled down at his heart.

ELEVEN

As I stood over Stackhouse, who was groaning on the cracked and grayed asphalt, two patrol cars pulled up ahead of the lead SUV. They blooped their sirens and put on their light bars. Gutiérrez stepped out of the first car with a shotgun. Other officers I didn't yet know came from the other doors. They were all armed.

I made a mental note to learn the names of every police officer on the Lansdale force and to buy them all a beer.

The truck door opened, and Hector shouted, "You all right?"

"Yeah," I answered. "Stay there. We're going to want to go quick when we go."

He climbed back into the cab.

For the sake of the watching DEA agents, I lifted and then holstered my weapon. They relaxed but didn't disarm. Not that I expected them to.

Kneeling beside Agent Stackhouse, I pushed his head to the side with one finger. He had a growing lump and road rash above the ear. "You're going to need that looked at," I told him.

He moaned but said nothing more.

"We need to talk again," I said like I was chatting with an old friend. "To make sure we do—" I lifted the gold shield from where it was tucked between his body and the road. For a second I examined it. Then I pulled at the chain holding it around his neck.

Agent Stackhouse hissed his pain as the wound on his head grated on the blacktop and the chain broke.

"You can come get this from me anytime. As long as you ask politely."

I took my prize and climbed back into the truck. "Come get your man," I shouted to the glaring agents. To Hector, I said, "Let's get back to town."

He hit the gas hard. We shot across the road and onto the dirt shoulder, where we passed around the cruisers. They followed with their lights on all the way back to the station.

* * * *

I was seated behind my desk with the office door locked before I took a genuine breath. We had hardly talked on the drive back to the station. Hector did manage to communicate how he'd texted Gutiérrez, and she had come to back us up. That wasn't the only news. Baron Wood and his girlfriend had been found alive and well and only partially dressed in the waters of the Rio Grande. They had indeed been picnicking. His father was still missing.

As I sat with my feet up, I fiddled with Stackhouse's badge. Taking it was one of those impulse things. It was like counting coup on an enemy. Sometimes you just needed to let them know that the ground under their feet was not as steady as they thought.

Now I had it, though, what to do with it?

I locked it away in a desk drawer, amazed at the idea of having a desk, let alone one that had a lock on it. That was part of the problem, though, wasn't it? I had the toys and the tools but not the experience to know the difference between them.

Once the badge was secured, I puzzled together the pieces of my phone and waited.

Nothing happened.

I couldn't tell if that was a relief or a worry. For over an hour, it sat there silently, daring me to pick it up and make the call myself. I didn't. I was afraid that like Stackhouse had said, things were bigger than me. That wasn't true. Things had been bigger than me, and I'd been aware of our relative importance, many times. I'd just never cared before.

When the phone finally rang, I let it wait through three rings and then picked up.

"Yeah?"

"The fuck, Paris?"

"Good to hear from you too, Milo."

"Screw that. Just what do you think you're doing?"

"To tell the truth..." I took a breath. "I'm doing the best I can."

Milo took a breath too. "Yeah. Look, I understand it's not easy. But you can make it easier by keeping this phone on and staying in contact."

"I can't do anything with you calling me all the time."

"I wouldn't call you every goddamned hour if you ever once picked up when you should. Or call me. Is that too professional for you? We don't need a rugged cowboy out on the lonesome prairie; we need a cop."

"That's the thing—" I stopped. I didn't mean to or want to, but I did. It would have been easy to admit that I wasn't a cop. I'd tried to come clean with Stackhouse. But that had been more about the end result. Trading truth for justice against the Machados. I didn't have reason to believe that the DOJ would do more than the DEA. Even worse, I'd be an embarrassment to Milo and whoever his bosses were. They would work hard to bury me and everything I touched.

I didn't go on.

"What?" Milo made the question both a demand and a challenge. "What's the thing, Paris?"

"Desert," I said.

"What's that mean?"

"We're in the desert here. The prairie is way north."

"Tell you what, big boy," he said, sounding deadly serious. "Why don't you fold your geography lesson up until it's all corners and cactus and then stick it up your ass?"

"I don't know what I'm doing here," I admitted. "Everything is a mess, and all the ends seem to tie La Familia de los Muerto to some DEA—"

"Screw the DEA," Milo butted in. "And damn sure screw the family...whatever thing. You're there for the money and the dirty department. You're there to find the link between the cops, city officials, and all the disappeared grant money. And a big part of that is being there to pick up the phone when I call. Now are you going to do the job, or are we going to have to make changes?"

"Relax, Milo. I know what I need to do now, and I'm on it."

"Anything you want to share?"

"Not yet." I wasn't lying. When Milo mentioned disappeared grant money, it was the confirmation I needed that I was on the right side of the street. The problem was he seemed to think it was a town problem. I took a deep breath and let it out slowly. Milo could probably hear me, but I didn't mind if he knew I was being careful. "Will you listen to something you don't want to hear?"

Even when he was silent, I could hear him cursing me. In the end, though, he said, "Tell me."

I gave him a short version of what had gone on that day. I included Stackhouse and his crew. I even told him about the offer I had made. I didn't tell him how I had the information I tried to serve up on the Machado brothers.

"Let me get it all straight," he said. His voice was uncharacteristically even. "You believe there's a connection between your investigation, a drug cartel, and rogue DEA. And your first move was to run over a federal agent and steal his badge?"

"Well, when you say it like that, anything is going to sound bad."

"Someday you're going to have to tell me the story of how you ever got to be a cop."

"It's a good one," I said. "You'll get a kick out of it."

"No. I don't think I will," Milo answered.

"Would you do something for me?"

"What?"

"Can you run some names for me? Look for connections."

"Run your own names. Investigation is your job."

"You can go deeper than I can. And I'm not sure of the security of the system here."

"Why? What's wrong?"

"Nothing." I thought about that, and then I said, "That's part of the problem. This town lost the chief of police, and then the replacement was killed. The mayor is dead. And things just keep right on going."

"You think the people in charge are not the actual people in charge?"

"Something like that," I answered. "And most of the names I'm looking at are cops."

"What are the names?"

It was a long list. I gave him Bascom Wood and the Machado brothers. Then I went through the cops: Mark Walker, Bronwyn Gutiérrez, Darian Stackhouse.

"Anyone else?" he asked.

"Buick Tindall."

There was a beat of silence from the other end, and then Milo said, "I'll get back to you. And you have that phone on." He disconnected with his usual abrupt charm.

If I had taken a moment to think, it would have turned into hours of worry and brooding. I was lucky I had the thought to call the funeral home about Paris's—Longview's—body. It turned out that the DNA was a match, and no one questioned which of Buick's sons was dead. The funeral director told me the body had been released, and they had Paris onsite. The funeral could be scheduled at my convenience. It led me to ask a question I swore that I wouldn't. "Has Buick Tindall been in to ask about the arrangements?" There was a long silence from the other end. Before it could be broken by an apology I didn't need, I said, "Never mind."

There was another silence. I didn't know how to fill that one. Before I had to try, the man on the other end asked me about clothes.

It was something I'd never considered. I had an instant solution though.

"A man—*a friend*—will be there tomorrow. His name is Hector Alazraqui. From now on, he will be responsible for everything about the funeral."

I got off the phone and checked the papers littering my desk. Sure enough, one was the vacation schedule I'd asked for. I put Hector down for a week's vacation starting the next day. With the paper in hand, I wandered out to the main office looking for Gutiérrez.

She wasn't in the office. I checked with the dispatcher. She was the same black officer who had given me that quiet ride.

"Officer Gutiérrez is not scheduled on until three," she told me. "But you called her and Officer Alazraqui in this morning." She didn't say more about it, but the message seemed to be that I was messing with schedules.

"What's your name?" I asked. I had been told the first day but hadn't paid real attention.

"Sunny Johnson," she answered.

How could I not smile? She was a black woman who was both slim and challenged in stature. I could see why she was working the desk.

"Have I been making your life harder, Officer Johnson?"

"You have, Chief."

No smile. She wasn't joking, and she wasn't letting me off the hook just because I asked the question.

"You're full-time dispatch, aren't you?"

She nodded.

"How do you feel about that?"

"It is what it is."

"Fair enough. Would you change it if you could?"

She nodded again and then added, "Some people don't think I belong off the desk because of my size."

"We're not those people, are we, Officer Johnson?"

"No, sir." She smiled that time.

I handed her the vacation form. "Give Hector a call, and tell him about this vacation. You can take his patrol shifts while he's gone, but I want you to make a workable schedule to keep someone on dispatch. Can you handle that?"

"Yes, sir."

I felt like I'd made a friend, and a realization slowly settled on me. I had more cop friends than crook.

"I need a drink," I said. Then I thought about it and added, "I really need a drink. So, Officer Sunny. Sunny smile and sunny disposition. Where should I go?"

"Are you flirting with me, Chief?" She didn't look angry. She wasn't smiling though.

"When I flirt with you, you'll know it." I grinned to show how charming I was.

"Because that wouldn't be right." Her face was open. The brown sparkle of her eyes was centered on mine. "And it would make my life harder."

I deflated. Being a professional was not an easy transition to make. "No," I agreed. "No, I'm not flirting," I lied. "I'm just…"

Officer Sunny saved me from further embarrassment by asking, "Where can you go, or where should you go?"

"What?"

"You said you needed a drink. Then you asked where you should go."

"Yeah."

"Well—" She hesitated; then the decision showed in her eyes. "You've been here almost a week. I'd bet you hardly know a thing about your department."

"Go on," I encouraged, keeping my gaze square on hers.

"If you want a quiet beer, go to Ernesto's."

"Ernesto's."

"It's the taqueria where you got into the fight."

"I remember. But if I want a little eye opening with my beer?"

"Go to the Border Crossing."

I must have looked a little blank. A lot blank maybe.

"The Border Crossing is that place out on the edge of town," she explained. "By the new bank."

I had seen the place that first night I had come to town. It was basically a shack with trailers out back, cribs for the working girls.

The blank look on my face must have filled in because Sunny said, "Yeah. That place."

* * * *

The Border Crossing was busy even in the middle of the day. Outside the sprawling, tin-roof joint was a dirt parking lot. That lot was filled with big rigs, bikes, and rattletrap pickup trucks. Inside, it was dark and loud. What light there was had a decidedly red cast to it from the miles of red neon beer signs covering the walls. The few spaces left free of beer lighting were filled with paintings of women with big hips and breasts that were both unreasonably large and impossibly high. Because they were painted on black velvet, the women seemed to float in the red atmosphere.

I half expected a Wild West moment where everyone fell silent and turned to look when I walked into the room. That didn't happen. Nothing happened. No one noticed or cared that I had walked in through the thick green door. The steel mesh bolted over the window was a nice touch.

To one side was a cluster of stand around tables. To the other were pool tables surrounded by salvaged church pews. Past the games was an even darker area full of tables and chairs filled by men and trafficked through by Mexican women bearing trays of beer. On a small stage, there was a girl. Pale skinned and bony, she was grinding against a brass pole with the kind of expression usually reserved for toilet plunging.

"What are you doing here?"

I turned toward the question to find Gutiérrez glaring at me. "Maybe I should ask you the same thing."

She tossed up her hands and shook her head. It made me feel the same way I had when impatient teachers tried to get me to understand algebra by jabbing fingers at equations and then moving on to better students.

Gutiérrez walked off, and I looked around. My eyes were adjusted to the darkness by then, and I was able to get some of the finer details. One of those details was an overstuffed seersucker suit. Detective Mark Walker was sitting close to the stage, watching the skinny girl hump the pole.

"Get over here," Gutiérrez called from the bar.

"Is this what you do with your time off?" I asked as I took the stool beside her. Removing my straw hat, I sat it on the bar with the crown down. I needed to keep all the luck I had.

"What are you doing here?"

"Homework."

Gutiérrez looked like she was considering that. She took a sip of beer from a bottle and asked, "So, school's in session. What have you learned?"

"Walker is here when he's supposed to be on the clock."

"Obvious. What else?"

"Those two guys playing pool." I tilted my chin at the pair of big men with tattoos and long hair. They were not looking our way and being careful about it.

"What about them?"

"They're DEA. Part of Stackhouse's crew."

"You've seen them before?"

"They may have been on the road today." The bartender put an open bottle in front of me and then moved on. "But that's not why I make them."

"Okay..."

"They look like cops."

"What do cops look like?"

"Mostly like smug thugs. Like they have a right."

"What right?"

"All of them. Cops like rules that everyone else has to follow. Order. Those guys have tattoos that only show if their sleeves are rolled. They have ankle holsters, and they haven't looked over here once."

She shoved my beer over closer to me and took another drink from hers. "Why should they look over here? Are you that interesting?"

"Nope. But you are."

"I'm not sure if that's a compliment."

I shrugged. "I'm not as good at complimenting women as I thought I was."

"A man should know his limitations. What else?"

"I'd bet a nickel that most of the other men in here work for the Machados."

"Most of the men in town work for him one way or another."

"Yeah, I get that. These guys are a little more directly involved."

"How do you know?"

"You, me, Walker—all local cops. The pair of feds. If I can make them, anyone else can. That's five cops in here."

"If you say so."

"Five cops. No one cares. They're all protected."

She took another drink with her eyes open and gaze fixed on me. When the bottle was empty, she said, "Maybe you're just a little sharper than I was giving you credit for."

"Even a broken clock…" I said, toying with my sweating beer bottle. "How many sides are at play here?"

She was no longer looking at me. She had turned to look at the mirror in the bar back. I couldn't tell if she was inspecting her reflection or the condition of the glassware. I did notice that there was good reason to take your beer from the bottle at the Border Crossing.

"Just when I think you might have a little edge, you turn into a big blunt hammer again."

I slid my untouched bottle over to her hands. "What I lack in subtlety I make up for in other things."

She took the beer. "What things?"

"I was hoping you wouldn't ask."

She took a drink.

"You didn't answer my question," I said as she sucked down a long drink of pale lager.

"Getting sharp again," she said, setting the bottle down and keeping her eyes forward.

"Sides," I said. "And who plays for which team?"

Gutiérrez raised the beer again stopping before it got to her lips. "That could be a fluid situation," she said. Then she pursed her lips and pressed the bottle to them.

Off to the side and beyond the bar, I caught some movement. Detective Walker was standing at a table talking with a group of Hispanic men. I'd seen one of them at the gun club. Joaquin. The doorman who'd let me in. They looked a lot closer than one would expect.

I left Gutiérrez with her beer and her reflection.

"Detective Walker." I didn't quite shout it across the room.

He lost his smile quick. "Chief?" Walker asked.

Joaquin didn't even turn to look at me.

"Walker." I made sure to sound happy to see him. "Great work you've been doing."

"What?"

"All the information you've been gathering."

"Chief…" Walker had a little warning in his voice. "I'm just—"

"Don't explain. I don't need to know why you're here. Are these the men you told me about?"

Joaquin looked at me. Then he looked away. The three other men at the table never even glanced up. They tried hard to act like I was invisible. The guy on the end was the most nervous. He looked familiar too. At first I couldn't place him, but it occurred to me that I'd only ever seen him from behind. There was no way to be sure, but I thought he might be the guy who had kicked in the motel door two nights ago.

Walker was outright scared. "No," he said. "I mean there aren't—what are you talking about?"

"Don't worry. It's just between us chickens." I laughed, but no one joined in. Then I pointed to Joaquin. "Is he your informant?" I shifted my finger to the man on the end. "Is that the guy from the motel?"

Walker went a little pale. All the men at the table leaned away from each other, adding a tiny bit of distance between everyone. The doorman scooted back in his chair as if to rise.

"Stay where you are, Joaquin," I said. I wasn't laughing anymore. Then I turned to Walker and tossed my arm around his shoulders. "Come here with me. I want to introduce you to a couple of our friends in the DEA." I dragged him to the pool tables.

The bar was very quiet as we walked the few steps over. The two feds were leaning on their cues staring bullets at us—at me.

"What kind of crap are you trying to pull?" the bigger one asked.

"Tell me something," I said. "You ever been fishing for sharks?"

"You've gone fucking crazy," the smaller one said.

"No. I'm just fishing. And if you want to catch sharks, you gotta get some blood in the water."

I turned toward the bar and looked straight at Gutiérrez. Her beer bottle was empty again. "Ain't that right?" I hollered.

She didn't reply. She didn't even look.

The big fed pointed at me with his cue and said, "I don't know what kind of game you're playing here—"

"Game?" I cut him off loud and clear. "Yeah. Speaking of games—which one of you was in on that game down in Juarez?"

The change in their faces was instant.

"That was some bad action down there." I checked to make sure the table of Machado's guys was listening. They were. "But I hear someone got away with a load of cash."

The feds were split. They wanted to go at me with their pool cues, but they were afraid to take their attention away from the four men at the table.

I turned to Walker and told him, "Get out of here. It probably wouldn't be wise to come back to this place. In fact, if I don't see you again, you can consider your resignation accepted."

He left without looking back.

I walked across the room. Even the gloom seemed to be holding its breath. When I got to the bar, I picked up my hat and set it in place. Then, to Gutiérrez, I said, "Now, that's what a hammer does."

TWELVE

I didn't go back to the station. I didn't go home either.
Without a plan or destination in mind, I twisted the wheel and hit the truck's gas pedal. It responded with a surge of speed that shot me out of the gravel lot and onto asphalt headed out of town. I passed the entrance to the gun club and kept going until I was well into Big Bend National Park.

Main roads were not what I needed. The first unpaved cross road I came to, I took. It reminded me of the dirt track I had traveled that night I escaped my grave. That was a thought I tried hard not to linger on.

The trail took me into a spit of desert that drooped as if melted into a ravine that spread into a tiny valley. In the sheltered walls, water collected when it did rain. Mesquite and junipers grew in clumps. Along the path of drainage was a line of pecan trees.

When the road petered out over the slope, I stopped and let the truck rest. Metal ticked under the settling dust. An idea was already forming in my head that could tie some questions together. But thoughts as hard and black as mine were didn't give much peace. I was feeling worse, not better. Everything was a nagging grievance: my outlook and attitude, the pain in my spine, and the taste in my mouth. The day was ugly and bad. It needed an ending that didn't suck quite so hard.

With a last glance, I left the little valley behind me. At a roadside joint that was both restaurant and gas station, I picked up a heaping box of fried chicken. To that I added a tub of black-eyed peas, mashed potatoes with a steaming quart of gravy, cornbread, and a six of Victoria. It wasn't until I was about to leave that I noticed a galvanized trough full of ice and Big Stripe watermelons. How could I resist? Good food, home food, was one of those things that could raise any spirit.

On the way back to the Desert Drop Inn, I called Officer Sunny. I asked her to make a general radio call putting everyone on notice that the Border Crossing bar was off limits to all officers.

She told me, with remarkable patience, that we didn't use the radio for such things. Then she said, "I guess you're learning a thing or two."

"Yeah, a thing or two," I answered. "Put it out anyway. And type it up to hang on the bulletin board too."

"A staff meeting might be a good idea," she said. I appreciated that she didn't make me feel like an idiot about it.

"What do you think, once a week?" I asked.

"Monthly has always been enough."

"I buy that. Thank you, Officer Johnson."

"Thank you, Chief."

I hung up feeling a tiny bit better about my job.

The day was slipping into amber when I got to the motel. Another magic hour in south Texas. Who would have ever thought barren could look as beautiful as it did? I laid out my feast on a couple of the pool's umbrella tables.

While I worked, a car pulled off the road and into the lot to park beside my truck. Hector got out.

Hector stood on the other side. "I got your message about vacation. What's that about?"

"I'd like you to do something for me."

Hector leaned over to get a look. "Having a party?"

"You want some chicken?" I asked him.

"What do you want me to do?"

"Paris's body is at the funeral home."

Hector stiffened his back and set his gaze on my eyes through the galvanized wire diamonds of the fence.

"I want you to go."

He dropped his eyes to the ground and started to say something.

Before he could speak, I added, "I want—need you to take care of it for me. I can't go. The funeral director is expecting you. Paris needs a suit. He needs you to be there."

"I don't know," he said, still evading my gaze.

"Why?"

"I don't know how he felt."

"You mean—"

"About me. We didn't talk about feelings. Maybe…maybe I was projecting my hopes more than reading his."

"I don't know what to tell you about that. I can say don't worry about doing it for him. Or me. Do it for you—for how you feel."

"Maybe." He looked up to meet my eyes.

"Tell me something."

Hector nodded over at the table. "Give me a beer."

I fetched two bottles and opened them both, tossing the caps away.

"How you met Paris."

"About two years ago. He said he was in Lansdale on Ranger business checking on something."

"Did he say what?"

"No. But it had something to do with the other one."

"What do you mean?"

"There was another Ranger. Old school—you know the kind. He was here a lot around then. Kept meeting with Chief Wilcox."

"Why do you say Paris was here about him?"

"Timing mostly. The old Ranger would show up. Paris would be here soon after. That and the fact that Paris wouldn't talk about it. Not at all. But you could tell how bothered he was about it."

"Wilcox was the old chief, right? Everything started with him."

Hector shrugged and took a drink of his beer. "We found him shot in the head with his car still idling down by the river. Whatever he started, it finished the heck out of him."

"Tell me about the replacement chief."

"What's to tell? He was here a month, and he turned up dead."

"By the river again?"

Hector shook his head and used his bottle to point off into the coloring west. "Out in Big Bend. But otherwise the same. Bullet. Head. Parked vehicle."

"You know about the money?"

"What money?"

"Grants. Homeland security, border protection, economic development—anything like that."

Hector upended his beer and swallowed the last of it. Then he tossed the empty at a trashcan like shooting a free throw. He made the point. "Over my pay grade," he said. "I'm going. I need to see him."

"I'm glad to hear it." I dug into my pocket and pulled out a wad of cash. "Here. This is for a suit. Anything else that comes up."

"Are you sure—"

"I am."

He shoved the money in his pocket without looking.

I thought he was going to say something else. He didn't. Hector went to his car and left. I remained alone by the pool for a while with too much food and too little beer.

After a bit, a family, a man, his wife, and their little boy came from one of the rooms to the pool. Nothing like a four-year-old determined to have fun to pull the chill out of one's thoughts. I sliced up the watermelon, and they helped me polish it off. By then the evening had become night.

The family left me. I stayed by the pool watching stars and then turned out, drifting off to sleep.

I woke in the metal chair with a crick in my neck. On the table beside me was a burning candle within a glass cylinder. On it was painted the image of La Virgincita. Sitting beside it was the last beer.

After I'd twisted off the bottle top, I took a quick swallow and continued what seemed to be the natural next step: stripping. There was no thought behind it, like the moment was a continuation of a lost dream, a dream in which being naked in a lonely, dark world was the most normal thing possible. Once bare I dropped into the water.

Just like the beer, still in my hand, the water was blood warm. Sitting in the chlorinated bath reminded me of being back in my grave. I would have climbed right back out, but Lenore stood at the gate watching me. She held a sixer of cans cold enough to be misting.

"This is my favorite time of the day," she said, kicking off her sandals.

"Night?"

"Hot night." She pulled a can from the rings and opened it. Lenore tossed her hair and put the cold can against her skin, just below her throat. She kept it there, riding her breaths, as she unbuttoned the shirt with her free hand.

"The heat of the day is not yet spent on the stars," she said. "Night, desert night, is hot early, cold later. Life and death. There is no fighting it. But we can love the heat while it lasts."

When she shrugged the garment off, her skin came alive. It was as if she had been painted with magic pigments that showed only under starlight and ice. With the can still pressed to the hard bone of her chest, she made sure my eyes were watching. Then she trailed the dripping can lower, between her breasts, and began rolling it side to side. To her left, it watered the flower tattooed on her skin. To the right, it rode over and then rested on her nipple.

"You want a taste." It wasn't a question. Nor was it a statement. It was almost a command. With her left hand, she cupped her right breast. With her right hand, she tilted the can's mouth over her thick, puckered nipple. She bathed it in frigid beer.

I was ready to climb from the pool to taste it all, the froth of beer, her skin, her mouth. Lenore beat me to the moment.

She came to the edge of the pool and knelt. She dropped the can as she reclined on the rough concrete, extending one arm over her head and offering her breast with the other. When my mouth found her skin, I think we were both somehow swallowed.

I tossed an arm over her bare waist and pressed my face to her. I suckled like I was starving and she was Rose of Sharon. My teeth raked, and my tongue caressed, urging the warmth of her body to melt into me.

Lenore put her arms around my head and pulled. She was forcing herself into my mouth like she could disappear if only I found the right way to swallow her. We were so tightly bonded that for a moment we were one creature, the snake eating its own tail.

Her chest shook, and sounds, indistinct but meaningful, were communicated through our bones.

Sucking her nipple, I worked it into my teeth and bit.

Lenore pulled her embrace tighter and that time moaned at the contact. Then, like a distant echo of the sound, she whispered, "Yes."

She rolled to me, and I pulled. Wrapped up with me, she tumbled over and carried us both into the depths of the shining water.

We broke apart. The distance was an instant of clarity. And for some reason I could see her better underwater and lit by pool lights than I could when she stood before me under stars and neon. In the water the bats inked onto her right arm appeared to flitter and fly. Her black hair was like a living thing that both reached and ran from me. The jeans she still wore were a blue skin that covered her kicking legs. When she twisted away, I saw the colors and art of her back. Between her shoulder blades was a crucifix bearing a bleeding Christ. It was all in shades of gray but the blood. Where it poured grew flowers and skeletons. Low on her hips was the band of grinning skulls I had seen before. On her ribs, curling from front to back under her left breast, was a series of lines, words, like a verse tattooed so it would always be singing to her.

I was torn between reaching for her again and reaching for breath. She wasn't. Lenore snuggled her back against my chest and wrapped my arms up, holding my hands to her breasts. I could have drowned happy. I almost did.

Thrusting my hips to her backside, I let her feel my arousal. The denim I pressed against flexed. She ground back at my erection.

That was when something outside the water flashed. It was a comet of light, flaring, streaking, and then dying in the space of inches and instants.

Lenore released me and kicked. I followed upward, gasping in the air for breath. My arms reached for her. But she was already climbing from the pool.

"Lenore?" I called. It was hope without urgency because I could already feel her fading from me, pulled into another orbit.

The air around where the light had flashed was still swirling with blue smoke. I caught the scent of spice and chocolate. Someone had lit a cigar, one characteristic of tobacco grown in the San Andrés Valley.

Twisting my body around, I placed both hands on the deck and pushed myself up into the cold air. I scrambled for my pants but chose to hold them up before me rather than take the time to put them on. I was more concerned about the pistol clipped to the belt than my modesty.

When I turned back, I was alone. Lenore was nowhere to be seen. I think I saw the door to the office moving the last inch to close. I couldn't be sure. There was no point in trying to follow. If she was alone, she didn't want me there. If she wasn't...

Screw the pants, I decided. I looked around for the beer she had brought. It was gone. I sat on the concrete deck and pulled on my boots. Shod but bare assed, I sat under stars as the night cooled and my mind stilled. Thoughts chased me from dark corner to even darker corners. Inside I was all hollows and blackness. That grave I had escaped had somehow dug itself within me. I could feel it there, a shadowed emptiness demanding that I fill it.

The beer Lenore had poured on her breast and dropped was close enough to reach if I stretched. I did. There wasn't much left in the can, but it was still cold.

THIRTEEN

The next day was Saturday. I had no idea until I showed up at the station—late. The work of being police chief had turned into a job. As much as that galled me, there was nothing for it but to keep doing what I had to do. I could have still bailed on everything and run. I think by then, I knew that was a fantasy. Or at least it was a last resort. I was in the middle of a tangle that needed straightening. And I was there not just because I had the job. I was in the middle because of Paris. And because of our father.

The night before, Hector had mentioned an old-school Texas Ranger Paris had been interested in. There was not a chance in the world that Ranger was not Buick Tindall. It fit. I already knew he had been in Lansdale—the grants, of course. And Paris. I wondered if he had become involved by accident or because Buick had tried to bring him in. Put that together with the people who kept trying to kill me, and there was no wonder I wanted to spend Saturday surrounded by cops.

The first thing I did was to dig up Bascom Wood's home number and call. Baron had been found and sent home. It was time for the councilman to talk.

His phone kept ringing without going to voice mail. I called his office. A machine picked up. It directed me to a switchboard number. I decided to wait and try again later.

I didn't wait very long. The tedium-inducing desk work of a chief of police had me squirming. Aside from that was the feeling

that whatever I had to do in Lansdale needed to be done quickly—
before I ran out of whatever luck had gotten me to where I was.

I called Wood's house and office again with the same results.
Then I checked in with the officer who had picked up Baron and
taken him home. He reported leaving the kid at the house and
not seeing Bascom Wood. But he hadn't gone in.

An hour later I made the same calls again. By then I was
completely convinced that there was no paperwork to be found
onsite about grants or outside money. I gave up the paper shuffle
and went out to my truck. I felt safer and much more in control behind the wheel than behind a desk. Leaving the station,
I passed the city hall. I didn't see Wood's car. I went on. At the
councilman's house, I rang the bell and pounded on the door.
No one answered. I went around the entire house looking into
windows and trying the doors. No one home. And there was no
car in the garage.

Still having not programmed the nonemergency number
into the phone, I called 911. The officer on duty didn't sound
happy, but she said she would issue a BOLO, be on the lookout,
for Councilman Wood and his car. I also asked for officers to
start looking for Baron Wood. I suggested they start with finding
Louisa Rey.

While they were doing that, I went drove by the gun club. I
didn't go in. I asked about Wood at the gate. The gunman seemed
bored by my question. I believed him when he said Wood wasn't
there.

That time the DEA team didn't run me down when I left.
I had to go looking for them. It took a couple of passes before
I found an SUV hidden just off the road. There were two men
inside, the same pair of big guys who had been at the Border
Crossing glaring at me over pool cues. They weren't happy to see
me pull up.

"You need to get away from here, Sheriff," the driver said.

"Chief," I said. "I'm the chief of police, not a sheriff."

"Whatever." He spat. It could have been dust. I didn't think so. "You need to cowboy up your shit and mosey on. We're working here."

"What exactly is that work?"

"Hey. Fuck you," the man in the passenger seat yelled.

The driver, trying to look like the reasonable one, held up a hand to his partner without taking his attention from me. "What do you want, *Chief*?"

"I'm looking for someone. He probably went to see the Machados."

"Your councilman hasn't been up here."

"You seem well informed."

The guy in the passenger seat reached out and did something on the dash I couldn't see.

"Word gets around," the driver said.

"Yeah. Tell me something. Are you watching the Machados or keeping watch for them?"

The driver spat again. He followed by raising his middle finger.

I drove on. I had gotten two bits of information from them. They had already known I was looking for Wood. And they were monitoring city police transmissions. When the passenger fiddled on the dash, I was sure he had been turning off a police-band radio. It hadn't been to keep me from hearing what the DEA had to say.

After that I circled the town. I cruised through the Desert Drop parking lot to see if he was there looking for me. The whole exercise had me bored and pissed and worried. There was only one answer for that—tacos. I went to Ernesto's for lunch. I had tea, no beer.

The weekend feeling of the taqueria got me thinking. Even a man pretending to do a job needed time off. I was on edge and needed a way to clear the wasps out of my brain. In my experience the best thing for taking reality out of my life was to drop a hook into the water.

Stuffed with too many tacos, I went to equip myself at Walmart. There I bought a two-piece cane pole that came with line, hooks, a float, and sinkers, all for less than five dollars. I added a tub of night crawlers, a bag of ice, and a six of beer. Out in the parking lot, I tucked the pole in the back of the truck. I dumped the ice into my cooler and stored the worms and beer inside. Then my phone rang. I expected Milo. It was dispatch.

It took a little driving around and two more calls to the station for directions to find the rutted track off a county road that took me to the water. Under a copse of cottonwoods and pecan that ran right up to the crumbling river bank were two cars. One was a Lansdale police cruiser. The other I recognized as belonging to Councilman Bascom Wood.

As I parked behind the cruiser, Officer Sunny leaned away from the open driver's-side window of Wood's car. Her head was canted over as she spoke into the mic at her shoulder. She kept talking and taking notes as I approached.

When I got close enough, I heard the flies. The front glass was sprayed on the inside with blood and gray matter. I didn't bother to get much closer.

She finished what she was reporting to dispatch and looked right at me.

"His son?" I asked. "Baron?"

"He's not here," she answered. "Only Councilman Wood."

I looked around the grove, grateful for that bit of news. "This isn't in city limits, is it?"

"Is this going to be about jurisdiction?"

"Is *what* going to be about jurisdiction?"

"The reason I have to leave this alone."

"Who said you have to leave it alone?"

When I didn't say anything more, she shook her head. "No."

"No?"

"This isn't in city limits."

"But Bascom Wood is a city councilman."

Sunny nodded.

"I'm guessing there's an issue with going to the county sheriff."

"Same as in town," she said. "Sheriff hasn't been seen in a couple of months. If we take it there, things end up with the feds. Their...*support* is all over this county."

"What do you suggest?"

"You're asking me?"

"I'm the new guy."

"You're the chief."

"Fair enough. But I'm still asking."

"There is a county coroner but no medical examiner. Forensics work is done through that office. There are...*problems* in the system."

"So?"

"So we should double up on evidence collection where possible. Keep a set in our custody."

"Who can I trust?"

She seemed rattled by the question. "With evidence? I'd say—"

"I'm not talking about evidence, Officer Johnson."

"I know."

"Who?"

She shook her head.

"Hector?"

She nodded.

"Gutiérrez?"

Sunny opened her mouth as if to say something. Then she closed it. I was about to press for an answer when she said, "She's a good cop."

"But?"

She shook her head. It wasn't a negative. It was more a gesture of confusion.

"You don't trust her?"

"Trust is hard to come by in Lansdale these days." She didn't seem confused about that.

"Other officers?"

"They're okay—mostly."

"Mostly?"

"They don't like you and sure don't trust you."

"Because I'm from outside?"

"Because you suck as a chief."

"Yeah," I agreed. "I get that."

"What are you going to do about that?"

"Hell if I know." I shrugged. "But for now, call in whoever you trust and need."

"What are you going to do?"

"I'll do what a chief does. Handle the problems when they show up."

"What does that mean?"

"I figure you'll know in just a few minutes." I pointed at a fork in the trail that led down to the river bank. "I'm going to move my truck there, behind those trees."

"Why?"

"I think it might be best if the problems don't see me first."

She shook her head again, more confusion with a bit of dismissal. Still, she went back to the work at hand.

I backed my truck and then angled it into the fork. I parked behind a screen of brush and hardwoods. Close by was an eddying pool with a pair of rotting logs sticking from the dark water. I pulled out my pole and worms. No sense in wasting the waiting.

From where I leaned against a tree, I could hear and catch glimpses of city cruisers rolling in. I counted three. About twenty minutes after I got a hook in the water, I pulled in a channel cat. The fish was a fighter but too small to keep. When the hook was free from his mouth and my catch had returned to the river, other vehicles were gunning up the trail.

They weren't city cars. Even from a distance, I could hear the growl of big engines and the grind of knobby tires on hard pack. I rolled my line up on the pole and carried it with me as I took position behind a cottonwood well back from where the cops were working the scene.

Two big SUVs roared past and slid to a stop in a fury of dust and noise. Someone was trying to make an entrance.

There were seven of them, including Stackhouse. Two were the guys from the pool table at the Border Crossing. The rest I had seen blocking the road when I left the gun club. They were pros. Even before the vehicles were stopped, the doors were open, and men were flowing out. Without words, they spread in a broad semicircle centered on the bloody car and the four officers taking pictures and tucking samples into baggies.

As they piled out, I slipped closer, keeping the brush between them and me.

Of the DEA team, five carried M4a1 carbines, and one had a tactical shotgun at the ready. Stackhouse strode into the half circle with only his holstered Glock. He was trying to look like the reasonable one.

"You're out of city limits, aren't you?" Stackhouse called to the officers.

"And you're out of the zoo," Sunny Johnson called back. "We won't tell if you don't."

"Funny." The way he said it sounded like he'd never actually found anything funny. "You're kind of small for a cop, aren't you? You can't weigh more than a buck."

I expected to hear some kind of smart comeback. Instead, Sunny said, "Kiss my beautiful black ass."

It wasn't funny, but it got a titter out of the macho guys surrounding her. Stackhouse shut them up with a glance.

I decided that was my cue to be ready. I unwound my wrapped fishing line. At the same time, I eased forward, out of my wooded cover.

"We're taking over this scene and this investigation," Stackhouse said, speaking up for everyone to hear. "You're going to leave all your evidence, turn over all notes and files, and clear my perimeter."

"This isn't federal," Sunny said. "Murder is local."

"This has jurisdictional overlap written all over it, sister. And my swinging fed dick carries more weight than your black ass. Clear my scene."

"No."

Officer Sunny Johnson was a hell of a woman and the kind of cop you wished they all were. These guys must have been impervious to her charms, though. Someone pulled back a charging bolt on his weapon.

"I don't think you understand," Stackhouse said.

That was when Sunny and the other cops first looked scared. They were the police. Until they heard the edge in Stackhouse's voice, they didn't believe they could be in danger from fellow officers. I could have told them they were giving the feds way too much credit.

At the end of the DEA line closest to me was the man with the shotgun. He was holding it at port arms. I snuck up and to his side as close as I dared.

I pulled back with my cane pole and whipped forward with my line. The hook and sinker wrapped around the barrel of the weapon and the man's forearm. When I jerked, the barbed hook dug in. The sudden bite and pull caused him to discharge the shotgun, narrowly missing one of his partners. Once the gun went off, I dropped the pole and pulled my .45. In three steps I was right behind the shooter and kicking hard into the back of his knee. He dropped, and I smacked my pistol against the side of his head as he went.

He sprawled out with his badge face up in the dirt.

I kept my weapon sighted on the center of his back.

"Tindall," Stackhouse shouted.

I almost looked around for Paris.

"This is a DEA operation. Step away from my officer."

"Show me your badge," I said. One of the men pointing weapons at me snickered, but not for long.

"I'll show you the goddamned morgue if you don't back away from my officer."

"Your officer?" I bent down and took a closer look at the man's badge. "Why's he wearing a treasury badge?"

"Joint operations."

"There you go," I said, sneering up at Stackhouse. "Bragging about your joint again. I think you owe my officer an apology."

"He sure as hell does," Officer Sunny said. She had her weapon out and aimed in a two-handed shooter's stance. My other three officers were in the same positions.

"We're all on the same team here." Stackhouse tried the reasonable route again.

"You're DEA, he's treasury. What about these other guys?"

No one said anything.

"Well, never mind. Our place on the team is filled."

Then Stackhouse asked me, "What do you want?"

"Information," I answered. "Inclusion."

"You're not cleared."

"Have you reported your badge missing yet? I know a guy in the DOJ might be interested."

"Whatever." Stackhouse turned to his men. "Lower your weapons." He pointed to the treasury agent still on the ground. "Help Connors." Turning back to me, he said, "I'll be in touch."

"Why seven?"

I could tell by the look on his face that Stackhouse knew what I was asking. He tried ignoring me.

"Six of them and you. It doesn't seem like a good number for a team. Awkward."

"What would you know about it?"

"Now I know you have someone undercover."

"You're a fucking bomb in a convoy, you know that? All chaos, no tactics."

They left. They didn't go happy. The officers of the Lansdale Police Department looked proud of themselves. I was darn proud of them too. They went back to work, and I untangled my line and headed back to the river. That time I didn't fish. I opened a beer and leaned on the bed of my truck to concentrate on keeping my hands and breathing steady.

Officer Sunny Johnson looked me up when they were ready to clear the scene. "I called a tow truck for the car and the coroner for the body," she told me.

"You don't sound happy about it."

"I'm not. At least not about the coroner."

"Anything we can do about that?" I asked, opening the cooler. I might have pulled that second beer if she hadn't looked at me the way she did.

"We can send the body to Houston for autopsy." She sounded ready for disappointment.

"Think it will do any good?"

"Probably not."

I nodded. "Then why do it?"

"Sometimes you just want them to know you're doing your job. They don't own you no matter what they think."

I picked up the cane pole from the truck bed and handed it over to her. "Like sometimes you need to go fishing more than you need to catch fish."

"Maybe." She handled the pole with no trepidation at all. "I don't know. That whole thing—those feds—that pisses all of us off."

"Then do what you need to do. Unless you need me to bait your hook?"

"I can bait my own hook. And I can take the fish off the line too. Even clean them and cook them. My daddy didn't raise no prissy girl."

"I don't doubt that at all, Officer Sunny."

* * * *

I didn't get to go fishing again. I didn't get any weekend at all. The rest of that day and the following Sunday kept me busy. It was routine stuff and a lot of phone calls. The machineries of murder were remarkably mundane. And it was murder. I had been concerned that Bascom Wood might have killed himself. Officer Sunny Johnson set that to rest when she found the gun tossed into weeds ten feet from the car. It wasn't rusted and had recently been fired—not much chance it was anything but the murder weapon. It was a drop piece. It wouldn't lead us anywhere unless someone had been dumb enough to leave a fat fingerprint on it.

Early Sunday morning we finished the onsite investigation. That didn't mean we stopped. Bascom's car was towed back to our vehicle impound. I had it locked into the garage and then set two officers to dismantling the interior. They were guys with a lot of experience pulling apart drug cars. It wouldn't be much of a car when they were finished. But if there was anything to be found, they would search it out.

We tracked Baron Wood down to another river hangout. He was with his girlfriend and friends. They were wading and splashing in shallow water and sunning on towels spread over the dirty sand shore. I went to talk with him.

When I arrived, the kids tried to hide their beer. Some called warnings. Everyone stopped their fun to see what the cop wanted. Baron watched me from a knee-deep pool. Without stopping at the waterline, I walked right into the river and to the boy. He nodded at his girlfriend as I approached, and she angled away from us and took up position on a sandbank.

"Are you coming to drag me home again?" Baron asked me. "Is my dad freaking out again?"

"Not this time," I said. I stood with him in the same pool of water. The water was the temperature of a bath that had sat too long.

"You should go looking for him. He's the one who didn't come home last night. Or is he blaming that on me too?"

"No." I shook my head and tried to think of what to say. "He's not blaming you for anything."

"That's a first. My father—"

I don't know if he saw something in my face, but I saw the world shift in his. Baron swallowed hard. He looked around at his friends, who were staring back. Then he looked back at me.

"That's why you're here," he said. "Because he didn't come home."

"I'm sorry, Baron."

"Was he drinking?"

"Drinking?"

"Sometimes he has a few beers. When he gets caught, the cops would let him off because of his job."

"Baron." I held his gaze and hated every word I could think to say. "It wasn't a car accident. I'm sorry. Someone killed your father."

His face broke first. Then the strength in his legs gave. I caught him by the arms and forced him back so he could sit on the shallow edge of the pool.

"Why?"

"We're trying to find that out." I waved the girlfriend over. "Louisa's going to sit with you." Her eyes were huge with worry, but she had the good sense not to ask questions. She settled into the water beside Baron. "Do you know anything about your father's work?" I asked.

Baron shook his head staring into the murky water. "No. He talked about it a lot. I never listened."

"It's all right."

"Now I wish I had."

"I know. He wished he could talk to you better too."

"Really?" Baron looked up from the dark water to me. "How do you know?"

"Because he talked about you. He was sad he couldn't make things perfect for you."

He nodded and looked back to the water. "He liked things perfect."

"He said you were going to be in a play."

"That pissed him off."

"I get it. I bet he would have come to the show anyway. What do you think?"

Baron nodded again, and I saw something drip from his face into the river. "Yeah. He would."

"Some fathers want their sons to do different things. Some want different sons. Maybe you were luckier than you thought."

He was crying openly. Silver tears fell into brownish-green water and disappeared. "Maybe," he said. His voice was thick, and he wiped his running nose with the back of his wrist.

"I have to ask you: Do you know of anyone who would want to hurt your father?"

He shook his head and wiped his nose again. "No. He was just a guy. Nothing special. Just my dad."

"I understand."

"What do I do now?"

"Do you have family that can come be with you?"

"My uncle and aunt."

"We'll get you home and stay with you until they can come."

"Do I have to go with you? I have a ride."

Baron's head was still down facing the dirty water. Louisa looked at me though. She had the same question.

"That'll be okay, I guess. Someone will be waiting for you at home. Don't take long." I left the pair huddled together and sloshed my way back to shore. From there I went right to the beer that had been hidden when I arrived.

"Hey," someone shouted when I lifted the cooler.

"Shut up," I snapped without knowing which one I was warning. "If I come back and find more, it won't just be the beer I take in."

I tossed the cooler in the back of the truck and left the river, feeling like a man with battery acid in his gut. The rest of the weekend wasn't any better. I called and got hold of Milo. He didn't have information for me, or at least not any he chose to share. I told him about the latest run-in with Stackhouse. It didn't make him happier with me. I also told him what I suspected about the team—that there was someone unaccounted for.

When I got into the station Monday morning—late again—I was still filled with anger and acid but almost felt good about the job. I decided to share my mood with the police department of Lansdale, Texas. The first thing I did was to call Gutiérrez into the station to promote her. It's not as stupid as it sounds. I knew squat about being a cop, let alone being chief of police. And surprisingly enough that was starting to bother me. Gutiérrez, I was convinced, knew everything necessary and more besides. Making her the assistant chief solved the problem of running a department and giving her additional duties made it that much harder for her to get in my way. At least that was my thinking. I still didn't know what side she was working for. Keeping her busy for me was the best solution until I figured it out.

Officer Bronwyn Gutiérrez was not happy about the promotion.

"What the hell do you think you're doing?" It was, I think, the third time she'd asked the question.

"It's a promotion."

"It's a trap."

"In what way?" I smiled as I asked the question.

"I don't work for you."

"You want to put that to the test?"

"You don't know what you're doing."

I smiled a little broader.

"Are you trying to make my life impossible?"

"Not me. I'm taking advantage of an officer's valuable experience."

"You're impeding a federal investigation."

"What federal agency?"

"I can't tell you."

"What are you investigating?"

"Again—I can't tell you. Isn't it enough that we're on the same side?"

"Are we?"

Her answer was the kind of look that, from some people, would contain daggers. In her eyes, I saw something more like dull and rusty mower blades.

"I noticed that Detective Walker hasn't reported for duty this morning," I said. "We need a detective, don't we?"

"Walker is over in old Mex, either drunk or dead. If he's drunk, it just means they haven't bothered to kill him yet. You put him in that situation."

"Nope. His choices. His ending."

"It's on you." Her voice was as cold and flat as a Kansas Christmas.

"What about Hector?"

"Hector?"

"In the detective position."

"He's not ready."

"That's why you're going to be his supervisor."

"I thought I was the assistant chief, whatever that is."

"You're that. And supervising detective and the official lead on investigating the murder of Bascom Wood."

"Hire from outside."

"Nope."

"What are you trying to do?" She flapped her arms in an exasperated display.

"I'm trying not to leave behind a mess for once in my life. You're going to help with that, like it or not."

I'd made Gutiérrez the official lead investigating the murder of Bascom Wood. I didn't tell her I was putting my own heavy emphasis on the word "official." I was going to do some work of my own in that direction because I was sure it had everything to do with everything else I had found. The place to start, I decided, was the councilman's office in city hall.

Outside, the 125-year-old building was solid limestone. Inside, it was a ghost with polished brass. There were records offices open, the business license, building permits, and city tax windows all serviced by one blue-haired lady. Everything else was closed, and the lights were out. I climbed broad marble stairs to the second level.

All the doors were closed and the lights behind their pebbled glass dark. I stuck my head into the mayor's office. It looked as if it hadn't been touched in years. I crossed the hall to Councilman Wood's office. I needn't have seen the order of his home to know that the councilman had not left his office in such disarray. On the floor were binders pulled from bookshelves. Loose pages were scattered. Every drawer and cabinet door stood open. Someone had been looking for something.

I spent a few minutes digging through the mess before I noticed that one of the desk drawers was splintered where it had been pried. The paperwork spilling out of it was all bank related, mostly statements and cancelled checks. Heading the pages were the names of two banks. One was Bank of the Republic. It was a Texas institution that had been around for forever. Bank of the Republic was the kind of place a city would keep its funds. Those pages were still in piles on the carpet. Other papers, scattered widely and crumpled, were all topped by the name Bank of Lansdale. I didn't need a road map to tell me the Bank of Lansdale had a shiny new building outside of city limits and directly across the road from the Gun Hills Hunting Lodge and Private Club.

"Is there something I can do for you?" The question came with the flash of lights coming on. It was asked by the frail-looking old man at the door.

From behind the old man's shoulder, the blue-haired lady peeked. "Tell him we're calling the police," she said in what she might have thought was a whisper.

"Who are you?" I asked.

"You're the one where he's not supposed to be," the old man said defiantly. "You answer my questions."

The lady punched him in the ribs. I couldn't tell if it was to say "good job" or "shut up." Not that it mattered. He ignored the jab.

"I'm Paris Tindall," I told him. The name still felt like a rock in my mouth. "The new chief of police."

"Well, it's about time," he said. The old gentleman held out his hand and advanced. "I'm Spencer Toomey. Last of the city council." We shook, and he nodded over at the woman. "This is Mrs. Toomey, my wife. She's city manager."

"What are you going to do about this?" Mrs. Toomey asked, coming out from behind her husband. She pointed around the room. "This. This mess and destruction."

"I'm working on it, ma'am."

"My wife gets excited, Chief," Mr. Toomey said. "It is not a good time for city government in Lansdale."

"It's a criminal time," she corrected him.

He shook his head thoughtfully. "We found the mess this morning. It must have been okay when that lady officer was here, or she would have said something."

"Lady officer?"

"The tall blonde with the muscles."

"Spencer likes her," Mrs. Toomey said. "Thinks she's feisty."

"Please, Norma," he said. He'd gotten that teasing a few times before.

"When was the lady officer here?"

"Day before yesterday. The same day poor Mr. Wood was found," he answered.

"She's the one told us he was dead," she added.

"Family business?" I asked.

"Family burden, you ask me." Mrs. Toomey nudged a pile of paper with her sensible slip-on shoe.

"What my wife means is that we're it for city government. Between deaths and resignations, we're the last holdouts."

"We know who did it," Mrs. Toomey said, almost gleefully.

"Now, Norma."

"Everyone knows," Mrs. Toomey said boldly.

"Not specifically," Mr. Toomey said. "But you can bet it was someone sent by the Machados."

"Yeah," I said. "That's a theme around here. You have ideas why?"

"Why they are eating our town alive or why they are getting away with it?" the Mrs. asked.

Mr. Toomey shook his head. "Power. That's what evil people always want, isn't it?"

"Power?"

"Look at the town." Mr. Toomey gestured around as though the town were in the room. "Mexico on one side. Big Bend on the other. Nothing but farm roads and county blacktop north for a hundred miles. The nearest city is Del Rio. That's about eighty miles across Mexico and desert. Twice that on a road."

"If you wanted to take over a place and have no one care"— Mrs. Toomey pointed a bony finger at me—"Lansdale is the one you would choose."

I nodded. I looked back at the torn-up room, and something niggled at the back of my mind. "When was Gutiérrez here?"

The pair looked at me with four raised and questioning eyebrows.

"The lady cop with the muscles," I said.

"Saturday." Mr. Toomey looked at his wife. "It was probably about five?"

"About," she said. "We were just ready for dinner when she came."

"City hall is open that late on Saturday?"

"No," he said. "But we were here catching up on things."

"There's a lot of work backing up," she added. "Business licenses, health certificates—things don't stop because there's no politicians."

"And you keep things going? All the important papers?"

"The Mrs. is a notary." Mr. Toomey sounded proud of the fact.

"Councilman Wood had some important papers. They were what someone broke in to take. We need them to help us find his killer."

"Mr. Wood was a careful man," Mrs. Toomey said.

"Yes, he was," I said. "Too careful to leave anything that important in a desk drawer."

She grinned with excitement. "Oh, no. All the important stuff is in the safe."

The safe was a green steel box. It was old and worn to the point all the lettering was rubbed from the face and the combination dial was almost solid black. Mrs. Toomey didn't seem to need the numbers to twist out the right sequence. The heavy door swung open on oiled hinges. It was a great first step. The second one was on the bottom shelf. It was a metal fire box with an alphanumeric combination pad that looked like the keys of a phone.

"That's his," Mr. Toomey said pointing at the box.

I pulled it out and onto the service counter. Science fiction movies weren't going to help that time. But even without pop-culture obsessions, people are generally predictable. There's a reason that "Password" is the most common password. I thought about Bascom Wood. I didn't know much. There was one thing—*Baron*. The man was probably corrupt, and he might have been an unsympathetic father, but he loved his boy. I punched the name in, and the display lit up in red letters.

Nothing.

I felt a huge letdown. I had thought it would be easy. And I didn't have any other ideas.

Mrs. Toomey did. She opened a drawer and pulled out a claw hammer. "How about a key?" she asked, grinning.

I grinned right back at her as I took the tool. On the first try, the display went dark. Two more, and the top popped right open.

It was one thing to believe the worst of your father. It was a steel-toe kick in the balls to get actual confirmation. Buick's name was all over the documentation in the box.

Buick Tindall had consulted on and filled out paperwork for at least four homeland grants. They included money for border-security manpower, rapid-response training, and armaments to combat drug trafficking, antiterrorism task-forces and equipment, and the cake topper, a commercial transportation-security screening facility. From what I could tell, that was $22 million for basically a big truck x-ray machine and bomb sniffer. There were no major highways and no border crossings in Lansdale. What could that be for?

There was more. I found economic-development grants as well as refugee support and resettlement grants. None of that made sense. Buick didn't know anything about stuff like that. He had signed many of them, though—even the ones he hadn't signed looked like his. On several pages, I saw the exact same language as if entire segments had been cut and pasted from other documents. I found other signatures too: the dead chiefs, Wilcox and Sawyer; Bascom Woods; and the kicker—Darian Stackhouse.

As I pawed through the stack of papers that represented millions of dollars stolen from the government, my phone rang. It was Milo.

"Hang on," I told him and then set the phone down on the table while I scooped pages back into the fire box. The safest thing I could think to do with everything was to put it right back where I'd found it.

After closing the box lid and making sure it was secure, I picked up the phone. "You still there?"

"What the hell—"

"Keep holding on." I covered the microphone with my hand and thanked the Toomeys as they closed the safe and twirled the black dial. "Okay, we can talk," I said to Milo as I walked out to my truck.

"A little goddamned phone etiquette wouldn't kill you," Milo told me. He didn't sound as mad as usual.

I told him what I'd found in the safe. I topped it all off by sharing the name Darian Stackhouse. Then I asked him, "How's it possible? You're DOJ. All federal agencies report to you. How did you not know any of this?"

"First of all, you can kiss my hard black ass if you think I'm involved in this shit. And second, do you know anything about DEA Special Operations teams?"

"What's to know? Door-kicking hard-asses."

"Nothing that easy. SOTs operate mostly in secret with classified mandates and missions."

"They're not just cops?"

"No. They operate under the oversight, if you can call it that, of the DEA Special Operations Division, but the SOD is made up of agents from partner agencies that include CIA, NSA, Homeland..."

"One of the men I saw had a treasury badge."

"SOD is an intelligence network. They don't play by cop rules either. They're known for illegally collecting evidence and entrapping suspects."

"How did Buick get involved?"

"Look around your town. If the money hasn't been spent for the listed purposes—and if Homeland hasn't been pitching a fit—millions in cash is being funneled to your SOT or someone else. All the dead people are the ones who might have asked questions."

"There is something going on between La Familia de los Muerto and Stackhouse's team," I said.

"I have two more pieces of the DEA picture. The other agent you asked about. Right again. Bronwyn Gutiérrez is DEA internal investigations."

"She's not here for the same reason I am?"

"Remains to be seen. Her job is keeping an eye on DEA operations that are suspected of crossing lines. The funny thing is that SOD doesn't have lines. If she's there, someone is worried, and she's been there over a year."

"The other piece?" I asked.

"Cesar Barcia."

"I don't know him."

"You asked me to find out who was missing from Stackhouse's team."

"Is this the guy undercover with La Familia?"

"More like underground."

"Dead?"

"Cesar Barcia is the only name other than Darian Stackhouse I can get for the team because he was reported missing, presumed dead."

"When?" Even as I asked, I was doing a little addition of my own, and two plus two was Cesar Barcia.

"A couple of weeks ago."

"The laughing guy."

"What's that supposed to mean?"

"It means you're right. These guys don't care about crossing lines or being cops."

FOURTEEN

The nice thing about being the boss was being able to ignore my own rules. That afternoon I went to the Border Crossing. I sat outside parked in the shadow of a tractor trailer, watching the door for a few hours. I saw a couple of familiar faces. Not the one I wanted. The sun had gotten low enough that I didn't complain when the truck driver returned and took my shade away. It turned out not to matter because the man I was watching for entered the green door. It was the treasury agent, Connors.

I went inside and found him at the bar. He saw me too and made a good attempt at keeping his face under control.

"Sorry about that fishhook thing," I told him as I took the stool next to him.

"Whatever."

The bartender sat a bottled beer beside Connors. I raised a finger for my own. "Buy you your next beer?"

He tilted his beer up and took a long drink, keeping his gaze locked to mine. He didn't have to say "fuck you" to get the message across.

I gave an exaggerated shrug as my beer showed up. "Suit yourself," I said. "We're both just doing our jobs."

That got him. "Doing our jobs? Do you even have a clue what the job here is?" He shook his head with the bottle poised. "I don't think so." He finished the bottle.

"You're right," I said. I pushed my bottle over to him and raised another finger to the bartender. "I don't know your job. But I think I know mine. And that's what I'm doing."

Connors puffed a breath through loose lips, making them flap dismissively. Then he took my beer.

I waited for him to have a good mouthful before saying, "They put you on shotgun because you don't have as much tactical experience."

He didn't spit, but he stopped drinking.

"There's no shame in it. You're a treasury agent, after all."

"What's that supposed to mean?"

"Your experience with banking and money is more important than your trigger finger."

"Go pump another well." He saluted with his bottle. "I'm not giving you anything."

I waited for him to raise the beer to his mouth again and then said, "That FBI agent is a real shooter."

Connors managed to smirk and keep sucking suds. Apparently I guessed wrong and the FBI was not part of the team. "You're an asshole," he said as soon as he swallowed.

"Maybe. But I don't have to take crap from Homeland."

There was no smirk that time.

"And how did a respectable guy from treasury get stuck in a black-bag op with the CIA?"

That time he leaned in and put everything he had into telling me, "Fuck you." Everything but denial. Connors picked up the waiting full beer. He walked away, telling the bartender, "He'll pay."

I paid, and I tipped well. Then I left.

* * * *

The first thing I did the next morning was call Gutiérrez into my office. She came but she didn't look happy to be there.

"Still mad?" I asked.

"In many ways."

So much for easing into things. "Who or what are you investigating?"

She gave me the kind of look I usually only see when I'm drunk and hitting on a woman way out of my league.

"Is it Stackhouse or all of them?"

Gutiérrez raised her eyebrows in surprise but otherwise gave nothing away.

Still, I knew I'd scored a point. "Are they taking the money for themselves?"

"We're not having this conversation."

"Which one would you like to have?"

"None. Are we finished?"

"Why'd you toss the councilman's office?" I tried to make it a casual question.

"Who says I did?" She tried to make it a casual answer. But she let herself fall back against the doorframe.

"You made a mess."

"You're throwing darts blindfolded."

I shrugged and leaned back in my chair. "Maybe. Maybe not. They're connected, you know."

"What's connected to what?"

"Your special operations team is connected to the money going through the town of Lansdale. And both are connected to La Familia de los Muerto."

"It's like you have a box of words, and you keep throwing them in the air hoping they land in a way that makes sense."

I didn't say anything. I waited.

After she got tired of staring at me, Gutiérrez nodded, the kind of slight bobble people sometimes do when they are answering themselves. "If I was to give you anything. *If.* It would be to shut you up and get you back to your own target."

"If."

"Yes," she said. "If."

"Please," I said, spreading my hands to receive. "Help me get back on track."

She laughed. "You are a man without shame, aren't you?"

"You have no idea."

"You do your job," she said. Then she hardened her face and added, "Whatever that is. I seem to be doing most of it for you. And when I'm not covering for you, I'll do what I was sent here to do."

"Spying on the SOT."

"I'm not spying on anyone."

"That team is a strange mix."

Gutiérrez stood rigid. Her gaze sharpened on me. With a new, quiet intensity, she asked, "What do you know?"

"I know that on a team operating within US borders, there is CIA but no FBI presence."

"Okay." She deflated. "Who told you?"

"Well, I have a source. You were my confirmation."

"This is all classified stuff that you don't need to know."

"You won't share with me?" I stood behind my desk and picked up my hat. It had been sitting crown down. Bad luck.

Gutiérrez opened her mouth to say something but seemed to change her mind. She backed away toward the door, keeping her eyes on me.

"Hey," I called as soon as she passed the threshold and turned her back to me.

She stopped.

I settled my hat on my head as I stepped through the door. The dispatch officer and our civilian receptionist, plus two other officers off patrol, all turned to look at me.

"Tell me about Cesar Barcia," I said.

Gutiérrez turned to me, and everyone else turned to her. "What?"

"Cesar Barcia," I said the name carefully. "Would you like me to take you to the body?"

Her pale skin flushed red from her collar up into her hair. "Let's talk," she demanded, pushing past me and back into my office.

I might have learned something if my new cell phone hadn't started ringing.

"Let it go," Gutiérrez said. "You wanted to talk."

I did want to talk. But I wanted to take this call too. "Hector," I said as much to the people in the room as to him.

"This is important," Gutiérrez told me.

"So's this," I said. To Hector, I asked, "When's the funeral?"

"That's why I'm calling." Even over the cheap phone, I could hear the edge in his voice.

"What's wrong?"

"I'm sorry, Longview."

"What?" I don't know if it was the sound of my voice or the language of my body, but Gutiérrez looked at the floor. "What happened?" I asked again.

"I didn't understand," he responded in a low voice.

"What are you saying?"

"I was the only one."

"What does that mean? The only one what?"

"We had the funeral. I'm at the cemetery. He's being covered up right now."

"Is Buick there?" I don't know why I asked. I couldn't imagine that it would have mattered, but...

"I was the only one," Hector said. "No one else came. Just me."

What came from my mouth wasn't a word. I don't think it was even a sound. Meaning and air were all there was to it. No one had come to my funeral. I couldn't help but wonder how many would have shown up had they known it was Paris in the box. Then I felt horrible for thinking it.

"Longview?"

"Thanks, Hector. It means a lot that you were there for him." My voice sounded like someone else speaking from a million miles away.

"I'm sorry," he said.

"Don't be." I broke the connection. That was one of those times I wanted to drop the badge I was wearing on the floor and show the world my back. I didn't. Gutiérrez was waiting. "So—" I stepped back to my office, where she was holding the door open. "Cesar Barcia."

She pushed the door closed behind me. "He's DEA. He's bad news. And he's missing with millions of La Familia cash."

"He's not missing. He's dead."

"I figured that out when you offered to show me the body. What happened, and how do you know about it?"

"It looks like we both have stories to tell."

She kept her face immobile, waiting on me to make an offer.

"You go first. Tell me all you know about the team and what they are doing."

Gutiérrez didn't even blink. "I can't do that."

I adjusted the hat on my head and eased the door open again. "Call me when you can."

Outside the building the day had become another inferno. The hat I was wearing was a summer straw. Even so, heat immediately built under the crown. Sweat seeped under the band and ran in tiny rivers to my eyes. It stung. I blinked and wiped the moisture away with the back of my hand. To wipe my brow, I removed the hat. The loss of shade on my face and neck allowed the sun to work like acid on my skin. I reset the hat and climbed into the truck.

Despite the heat, I rolled the windows down and drove without the air-conditioning. I didn't go anywhere; I simply drove around town. When I'd finally had enough of the self-pity, I decided to take some of Milo's advice: "Suck it up, buttercup."

The answer to everything—the day, the heat, my mood, and the pity party—was cold beer and good food. I went to Ernesto's place.

I drank a bottle and ate an entire bowl of greasy chips with salsa before the enchiladas showed. I had the habanero sauce again to help burn my thoughts away. That, and a second beer helped. A huge bowl of carbs and habaneros didn't stop me from digging into the enchiladas with gusto. I told myself I was almost feeling good. Everyone knows I'm a liar.

My plate was clean. I was full. It didn't matter. I was still determinedly picking crumbs and salt from the bottom of the chip bowl when two men walked in and took stools at the bar.

I stopped licking salt. I checked the door with my eyes and my weapon with my hand. The men at the bar were my old friend Álvaro and the gun club doorman, Joaquin.

"Chief Tindall," Joaquin said with his back to me. "We like things clear."

"Joaquin, mi amigo—I can't begin to understand what that means. And I can't say much about your drinking companion. But—I'll buy each of you a beer. Maybe we can all be friends?"

"I think you've missed your chance to be friends with Álvaro here." He kept talking with his back to me.

"Not for lack of trying. We got off on the wrong foot. Or hand, you might say." I raised my near-empty bottle with my left hand and held it up in salute. My right hand had remained on the butt of my pistol. As I took a sip of beer, I eased the weapon out and held it under the table.

Joaquin turned as I lowered the bottle from my lips. "What do you know of La Familia de los Muerto, Chief?"

"On the list of things of which I remain ignorant, it is right at the top."

"I don't believe that." He sounded genuinely surprised. "You talk about our business freely. You know things most people fear to mention. And you make—insinuations."

"Insinuations? What are you trying to say—I hurt someone's feelings?"

Joaquin looked at me like I was a lost cause and too dumb to understand how I had screwed up. They rose from the bar stools and went back out the front door. Something about the way they went made me feel I was expected to follow.

I paid my bill and went to see. Sure enough, they were leaning on the front of my truck. When I stepped out, they watched but said nothing. If they were going to shoot, they would have already. I walked to the driver's-side door. "You fellas got something more to say?" I asked as I climbed in.

They rolled out to the sides. Álvaro went to the passenger door. Joaquin came around to my side. Each of them leaned in the open windows.

Joaquin held up his hand, showing me the back. There on the long knuckle of his index finger was a colorful grinning skull. It was fresh ink. "In La Familia, these are tokens of our usefulness."

"Notches on your gun butt. Classy."

"When it turns out that, somehow, we've failed. The token is taken away."

Álvaro raised his left hand, spreading his wrapped fingers.

"That empty space," Joaquin said, nodding at Álvaro's hand and the space where his ring finger was missing. "That represents a failure. You know what he failed at?"

"Marriage?"

"You're a funny man, Chief." He didn't mean it. "Álvaro was supposed to keep you from showing up here to take your job. He came to visit you at your brother's trailer."

A feeling of heat and ice, like I'd swallowed gasoline and a match, hit my gut. My brain replayed the night I'd found Paris in my home. I thought he had been murdered in my place. That was somehow easier, thinking I was the target—thinking it was my fault.

"Is he here to get his finger back?" I asked.

Joaquin grinned. It was a razor of an expression, all cut and blood. "You seem to know our business. Álvaro simply thought you should know a little more."

"Tell me something, Joaquin." I raised both hands and gripped the steering wheel. Hard. My knuckles were white, and my muscles burned. "What do you know about me? About our situation here?"

"Our—situation?"

"See?" I asked. Then I let go of the wheel. I used a finger to tap the badge on my chest. "It's a funny thing about the law and this badge. Everyone, the good people and the bad, all rely on the rules it represents. What happens when a bad man wears the badge?"

"Just like when my friend lost his finger," Joaquin said, still beaming that sharp-edged grin. "Even for cops there are prices to pay."

"I don't think so, amigo."

His grin slipped. Álvaro's back straightened.

I grabbed Joaquin's tattooed hand in my left. Álvaro reached through the window, trying to get to my right hand as I pulled my .45. With those hands, I don't know why he bothered. When I pointed the pistol at Joaquin, Álvaro pulled back. He put both of his bandaged hands on the window frame as if he was waiting to jerk the door off the truck.

I tapped my badge with the business end of the pistol. "Between La Familia and the feds, I'm all there is. I think I can do what I want. The only things I have to worry about are more assholes like you."

Joaquin's smile evaporated, but he still seemed to think we were talking. "What are you trying—"

"Let's find out." I thumbed the hammer of the gun back and put the barrel to Joaquin's cheekbone. "What would happen to me if I pull this trigger? Do you think all of a sudden the world would change, and I would meet justice? Or do you hope you would be revenged?" He didn't say anything. His eyes were pointed my way, but the pupils were constricted down to black points. I knew it wasn't me he was seeing. "The big men in their houses and suits—do you think they'll come themselves to settle things over, Joaquin? The best you can hope for is some other slouch like you and Álvaro there. And how's that been working?"

Joaquin didn't say anything.

I turned the weapon to the sky, easing the hammer down. Darian Stackhouse was standing behind Joaquin's shoulder, watching. "What's going on here?" he asked, as if he didn't know.

I let go of Joaquin, and he walked away from me. Not just from me—he left the parking lot without a glace back at me or Stackhouse. I took a look to my right. Álvaro was gone. Either they were afraid of the DEA agent, or…was it possible they were there working for him?

"Sorting out the good guys from the bad ones," I answered. "What do you want?"

"You still think you're a good guy?"

"No." I looked him square in his eyes. I noticed they were the color of old brass, muted but not lifeless. "But I'm a hell of a lot better than anything you offer."

"Keep telling yourself that."

"Again. What do you want?"

"I want to show you something."

"I'm not interested."

"You don't know what it is."

"I can smell a sales pitch from a mile. You're not the kind of man I want to get my used cars from."

"You're a smart-mouth son of a bitch," he said. There wasn't a lot of fire behind it. "But you're not as sharp as you like to think you are."

"That's no news flash. It's been the headline every day of my life."

"Come on." He jerked his thumb at the SUV parked nearby. "Let's take a ride."

My face must have given something away.

"What?" he asked. "Don't you trust me?"

"Does anyone?"

"I'm married. I have two kids and a dog."

"Do they trust you?"

"Mostly. Look, I'm trying to tell you I'm a regular guy. We're on the same side."

"Is this the honesty-if-nothing-else-works trick?"

"Kinda." He grinned. The expression was big and warm. Then he dropped the hammer. "How do you like working for Milo?"

I can't say it didn't have an impact on my stony resolve. But when you get hit, you have to get up and hit back, or guys like Stackhouse will eat you alive.

"I don't mind it," I said. "It beats having me and my whole team under internal investigation by my own agency." There it was. His eyes widened slightly before he glanced to the side. Stackhouse didn't know he was being investigated. That was a screw that needed twisting. "From what I hear, you have to fuck up good for anyone in SOD to start worrying about the rules."

His big friendly grin was frozen and hard. "How about that ride?"

"Why not?"

It wasn't a quick trip. We went to the border crossing and into Mexico. There we went onto a hard-packed dirt road looping almost back to where we'd been. We drove well over an hour to end up a couple miles south of Lansdale and the border.

It was almost dark when we found the town. "Town" was a big word for a collection of mostly industrial buildings, unpaved streets, and trailers tucked behind desert hills. A big word but evidently not big enough for the residents. There was a sign. Hand-painted red on bare planks, it read, Ciudad de la Sangre de Angel. City of Angel's Blood.

There was a war going on in Angel's Blood.

From where we sat at the top of a hill, I saw the far end of town lit with muzzle flashes. There was a force of maybe forty men in trucks. One of the pickups had a machine gun stand mounted in the bed. They were assaulting a blockade of no more than a dozen men, who were firing back with military-grade automatic weapons.

"This is what's happening two miles beyond our border," Stackhouse said.

"What is it?"

"Some write it off as a turf war. That's too simple and plain wrong. It's a revolution." He kept looking at me as I looked at the action. "And don't think it stops here. The border won't keep it out." In the deepening dusk, I saw movement on the crest of the opposite hill. Men were circling the conflict on the high ground and flanking the men in the trucks.

"Are you and your black-bag friends here to stop or help the revolution?"

"We're here to control it."

We watched. The trained men on the hill disappeared from sight as darkness grew over the desert. They reappeared as flashing firepower and tracer bullets cutting in from the side and behind the men and trucks. The pickup with the machine gun took a rain of glowing metal that wore it down to smoke and ash. No one escaped.

As the violence wilted to single shots of mercy, Stackhouse kept watching. I looked away. I'd had my fill of brutality and rage that day. Down in the City of Angel's Blood, the gloom of evening was cast away with the light of multiple fires. What caught my eye were answering flickers from the other end of the road. There, alongside the largest building, were parked three white commercial vans. On the side of each, in reflective vinyl, was the same company name I had seen on vans parked at the industrial development in Lansdale. They were contractors for electronics and IT systems.

"What's the end game here?" I asked Stackhouse.

He pulled his attention from the circle of fire that had been a battle a moment before. "I told you. Control."

"You can't control revolution. Isn't that the nature of the beast? Uncontrolled change of power."

"Tools."

"What's that mean?"

"Everything is a tool, if you use it to build what you want."

"I don't get it," I said, looking down at the town. The fading flames were leaving me literally and figuratively in the dark. "Revolution, war—those are your tools? To build what?"

"Mexico is the third world on our doorstep. It's at war with itself and sending the conflict over our border."

"Our drug habit, our war."

"That's an easy thing to say," Stackhouse said. "But like everything easy, it doesn't mean shit."

"Okay. You brought me out here because you want me to get the meaning. What is it?"

"Like everything else—money."

"Drug money?"

"Bigger than that." He pointed down at the dark buildings. "What you see down there is a joint operation of US forces and Mexican Federal Police against criminal organizations. The only thing they all have in common is money. Drugs and whores, guns, and extortion generate cash. What most people don't think about is the money in fighting it. Police, Border Patrol, DEA, Mexican police and military agencies on both sides: it's an industry that generates billions. Lawyers, arms dealers, manufacturers of ammunition, ballistic vests, handcuffs, assault vehicles—everything down to tactical boots. We can't afford to win the drug wars. The best we can do is manage it."

"With more war?"

"You use the tools you have."

"Take me back to town."

He started the SUV and then spun the wheel around to take us back the way we'd come. "Now you have a part to play."

"I wondered when you'd get to that."

"I need things to go easier with La Familia."

"I'm not your guy."

His reaction was to press harder on the gas. The big SUV sped over the rugged track, bouncing from peak to peak. "You are. Know it or not. Like it or not. You're the guy that keeps showing up and wiping his shoes on my plans. The Machados think you're part of my team. And they think you were involved in a mess your asshole brother got into. That giant clusterfuck in Juarez."

"You want them to blame Longview."

"Why would I want that?"

"Because it was Cesar Barcia's badge in the house. No one's found him or the missing money."

Stackhouse hit the brakes, and we slid sideways. Billowing dust made the night even darker. "Where are you getting your information?" His question came through clenched teeth. He didn't look at me either. It was as if he believed loosening any control would be to lose it all.

"Barcia was the poster boy for everything wrong with agencies like yours. And he was a piece of shit," I said.

"Maybe. But he was my piece of shit."

I didn't look at Stackhouse. I watched the dirt settle out of the headlights.

"I shouldn't have said that." His voice softened. "He wasn't the best of people, but he was a decent cop doing a hard job."

"I don't believe that."

"You don't know what you're talking about."

"I suppose he had a wife and two kids and a dog at home?"

"Fuck you, Paris Tindall."

"I think that's the first honest thing you've said tonight."

Stackhouse hit the gas again. I couldn't help but notice that he didn't say anything more to defend Barcia.

"Your brother was a drug runner for the Guzman DTO. They got taken over by La Familia de los Muerto."

"Longview Moody was a cash courier."

"A distinction without a lot of fucking difference." Stackhouse was practically snarling his words. "And your old man is a dirty cop."

"A dirty cop that works for you."

"As far as he knows, he works for La Familia."

"Viva la revolución."

"Look." Stackhouse turned to look at me for an instant. Then he shifted back to the road rushing under our tires. "People are dying. Good people. Bad people. If we keep it managed, we keep it down here."

"You want to keep good people and bad people from dying but not Mexican people?"

"My job is to protect American interests."

"You expect me to help you with that?" I asked.

"I don't think you have a hell of a lot of choice."

"Why didn't you just take me to the river and put a bullet in my head?"

"My team doesn't commit murder."

"Have you ever stopped La Familia from murdering?"

He didn't answer. The SUV did go faster. We traveled in silence through desert and impossible dark until we saw the lights of town and the border crossing.

"If you don't convince the Machado brothers that you aren't a part of my team—if you don't find a way to put their worries about DEA betrayal to bed…" Stackhouse didn't finish the sentence. He didn't have to.

Once we were back stateside, I asked him, "How long can you keep it up?"

"Keep what up?"

"You're partners with a criminal family operation. Your team is funneling money to them. You have a crew that commits murder and brutality, not to mention black-bag military operations in another country. How long can it last? Your own agency is investigating."

"That's the thing about government work." He was smiling again as he said it. "All you have to do is get the pieces in place. Politicians won't walk away from the money spent or open themselves up to scandal. Almost all my pieces are in place."

"All except me?"

He didn't say another word the rest of the drive back to Ernesto's place and my truck.

FIFTEEN

My truck had a bullet hole in the fender—either Joaquin or Álvaro venting after our talk. Who could blame them? I wasn't mad about it. It helped that it wasn't my vehicle. I climbed in and sat behind the wheel without twisting the key.

I was numb and tired, and my head was filled with everything but understanding. Time to go home, even if home was a motel room.

I pulled into the Desert Drop parking lot. The early-evening sun was still bright and yellow. It made long, angled shadows. In the deep shade of the motel alcove, along with the ice and vending machines, stood Lenore, almost as if she was waiting for me.

I parked and went straight to her.

Lenore leaned away from the soda machine and smiled at me. I ignored the scent of cigar smoke in the air.

"You look like a man carrying weight," Lenore said.

"You look like a wish."

She cocked her head and examined me with a crooked smile and off-angle eyes. It made me think I was the tilted one. It may have been the case.

"A wish come true?" she asked. The tease and promise were clear in her voice.

I took her hand and led Lenore up the stairs to my room. With the boards covering the windows, the room was dark. I turned the lights on and left them on. I'd had enough of darkness, and I wanted to see every inch of her skin. Lenore didn't complain.

Taking charge, she slid down my body, raking her nails as she went.

"Hold my hair," she told me without waiting for compliance. With her gaze locked to my eyes, she covered me with her mouth.

I did as I was told.

She smiled with her eyes as I watched every movement.

There were no words exchanged, but somehow she knew when I got too close. Lenore released me and laughed with pleasure.

My own laughter was in relief. I wasn't ready to reach an ending. Her hair flowed from my fingers, leaving them empty and lonely for contact. I reached for her, and she let me touch as she drew away. At first my fingertips grazed her face, then her shoulder. Lenore turned. My hands caught instants of her skin as she fell away from me.

Lenore spread her arms out and lowered her body to the bed with her back to me. Her thighs were open. All but her hips were pressed to the bed. The shapely swell of her ass was lifted. A new demand.

That time I didn't obey. Not instantly. I bent over her body to kiss and then bite the soft skin at her waist and worked my way down.

She made a feline sound in the back of her throat. It was urgent and rough like a tiger's purr.

I put my tongue to the base of her spine and licked upward. I pinned her arms and then used my legs to spread hers wider. When she raised her head to meet my mouth, I bit her hair and pulled. She moaned in response and under me, pressed herself up.

"I'm ready," she said.

I wasn't. I rose up on my knees and scratched her back with my nails. Then I touched. My fingers worked her back like the stations of the cross. It was enough to have my skin against hers.

The warmth of her flesh, the firm feeling of moving bones under muscle, her breath rushing cool into her lungs and racing out hot—that was everything I needed.

Lenore turned on her right side and exposed her breast to my searching hand. She arched her back when I pinched the nipple.

As I drew my hand away, it trailed over the lines tattooed on her ribs. I could read the words clearly.

> Yo soy la noche vivente.
> La oscuridad. El aliento de la muerto.
> En mi cama, la sombra reside—cada lado de mis ojos.
> Bajo la tierra, entre los muros de la desesperación.
> Mi santa viene.
> Mi protector me lleva a Jesús.
> Me convierto en la sombra en tu sangre.
> Derramar me para respirar.

The way I read it, the poem came out as this:

> I am the living night.
> The darkness. The breath of death.
> In my bed, the shadow resides—each side of my eyes.
> Under the earth, among the walls of despair.
> My saint is coming.
> My protector carries me to Jesus.
> I become the darkness in his blood.
> Spill me to breathe.

I didn't understand. Then it didn't matter. Lenore reached back to take my hands. She guided them to her hips. I didn't need more encouragement.

* * * *

I woke up to dawn creeping through a wide-open door. I wondered if Lenore had left the door open to make a gift of the sunrise or to leave me vulnerable.

Just in case I shut the door and put the security latch on before heading for the shower.

Clean and dressed, I felt good, better than I had in a long time. There was no mystery why. I was smiling as I went down the stairs to the truck. I was smiling still when I stopped at a café for breakfast because Officer Sunny Johnson was there.

She asked me, "Why the smile? You look like a dog that buried a bone."

"Did what?"

"You know what I mean," she said and then added, "And yeah, you did."

Her apparent disapproval brought my mood down but only a bit. "What do you say I buy you breakfast?"

"It's the least you could do."

"That's me," I said as I sat across from her. "Always the least I can do."

"You think that's funny?"

"I'm sensing that you're not sharing my good mood."

The waitress came over. Sunny ordered one egg, grits, and a strip of bacon.

I laughed. "How are you going to keep going on that?" Then I turned to our waitress. "May I have the short stack, please? With three eggs over medium, grits, sausage, and bacon on the side."

"How long do you expect to keep going eating like that?" Sunny asked.

The waitress left us without a word.

"You're a strange man, Chief Tindall," Sunny said as she examined me from across the table.

"What makes me strange?"

"Sometimes you seem like a decent person. Sometimes you seem like a decent cop."

"Other times?"

"Other times you're a psychopath." She didn't smile when she said it.

"Psychopath is a little strong."

"Violence won't solve all your problems." She said it without accusation. If there was anything in her voice, it was concern.

Our food began arriving. First came Sunny's diminutive meal. Mine took two trips.

I poured syrup on my pancakes but kept my eyes on her.

Sunny stared back at me like I was an idiot. Then she glanced down at my plate of pancakes.

I pushed them across the table, right in front of her.

Without hesitating, she cut into the most syrupy and buttery part of the pancakes with her fork. She held the big, dripping wedge up like a prize. "You're fooling yourself if you think violence follows you because you're a cop. It's because of who you are. Who you choose to be." She stuffed the bite into her mouth.

We dug in and ate in silence for a while. I couldn't help feeling a difference in my past night and the morning. It was a contrast that resided entirely in the women I was with. To keep from thinking about what I was feeling, I asked, "Is that who you choose to be—a cop?"

"Cop is something you choose to do." She pushed aside her empty plate. "That's different from who you are."

"If you say so." I pushed over the last of my pancakes to her.

"Tell me about you, your choices. How'd you become a cop?" She dug in.

"My father is a cop. And my brother—" I tossed the answer off before thinking about it.

"A family thing?"

"No." I must have put more force in that answer than I intended because she stopped chewing and looked at me hard.

"Why not?"

"We're very different people."

"Who?"

I thought about that one. Then I said, "All of us, I guess."

"You can't be that different."

"My half-brother, Longview, isn't a cop. He's a criminal."

"Complicated. But you must have some things in common. Did you grow up together?"

"My father kept two families. One real. One something else. My brother and I knew about each other but didn't meet until he was sixteen and had a driver's license. He came to our place and parked outside just—looking—for a long time."

"Looking at what?" Sunny had set her fork down and pushed the pancakes away.

"Differences, I think."

"I don't understand."

"He had a house and a car and a mom who didn't work."

"And you?"

"I didn't."

"And?" she asked, pushing me.

"And we got past it. We became friends."

Sunny stood. "Time for me to get to work."

I rose too, dropping cash for the bill. "Report in. Tell them you're on duty with me."

"Doing what?"

"We're going to that construction site by the Border Crossing."

"That's out of our jurisdiction."

I didn't say anything as I went to my truck.

"Why are we going there?" she asked as she followed.

"Call it investigation. Or call it fact-finding."

"Fishing," she said.

"Yep."

I got into my truck and she into her cruiser.

At the site, Sunny went straight in the main drive. I circled the far side and parked behind the contractor's trailer.

It was still early. There were no workers. Plastic tacked up on two-by-fours to shield the site from prying eyes billowed in a rising breeze. Where I parked was muddy even though it hadn't rained since I'd come to town. I picked my way around puddles to check the trailer before moving on.

Officer Sunny Johnson left her cruiser and went straight for the first, and largest, plastic-wrapped foundation. She thrust the sheeting aside and walked through.

I angled over to another unfinished building. That one had three standing walls. They appeared to be prefabricated pieces of steel and concrete. The floor was a smooth slab of cement. There wasn't much to see. I walked on to where Sunny had gone through the tarp.

"I'm a police officer for the City of Lansdale," she said, in a full, strong voice.

She wasn't speaking to me, but the volume was for my benefit, I was certain.

I backed away from the opening in the plastic and circled back to the side. There the draping was closed and taught, but it was still a glorified trash bag. I gripped the plastic and tore a hole.

Sunny was standing with her left hand out and her right on the gun at her hip. The man facing her was armed with a machine pistol. The only reason I didn't shoot him then and there was that his weapon was not pointed at her. He kept it angled into the dirt. His other hand was pointed out the direction she'd come.

"I can't leave," she said. "I need you to put your weapon aside and talk to me."

"No," he said right back. "You go."

I took a moment to look for other guards. There weren't any I could find. Taking another grip of the plastic, I pulled it apart until I had a hole big enough to step through.

Sunny could see me. I caught her glance. But it was just a glance. She kept her gaze and all attention on the man in front of her. "Drop your weapon," she ordered him.

He shook his head and pointed again at the flap in the plastic. "No. You must go."

I crept up, moving to my left until I was behind and to the man's left. That kept me clear of Sunny's line of fire and still out of his sight. Once placed, I told him, "Drop your weapon, and show your hands."

As soon as I spoke, Sunny pulled her revolver.

Instead of freezing or reaching for his gun, the man gave a long, tired sigh and asked, "Policia?"

"Yes," I answered. Then I added, "Sí."

He nodded and asked, "Tindall?"

"Yes."

He shrugged the strap from his shoulder and let the machine pistol fall into the dirt. Then he raised his hands and said, "Álvaro esta un culero."

"Sí," I said. "He's a big asshole."

"Are you going to shoot me?" he asked.

"I don't want to shoot anyone," I answered.

"Oh." He sounded disappointed.

"You want me to shoot you?"

"If you shoot me a little, it would go easier on me with La Familia."

"Show me your hands," I told him.

He presented the backs of his hands. There were no tattoos.

"Look at this," Sunny said, pointing into the building's foundation.

It was a rectangle of raised concrete rim with a slab floor poured within. The surprising thing was that the center of the pour was a long, wide ramp that dropped into darkness. It was a hole large enough to drive a truck through. Along the walls of the hole and rising up above the floor were conduits stuffed with wiring. None of it was the kind of cabling you expect to see for lighting or high voltage. It was all the thin kind of stuff that feeds computers and phones.

"What's going on here?" I asked the man.

He shrugged and said, "I keep people away at night."

Sunny pointed at the gaping hole and asked him, "Where's it go?"

He shook his head.

"Ciudad de la Sangre de Angel," I said.

"What's that?" Sunny asked, still staring into the shadowed tunnel.

"Blood of angels," our prisoner said with disgust. Then he turned his head and spat. "The angels come to towns like mine. They tell us we have jobs. You can't say no. You accept their money, or you take their bullet."

"Why don't you run away?" Sunny asked him. "Go back to your town?"

"They leave someone there to keep watch on our families. If you betray La Familia, your family dies. If you go home—the same."

"Come on," I said to Sunny. "We've seen what we need to."

"What about him?"

I turned to him and asked, "What about you?"

He shrugged again.

"He's not going to shoot us." I said it to her but kept my gaze on him. He listened carefully. "And I don't think he's going to tell anyone we were here."

"If they find out..." He dropped his eyes.

"We won't tell," Sunny reassured him. She turned and pushed open the fluttering plastic. "Shit."

"What?" I raised my weapon again.

"Cars," she answered. "And men."

"Workers?"

"Some."

I looked through the opening and saw, mixed in with workers, Joaquin and two of the men he'd sat with at the Border Crossing. "This has a big chance of getting messy," I said. "And by messy I mean dangerous and bloody."

When I turned around, Officer Sunny Johnson had the mic on her shoulder keyed. Her voice was quiet but firm. "Officers involved. Repeat. Shots fired."

"Help is on the way?" I asked her.

"That's the way it works."

"Remind me to make sure you get a raise."

"I promise."

I turned to look out the plastic again. The three men with guns were marching our direction. "Why did you say there were shots fired?"

"Turn around," Sunny said.

I was about to look when I realized too late she wasn't talking to me. The hammer of her revolved clicked loudly. That was when I turned. I was just in time to watch her shoot our prisoner in the back of the outer thigh.

"What the hell?" I shouted.

"We can't let him be found uninjured," she said to me. Then into her mic, she said, "Send EMTs."

I looked out again and saw the three men spreading out with their weapons at the ready. Before they could get around us, I pushed through the plastic gap. "Police," I shouted with my .45 aimed right at Joaquin.

He froze. His buddies didn't.

I spread my stance carefully and cupped my left hand under the butt of my pistol, taking solid aim, center mass, on Joaquin.

"Wait," he called, raising his gun to the air.

I'm not sure how much pull he had with the other two. They didn't shoot, but they didn't drop their aim on me either.

There was a long, excruciating few seconds before sirens could be heard approaching. At the far edge of my vision, the two gunmen put their weapons away and slunk back to a shining new red GMC pickup.

"You're making big mistakes, Tindall," Joaquin called over. "Screwing with things you don't understand."

I didn't answer. I was happy I could still breathe.

Joaquin rounded the hood of the truck and climbed behind the wheel. He slung gravel and dirt getting out of there as two Lansdale units pulled up. They were soon followed by an ambulance.

Sunny took charge. She set officers around the perimeter before ushering in the EMTs. The injured man was being taken care of as I went back to my truck.

SIXTEEN

My assistant chief, Bronwyn Gutiérrez, came tearing up the road with lights and sirens on. The odd thing about that was her direction. She didn't come from town. I pulled the truck around, slinging mud as I went, and cut her off before she could run from the car to where the EMTs were working.

"Get in," I told her.

"Where to?" she asked without moving to the door.

"Does it matter?"

"Yes," she said firmly. "It matters a whole lot."

"You don't trust me?"

"I don't think so."

"I trusted Stackhouse to take me someplace. You can trust me."

"I'm not sure that logically follows," Gutiérrez said, but she got into the truck.

I stood on the gas. Acceleration pushed us both into the back of the seats.

"Are we in a hurry?"

"I don't know," I answered. "Better fast than sorry."

I told her what was behind the plastic tarps at the construction site.

"Where does the tunnel go?"

"That's what we're going to see for ourselves."

I drove to the crossing and into Mexico, following the same route that Stackhouse had taken the night before. At one point,

I had to stop and get my bearings. There was more than one dirt road headed out of town and into the desert, and there were no road signs pointing the way to the City of Angel's Blood.

For most of the drive, we traveled in silence. I evaded one stone in the rut to strike another. The truck jumped. For a second we were free from the ground, and everything was smooth. When we settled back to earth, the shock was brutal. We bounced in the seats, restrained by belts and roof.

"You're dangerous. They shouldn't let you run around with a gun." We hit another huge bump too fast. "Or a truck."

I laughed. I was enjoying the drive.

"You outed me to Stackhouse," Gutiérrez said. The cab of the truck went silent.

"I didn't."

"Last night he made calls trying to find out about the investigation of his team. He asked a lot of pointed questions that included your name."

"I may have said he was under an internal investigation. I didn't mean...I never used your name."

"How stupid do you think he is? How long until he gets my name or figures it out?"

"I'm sorry." I meant it. "I screwed up."

"You're why people get killed."

"I said I was sorry. What do you want?"

"I want you to go away."

"That's not happening."

"Then you can fucking pay for my funeral."

Things were even quieter after that.

Ten minutes later we topped the hill above Ciudad de la Sangre de Angel. I pulled off the relative comfort of the dirt road and into the untracked desert and parked the truck behind a stand of cactus and rocks.

"What are we looking at?" Gutiérrez didn't sound less angry.

"That's the town—the City of Angel's Blood."

"Sounds cozy."

"I think Stackhouse and his crew built it."

"Why would they build a town?"

"I don't know. That's probably your job."

She gave me a hard look.

"But it's not a real town," I explained. "I think it's more of a depot. Or maybe it is a town. Maybe that works better for them. I don't understand any of this."

Again, she looked at me. Her expression was easy to read.

"Anyway," I went on. "What I do understand is that what starts at the construction site there by Lansdale comes out here."

"The tunnel?"

"More than that."

"A tunnel like that can move trucks full of drugs, guns, people. What more could they need."

"It has something to do with the bank."

"What bank?"

"Look…" I said carefully.

She took her gaze from the metal buildings below and gave me her full attention.

"I'm sorry," I said again. "I mean it."

Gutiérrez nodded her understanding. She kept looking at me, waiting for more.

"You've been looking at Stackhouse and his close relationship with the Machado brothers and La Familia. Am I right?"

She took a long, deep breath and held it. When she relaxed, it escaped slowly. Her eyes never looked away from mine. "They are building up La Familia, helping one DTO over the others. It's being done with the cooperation—with the help—of intelligence agencies on both sides of the border but without governmental oversight. It's not only putting millions of dollars at risk of misuse or outright embezzlement; it could be a huge international incident. The people who need to know, and who most need to be involved, are in the dark. That's why I'm here."

"Stackhouse said to me it was about revolution."

"Revolution?"

"He said they were controlling revolution. How do you do that?"

"I guess that depends on what you mean by 'control.'"

"Exactly," I said, feeling a little less foolish. "What he said made me think it wasn't about controlling battles or war. I think they want the revolution to keep going. They want to make use of it somehow."

"How do you make use of another country's revolution?"

"Money," I said. Then I pointed down at the big building. "That's where the tunnel comes out—I'm sure. If it was only for smuggling, that's all they need. But they're building a whole town."

"It doesn't look like much of a town."

"Which one of those other buildings do you think is a bank?"

The slower—saner—drive back to Lansdale took close to two hours.

* * * *

Back at the police station, I tried calling Milo. He didn't answer. Now I knew how it felt, and it pissed me off. I went to the impound lot to see what had happened with Bascom's car. It was in pieces with the interior now on the outside. The only thing to show for all the effort was a group of small plastic zipper bags. Each one had a slip of paper or a bit of dirt or a cigarette butt. None of the car's detritus looked very significant. The cigarette had been found in a heater vent and was so old the paper had broken into flakes when it had been recovered.

I tracked down Gutiérrez. She wasn't happy to see me, but when I asked about the councilman, she relaxed.

"Decided to be a real cop for a change?" she asked.

"I could ask you the same thing," I said right back. "But I'm the bigger man."

"Sure you are." She tossed a file over at me. "Here you go."

"What's this?"

"What you asked for."

I opened the folder, and within it were photos, forms, and handwritten notes all focused on Bascom Wood. "You've done all this already?"

"You sound surprised."

I skimmed over pages. There were notes detailing interviews with over a dozen people. "Not surprised. Impressed." I closed the file and dropped it back in front of her. "What's it all come to?"

"What do you think it comes to?"

"Nothing?"

"You win the prize. No one saw or knows anything."

"Maybe you're asking the wrong people."

"You think if I dragged one of the Machados in here, he would tell me everything I want to know?"

"I know a treasury agent you could ask."

Gutiérrez glared at me. "Why don't I just pull Darian Stackhouse in for questioning?"

"I'll drive."

The hard light in her eyes didn't flicker. I didn't press because I knew how useless it would be. Stackhouse and his team were protected by bureaucracy, and bureaucracy always had lawyers. If it was easy, Gutiérrez would have already done it. I left her and crossed the street to talk to Mr. and Mrs. Toomey.

They made the city hall seem like their home, and they were glad to have company. I asked, and Mr. Toomey opened the safe again. We chatted about the town and the situation it had gotten into as I made a more careful examination of the papers Bascom Wood had left behind. Conversation fell off as I laid out pages, organizing them into small piles grouped by type. I took notes and used my phone to photograph the bits that I thought were especially interesting. Those I e-mailed to Milo.

The largest pile was the paperwork for government grants. There were two other stacks in diminishing size. The middle one was banking information. Some were obvious receipts. Other pages were series of printed numbers with amounts listed. Those pages were on the letterhead of Bank of Lansdale.

"Wait a minute," I said. The sound of my own voice startled me; I hadn't realized I had spoken out loud. "I'm a stupid, stupid man." That time I was sure to say it aloud and let it sink in.

"What's wrong, Chief?" Mr. Toomey asked, setting a cup of coffee on the littered table.

"City councilman is not a full-time job here in Lansdale, is it?"

"Of course not," he said. "Even the mayor, when we had one, was part time. He owned the hardware store."

"Bascom Wood?" I pointed down at the banking papers. "Did he work at the bank?"

"The Bank of Lansdale is a family business. Bascom's father started it in 1966."

"And it started getting big just a couple of years ago?" I asked, but it wasn't a question.

"Yes. Bascom Wood has financed the entire boom going on in Lansdale." Mr. Toomey nodded his head sadly. "He'll be missed."

I turned to the smallest pile of papers. Those pages were crumpled and straightened bits with handwritten notations. Some were simply scraps on which questions and random statements were jotted. One was a segment of a computer print-out of more numbers with some familiar names written alongside them, names like Machado, Stackhouse, and my father's.

The last page was a sheet of lined notebook paper with names written and arrows drawn from some to others. To the side was a list that included Homeland Security, DEA, Policia Federal, and La Familia. Long looping lines linked the agencies to names and people to other people. It was a convoluted flowchart, maybe a representation of hierarchy or reporting order. Or maybe it was a series of guesses about the movement of money. None of it was clear to anyone but Bascom Wood. Maybe it wouldn't even have been clear to him.

One thing did stand out though. Between the name Darian Stackhouse and a circle bearing the names of the Machado brothers was a square with the name Joaquin D'Cruz in a little box. Joaquin's name was crossed out, and outside the square was a question mark. Was Bascom questioning loyalty or identity?

At the very bottom in a shaky black scrawl were three lines that left me feeling sick.

They know about Paris Tindall—

They know about me—

They know—

All along I had been assuming Bascom had been killed because he had gone storming up to the gun club making a scene about his son. It had nothing to do with that. He'd been killed because they knew something about him, and I was convinced what they knew about was this pile of paper. What was in the paperwork may not have been known, but someone was aware that he was collecting information. Was it blackmail? Protection?

And the big question—what did they know about Paris?

I photographed the chart and sent images to Milo.

* * * *

It was dark by the time I locked the papers back up and left with Mr. and Mrs. Toomey. The night was one of those startlingly clear desert infinites. There was no moon, but a river of stars overflowed its banks, flooding the sky.

When I pulled up at the Desert Drop, my headlights swept past Lenore standing at the office door. She looked like she was waiting for me to arrive. That may have been hope doing the thinking for me. She was wearing shorts of cut-off jeans and a threadbare white wifebeater. I could have read her tattoos through it if I were closer.

When I parked the truck and killed the engine, I looked for her again. The office was closed and dark. Lenore was walking slowly up the far steps. Her face was set straight forward, but I could feel her eyes watching me.

I went to the opposite staircase and started climbing.

My room door was standing open. The lights inside were off. When I got closer, I saw that the wifebeater was hanging from the doorknob, and the shorts were on the floor.

That night we didn't talk, and I didn't read the poetry on her body. We reached for each other in the darkness and held on as if all the needs in the world could be expressed by touch.

SEVENTEEN

In the coldest, smallest hours of morning, a fist pounded on my door. The sound, a threatening pulse, roused me quickly. Getting out of twisted sheets was less quick. I was surprised to learn that I was alone.

My pants and the .45 clipped to them were on the floor. I didn't open the door until both were on me.

The pounding didn't stop until the door pulled away from the hand that beat it. Hector stood with his fist poised to keep sounding his demand.

"What are you—"

"You don't answer your phone?" He cut me off with a voice as demanding as his fist.

I looked around, holstering my weapon as I did. "I think it's in the truck."

"Get your shirt and shoes on."

"What's going on?"

"Just do it," he said, already headed for the stairs. As he began tromping down, he called, "I'll be waiting."

I dressed from the discarded clothes.

"Where are we going?" I asked, dropping into the seat beside Hector.

He didn't answer. He slammed the car into gear and bolted onto the roadway. We traveled in silence until he jabbed the brakes and twisted the wheel, sending us into the same dirt track I had followed when I had gone fishing. That time I had found Officer Sunny Johnson with the body of Councilman Wood.

"Who is it?" I asked.

Hector didn't answer.

Through the trees, white lights strobed while red and blue chased circles. We rounded a rutted bend and came out into the same clearing in which we had faced down Stackhouse and his team. In the center of police cruisers was a circle of tape. It looked like every officer of the Lansdale Police Department was crowded up to the barrier. Some were in uniform and on duty. Many were in civilian clothes and had obviously been pulled from sleep just as I had.

Hector stopped the car in a grind of tires and billowing of dust. We both got out, but he stayed at the car, leaning against the open door. I looked ahead and then back at Hector. He shook his head and looked down. I went forward alone.

As I approached, officers made way for me. Some of them looked away. Some stared stones at me. Blame and shame.

I expected a car with another body slumped and blood spattered on glass and metal. Expectations are a bitch. There was blood. It had sprayed and pooled in the dirt around the woman's body tied to a young hickory tree. It was Gutiérrez.

Bronwyn Gutiérrez was dead.

She had been beaten. I imagine that had happened before she had been tied to the tree. Her clothes were soaked with thick blood not yet dry. The clothing was disheveled but intact. The violation that had been visited upon her was a different kind. Her tongue had been cut from her mouth. It was in the dirt and crawling with ants.

"Cut her down," I said.

"We haven't done our investigation," someone said.

"Cut her down. I know who did this."

"I want to help," one of the officers said.

"I'm in," another announced in a choked whisper.

"Fuckin' A," someone else said.

"We all want to help," Officer Sunny Johnson said. She was standing right in front of me. It was the first I'd seen her.

"You're cops." I lifted my head to include them all in my words. "You're all better than what I'm going to do."

"You're a cop too." Sunny placed a hand on my arm.

"If I was any kind of cop, she wouldn't be here."

I turned away, trudging back through the spinning lights and judging eyes to the car. Hector was no longer behind his door. He had moved forward to stand between the dirt ruts in front of his headlights.

I put out my hand and said, "Give me your keys."

Hector looked me right in the eyes. Nothing else about him or me moved. Our eyes watered and twitched. Finally, his head ticked a negative. He marched back to his seat behind the wheel and waited.

I climbed in, and we backed away, leaving the rest of the Lansdale police to take care of their own.

* * * *

There wasn't a single word spoken as we drove. I didn't tell Hector where to go. When we came to intersections, I pointed the way. At one point I pulled my .45. I ejected the magazine and the round in the chamber before checking the movement. Once I was satisfied that everything about the weapon was ready, I reloaded.

As we passed the construction area, I pointed at the sagging shack with trailers out back. Hector turned into the gravel lot of the Border Crossing and stopped sideways in a clear patch.

We both climbed from the car, and Hector said, "Hang on." He went to the trunk and pulled out a twelve-gauge riot gun. He racked the slide and then pulled a shell from the band on the stock and shoved it into the loading port. "Let's go."

Cars passed on the road behind us. Their tires made quiet tearing sounds on the pavement. Underfoot, gravel crunched. As we approached the door, music bled out. It was like everything else, though: sound without feeling or meaning.

This time there was no clear segregation. I didn't see Stackhouse, but most of his SOT crew were playing pool alongside soldiers of La Familia. Joaquin was there in the back. No one was surprised to see us.

I sidled right, toward the bar, with my hand on the butt of my pistol. Everyone was watching. I hoped that meant they wouldn't notice Hector creeping in and to the left with his shotgun at the ready.

They noticed.

Every man in the place—there were no women that I saw— was armed and weapons ready. When I stopped beside the bar, Stackhouse popped up from behind it with a gun at my head. Hector turned with his shotgun when Stackhouse showed. As soon as Hector shifted his aim, another man stepped from behind the partition wall and pressed a pistol to his temple.

Hector didn't flinch. He didn't lower his weapon either. His aim remained steady and fixed on Stackhouse.

"Good to see you, Chief," Stackhouse said. He was speaking carefully. I couldn't see, but I believed his gaze was on Hector, not me.

"I bet it is," I said, turning my pistol in slow motion to point right into his gut. "Looks like you expected me."

"Be prepared. I was a Boy Scout."

"You've come down in the world."

"You mind asking your friend there to lower the shotgun? It makes me nervous."

"Hector?"

"I'll play it how you say it." The fear in his voice couldn't compete with the resolve.

"Hold steady," I said. "Whatever we do, we shouldn't die alone."

A couple of the military types snickered softly. They thought it was bravado. None of the Mexican gunmen laughed. To a man, they eased back a step or two.

"You're in the wrong place," Stackhouse said.

"Where should I be?"

"Not here."

"Why not here?"

He didn't say anything.

I eased back a long step, clearing more room between Stackhouse and me. His gun followed me but nothing else.

"Hector," I said. "If you shoot him, the man with his gun at your head will kill you."

"I know."

"Will you shoot him if you have to?"

"Yes."

No one snickered.

"There are a few ways to play this, Stackhouse." It was gratifying to see the sweat beading on his forehead and rolling down the bridge of his nose. "Most of them end up with you dead."

"You won't survive it."

"That's the thing. That's your fuck-up here." I turned my attention from him to the rest of the room to make sure everyone was listening. Then I brought my gaze back to his eyes. "We're willing."

I let it set there, time for him to think it through.

"Put your weapons down," Stackhouse said. "We can talk."

"We like the conversation as it is."

"You're holding federal officers at gunpoint, Tindall. Do you think you can get away with that?"

"Tonight, you and your boys murdered a federal agent."

Some of the big military types looked at each other. It was a reaction of surprise. The Mexicans didn't respond.

"But I don't think everyone was in on it. Keeping secrets from the team?"

"No one knows what you're talking about." Stackhouse spat the words out in a desperate slur. "We've been here all night."

"See, Hector?" I stole a glance his way. Hector never took his eye from Stackhouse or the front sight he had centered on his chest. "He gave an instant alibi for something he claimed not to know about. What's that say to you?"

"It says guilty as fuck."

"We don't know what you're talking about. *I* don't know what you're talking about, Chief." The hand with which Stackhouse was holding the gun on me inched down. "Can't we deescalate this?"

I brought my pistol up rather than lowering it. His hand stopped.

"First thing you said when I came in, Stackhouse—remember?" I asked. "You were prepared. You knew. Question is—" I looked away from him and turned to one of the men. He was the same big pool player I had antagonized a few days ago. "Did you know?"

The man looked stunned but otherwise did not react.

"Officer Bronwyn Gutiérrez of the Lansdale Police Department. I know you knew her. You were standing right there when I talked to her at this bar a few days ago. She was murdered."

He glanced at Stackhouse.

"Don't look at him," I warned. "Look at me."

He did.

"The other question—" I pressed. "Did you know she was DEA?"

Whatever held his face in position cracked.

"You didn't."

"He's lying, Bart," Stackhouse told the man.

"Shut up." Hector's warning was like a feral dog's growl. Stackhouse listened.

"You didn't know your entire team was the subject of internal investigation?" I asked Bart.

He didn't answer.

"She was murdered tonight and her tongue cut out. Tell me, Bart, who gets that kind of treatment?"

"Snitches." He said the word, but it was simply a fact, not condemnation. Then he stole a look over at the nearest of La Familia.

"Is an undercover cop a snitch, Bart?"

He shook his head.

"You're flapping like a bird with broken wings, Tindall," Stackhouse said. "Noise and feathers, going nowhere."

"Keep telling yourself that," I said, with my gaze on Bart. "But it's not you I was talking to."

Bart was looking at his boss.

At the edge of my vision, I could see Stackhouse. His gun hand wavered. It was time for me to put up or get out. "Hector?"

"Yeah?"

"You ready to get out of here?"

"You want me to kill him?"

"No." I eased my .45 away from Stackhouse and returned it to the holster. "We're not going to kill them."

"Why?" he asked, sounding genuinely disappointed.

"Because La Familia is going to do it." That got a reaction. The Mexicans, who had been happy staying back, letting the whites and the cops threaten each other, became suddenly attentive. They looked at each other with questioning eyes and then looked at the cops around them with new malice. "And these guys are going to kill La Familia."

"What are you talking about?" With only one gun aimed at him, Stackhouse was sweating a little less and ready to be his asshole self.

"War," I said. Then I walked backward to the door and pulled it open. Holding it, I shifted my aim to the man holding his weapon to Hector's head. "Come on out, Hector. It's over for tonight."

"Tindall," Stackhouse called after me. "This isn't a little thing. This is big as hell. Government big. National economy big. Too big for a chief of police." He grinned, finally looking like a man back in control. "Too big for you."

We drove back the way we had come, still silent. In my head, I entertained myself wondering about the conversation Stackhouse was having with his men and the La Familia boys. There was something else rattling around in my brain—what he'd said there at the end, before Hector and I had made it out the door. Stackhouse had said it was big. Too big for me.

I was unable to shake the thought. It was like everything else that I had been trying to do since I had found Paris in my trailer. Nothing fit right. I had tried responding to events by becoming something I wasn't. Paris. I was trying to become bigger. Maybe the answer was to make things smaller.

When we approached the turnoff onto the dirt road, Hector had to stop the car and wait for the ambulance to exit.

"I don't need to go back there," I said. "Take me back to the motel."

"What are you going to do?"

"I need my truck."

"Then what?"

"Then I'm going to do what I do. And it ain't going to be pretty."

Hector turned the wheel and pulled back onto the blacktop. He passed the ambulance, which was traveling with lights but no siren.

EIGHTEEN

I didn't go back to my room or change clothes. Even though the morning was yet to begin burning in the east, I went to the city hall and parked out front. There I was alone with my thoughts as I waited. They weren't good company. I turned on the radio and listened to music. It was all about loss and fear and beer. Perfect.

The first sign of dawn was the pinkish glow on the underside of crawling clouds. It wasn't long after that another car pulled into the lot and parked alongside my truck. The driver was Spencer Toomey, and the passenger was his Mrs.

I'd expected them early, but their arrival with the sun was surprising. I stepped out of the truck and waited for them to disembark from the boat of a car Mr. Toomey drove. It wasn't quick.

Mr. Toomey climbed out first. He gave me a look but said nothing as he tottered around the car to open the door for his wife. It wasn't until she was out and the car door locked by key that they both looked at me again.

"Is there something we can do for you, Chief?" Mr. Toomey asked.

"We'll have coffee on in a minute," Mrs. Toomey said. "You can tell us all about it then."

"She's right," he said. "Ain't nothing that needs doing before coffee on a bright morning."

With her hand in his arm, they climbed the steps. He pulled a ring of keys tethered to his pants by a retractable chain. One by one he counted through keys until he found what he needed to open the big front door.

By the time we got inside and had lights on, I was ready to scream at the pair. When I had a hot mug of coffee in my hand, I was grateful and calmer.

First I told them what I wanted. They told me why it was impossible. Then I talked through a second cup and told them almost everything I knew about what was happening in their town. I told them about the morning just passing and the death of Gutiérrez.

"I wish we could help..." Mr. Toomey said when I stopped talking.

"We can," his wife corrected him. To me she said, "We will."

"We can't," he reiterated stronger. "It won't work."

"Why?" I asked.

"It won't be legal. It won't stand up in court. You would be doing it for nothing."

"I don't need it to be legal," I said. "In fact, getting into court is good enough. We want it all official, with records and publicity."

"You want to make trouble." Mrs. Toomey grinned.

"I do," I said. "The small problems of bureaucracy can build a big wall."

"Well, I always said it's easier to live with one elephant than a thousand cockroaches."

"He's right," Mrs. Toomey said. "He does say that."

"It'll probably take all day," he added.

"Tomorrow will be fine," I said.

* * * *

I pulled back into the motel parking lot with morning burning away behind me. I wanted a shower and clean clothes before I took another breath.

I scrubbed my skin pink in the hottest water I could stand. I used a fresh blade to shave clean and then a second one to do the job over until my face burned. Using my old brush, I worked my teeth over and over, stopping only when I spat blood into the sink. All of it was an exercise in removing stains that had settled into my bones and were never coming out.

Steam came out of the bathroom ahead of me when I opened the door and stepped out, wearing only a towel on my hips. Through the fog, I picked up cigar smoke. I had forgotten to set my two-by-four brace on the door, and Simon Machado was standing in my open doorway. He was dressed again in a western suit, this time lavender with a white silk shirt and matching neckerchief. It would have been easy to make fun of him if he wasn't holding Lenore in front of him like a talisman. In a stark contrast to his clothing, she wore only thin white panties and a red bra. Her hair was twisted in his hand, but she didn't appear to be uncomfortable or unwilling. She smiled with secrets in her eyes and on her lips.

Machado blew a gray cloud of smoke over her head and then removed the cigar. "You come talk," he said.

"What do we have to talk about?"

"This is not an invitation." He raised the cigar and took a long pull to savor the taste in his mouth. When he puffed the smoke out, he jerked Lenore's hair. She fell willingly against his body. "Do not mistake it."

"Are you all right?" I asked Lenore.

"Would you make me all right?" she asked as an answer. Lenore kept her gaze locked to my eyes, making sure I was seeing her as she ground her backside against Machado's hips.

He reached around with his cigar and put the wet end in her mouth. She drew in smoke and chuffed it out.

"You see how things are," he said. "Come. Talk. Someone else you know will be there. Learn what is happening. The truth."

He took his cigar from her mouth and put it back in his before backing away from the door. Lenore was dragged back by the hair. She wasn't fighting.

I left the door standing open as I dressed; then I accepted the noninvitation.

* * * *

I pulled up to the gate at the Gun Hills Hunting Lodge and Private Club. There was no banter or taunting. The man in the shack opened the iron gate. I proceeded through without a word.

The main door of the club was again covered by men with guns, but they were all new to me. I had hoped to have a few words with Joaquin. Once ushered to the inner door, I was disarmed. I tried to debate the issue. This time it was different. One man put a gun to my neck; the other took my .45.

Sitting in the center of the leather couch, taking it all but using almost no space, was Eladio Machado. To the side and around a corner, the sound of ice falling into a glass and pouring liquid alerted me that we were not alone. Expecting the brother, Simon Machado, resplendent in lavender, I turned.

I can't say which of us was more shocked, me or my father, when Buick Tindall walked in. For a second it looked like he might drop the highball glass in his hand. He didn't recover all his composure, but he saved the whiskey by taking a drink. Over the glass, his eyes, metal-jacket hard, stared at me.

His glass was half-empty when Buick took it from his lips and said, "What the hell?"

"My thought exactly," I said.

Buick looked back at the skeletal Machado brother. Eladio seemed to be ignoring us. "Eladio?" Buick asked. "You mind if I have a talk with my *boy* in private?"

"It is why you are here," Eladio said, staring off at nothing. "To talk some sense to your son."

"Come on," Buick ordered, pushing past me and going through the door to the big hall. I don't think he expected the men who had escorted me in to still be there. Finding no privacy, he kept walking. The riding heels of his boots intermittently clipped the floor, making his gait a quick leather-and-wood backbeat.

I followed without hurry. The confrontation was one I'd looked forward to. There was no reason now to make it fast for either one of us.

He looked back when he shoved open the outer doors. "You coming or not?"

I didn't answer, and he didn't wait for one.

Out on the big porch, he clomped from side to side as if trying to decide if it was private enough for his needs. Evidently it wasn't. Buick gave up the porch and jigged down the steps in a bandy-legged half hop. He looked back at me when he was in the middle of the drive. He said nothing, but the rage he felt from my lack of haste was projected through his eyes.

Buick crossed the drive and tromped out into the foliage of the landscaped front, where he stopped and waited for me.

For my part, I stopped on the bottom step and looked both ways like traffic was a big consideration. Let him stew, I figured. Then I crossed the drive.

As soon as I was in the grass, my father looked around, once more checking for other eyes and ears, and then turned on me.

I hit him in the mouth. The punch was not my best. It went off center because I hesitated, and Buick saw it coming. His response had no hesitation in it. He hit me high in the gut with a short jab that struck like a wrecking ball. I had no doubt that he held back. All the wind in me blew out, leaving my lungs empty and paralyzed. I stayed on my feet but bent and uselessly gasping.

Buick grabbed me by the collar and forced my head lower. Then he did the one thing I could never have predicted. He rubbed my back and leaned down, bringing his face close to mine. "Try to relax," he said. "You can't force it. Let it come."

Slowly, almost fearfully, my breath returned.

As if he didn't want to startle the air away, Buick kept his face close to mine and whispered, "What the hell have you done? Where is Paris?"

I didn't say anything. At first it was because I couldn't. Then it was because I hated the answer. When I was able to stand upright, I wavered on unsteady legs.

"Well?" he pressed.

The only answer I had was to stare until he got it. Realization was painful. Buick looked like he'd taken the fist to his solar plexus.

"No." He shook his head as if the gesture had the power to rework the truth. Then he said, "They killed him."

"Yes," I said, still out of breath and holding my gut. "Your friends killed him. They killed us both, you might say. But you don't care about that."

He moved in close until our chests almost touched. He didn't tower over me the way he always seemed to in my memory. "Are you all right?"

"I've been hit harder." Even to myself I sounded like a wounded kid.

He shook his head slowly as he stepped back and turned away. "You don't know anything."

It took me a few seconds, but I got it. He wasn't talking about the punch. The best I can say about the moment is that he was right. Still, I was gratified that he wasn't looking at me. I didn't want him to see my face because I had no idea what expression I was wearing.

My father ran his hands over his body, pocket to pocket, looking for something without ever finding it. When he gave up, he turned around and looked at me without fire. "How did you get into the middle of all this?"

I shook my head. "That's not the conversation I want to have."

"Stop this."

"You started it, and I want to hear it."

"What, boy? What is it you want to hear?"

"How did Paris get into the middle of it? Why did he die?"

"I just found out it was him."

"But you've got all the pieces. You know. If you say you don't, you're lying to both of us."

"It's my fault," he said. "You feel better making me say it?"

"No."

"Me either. It's the truth, but sayin' it is like pumping broken glass through my heart."

"How?"

"The way bad things always happen. I started something without looking far enough ahead. There was what I thought would happen. And there was everything else."

"You tied up with the Machados?"

"Not at first. At first I worked with Stackhouse. I helped him put together cash to finance a big op."

"Paris?"

"I told him. Not everything. Just enough to get him interested, I thought. It was going to be big, plenty of room for everyone and lots of easy money. You know your brother. He said easy money was always the hardest."

"He didn't take part?"

Buick shook his head slowly. "No. He didn't. And he didn't let it drop either. Why?" He looked at me, and the question remained in his eyes. "I thought he would let it go. I expected he would give it a pass. It was *me*."

"Maybe that's why," I said. "Because it was you."

Buick shot his eyes my direction and then fenced them off behind narrow lids. "I didn't ask him to do anything. Just gave him the chance. If he didn't want to, he shoulda…"

"That was never Paris, and you know it."

"Yeah, I know it." His eyes widened and softened before he looked away to the point of his boots. "What a man expects from his son is not about knowing."

"Sons can say the same about their fathers."

I expected a reaction—a curse or a criticism. It didn't come.

Buick kept looking at his boots as he said, "The SOT put me with the Machados. The DEA wanted La Familia to consolidate power and cash around Lansdale. I set up all the banking with a city councilman."

"Woods."

"Yes."

"Paris found out?"

He looked up and met my gaze. "I don't know what he knew. It was the Machados who told me he had come to town asking questions. They told me to take care of him. He wouldn't take the DEA money, but he pitched a fit at the idea of taking Machado money."

"How could you think Paris could be bought?"

"It was the only way by then. The things he was doing. The things I did. Everything was digging a deeper hole." Buick didn't look at me. He wasn't looking at anything outside of himself. Then he said, in a voice tinged with desperation and regret, "There was no getting out."

That sentence chilled me. "What did you do?"

"I told the Machados Paris was on the payroll."

"What the hell?"

"It was a way to keep him safe."

"That didn't work out the way you thought, did it?"

The flash in his eyes was weak. He didn't have a response. Instead he said, "I should have known better. I gave him every chance to be like me, and I was proud each time he made the better choice. But you…you were already like me. I tried to give you every chance not to be. I thought if you grew up learning what a bastard was, you might have a chance."

"Bullshit."

We stood there for a long time in silence, each looking away from the other. We were like castaways on a small island of grass in a sea of asphalt.

Buick squared his shoulders and said, "I knew that you were running cash for the Guzman Cartel. And I knew that La Familia was going to kill you when they took over."

He stopped talking. I waited for more, but he remained mute. That answered my question, but still I asked, "You didn't try to warn me?"

"They already knew about Paris. My position was on the edge. Trying to warn you would have been killing you and me and Paris."

"You left me hanging?"

"And I never worried for a second. Not until…" Buick kicked a divot of lawn out into the road. "Paris was the one I worried about. You're the hard one. I never believed that people like that could do you in. I told Paris to quit, get out, run. He was never as strong or as resourceful as you. And here we are."

"Here we are," I echoed him. Hearing him say anything positive about me left me feeling more winded than his fist had. If there was one man in the world I didn't want to forgive or cut slack for, it was Buick Tindall. "You didn't even go to my funeral."

"La Familia didn't know I was your father. It would have been a problem."

"Are you going to tell me you're a good cop just trying to do your job here?"

"Would you believe me?"

I opened my mouth to spit out my response. Then I closed it. "I don't know."

"Well, we have that at least." Buick squared his shoulders and pinched the bridge of his nose like he was damming back a weight rising behind his eyes. "Paris was the good cop."

"Yeah." I nodded and looked away. In part, it was to give the old man a little privacy in the moment. In part, it was because I felt a little sorry for him. I preferred hating him. "What're we going to do about it?"

Buick shook his head while looking across the asphalt at the big front doors to the gun club. "I'm on this one, and I'm tied to it. You can get out."

"I've been telling myself that, but here I am too." I'd had enough. I stepped out of the grass. The sun was so hot the road smelled of tar, and the black surface was tacky.

"Where are you going?" My father called after me. "We need to figure this out. We need to settle things."

I stopped in the middle of the street and turned around to look at him. He was still a lot smaller than I had always thought he was. "What things?"

"Us. Them. What's going to happen. Before you got here, there was another man with the Machados. His name is Joaquin."

"I'm not surprised." It was true. Joaquin kept popping up with the DEA and with La Familia. I was sure there was a good reason for that.

"He said you were talking about war between the cartel and the feds. He said you should be killed."

I nodded my understanding. "I think I've done my settling." I took a step and then stopped again. "Buick," I said, turning back to him. "There's one thing I've always wanted to say to you."

"Don't bother. I said it to my father. It's not as satisfying as you think it will be."

"Kiss my ass, you old son of a bitch."

"Feel better?"

"No." I turned and headed back to the clubhouse porch. At the door, I held out my hand to the man who'd taken my .45 and said, "La pistola, por favor."

Buick trod up the stairs. "We need to go inside. The Machados will want to know what's going on."

"You handle it."

"What am I supposed to say about you?"

"I have some things to do. I'll be back tomorrow and set everything right."

"You better be, boy. I'm the one with my nuts in the fire."

"I get it."

"I hope you do, boy. You want us to get out of this alive—you better goddamned get it and good."

"Tomorrow," I said. "I'll be here and sit down with you and the Machados to work things out."

"What's all the talk about war with the feds?"

"Tell them I'll give them the undercover agent in La Familia."

That got a reaction out of Buick. He looked a little scared. The two gunmen at the door stared openly at me. I clipped the .45 back onto my belt and then went down the stairs.

"That's his gun," Buick said to my back. "I gave that to him."

I never looked back.

NINETEEN

Driving into town, I pulled Paris's phone from the glove box. Milo had called back. I punched the contact icon, feeling tired and wasted. It was time.

"I got the images you sent," Milo said as soon as he picked up. "And I've been hearing things from other sources. What the hell is going on down there?"

"They killed Gutiérrez."

"Do you know who?"

"Yes?"

"Is that a question or an answer?"

"He'll tell me himself when I find him."

"Was it La Familia or..."

"Are you asking if the DEA's SOT could have killed one of their own?"

"Was it La Familia or the SOT?" That time his question had its spine.

"Both."

For a long few moments, he was quiet. "Which one pulled the trigger?"

"Both," I repeated.

"I'm not sure what that means."

"It means that she was mutilated and murdered by the SOT member working undercover in La Familia de los Muerto."

"Do you have evidence?"

"I don't need evidence."

"Don't go stupid on me, Paris."

"I'm not Paris," I said. "He's dead."

"Clamp that crap down and get your head screwed back on," Milo told me.

It wasn't the reaction I expected. It took a second for me to realize that he took my confession as hyperbole.

I was about to set the needle into the right groove when he said, "You're a good cop. I need you to see this through."

"Look—"

"And by me, I mean your country. This is important."

I didn't know which was worse, feeling good or feeling bad about that.

When I didn't say anything back, Milo said, "On the bigger picture..."

"Bigger picture?"

"I know how it sounds. I hope you know it's not what I mean."

As touchy as I was at the time, I thought I did know how it sounded was not what he intended. Saying okay was the best I could give him.

"What's happening?"

I filled him in on the basics, including the trips to Ciudad de la Sangre de Angel and the tunnel.

"What's it about?"

"That's more on you at this point," I said. "It's bigger than simple drug smuggling, and it's federal. I can't say I know what it is. But I will say you won't like what comes next."

"And what's that?"

"Killing."

It was Milo's turn to be silent. It didn't last as long as I expected. "That's not our job."

"Do you think you can arrest these people?"

He was quiet for a long time. Then: "What are you going to do?"

"You don't want to know."

I hung up, and Milo didn't call back. I called Hector.

He answered before the first ring was complete. "Chief?"

"I have a question."

"Yeah?"

"Where do La Familia get their tattoos?"

"There's a few places I know of."

"Where do they get the grinning skulls inked on their fingers?"

"There's only one place for that."

* * * *

Hector was waiting outside in his car when I pulled up in front of a dirty but colorful joint called Death's Head Tattoo and Body Art. There were also two bikes and a bright-red pickup that looked like it had rolled off the lot that day.

"What are we doing this time?" Hector asked.

"More of the same."

"Let me get the street sweeper." He opened the trunk and pulled out the shotgun.

"You know you don't have to do this, don't you?"

"I know."

"Thanks." I took a deep breath. "I mean it."

"Thank you."

"For what? I haven't done anything worth thanks since I've been here."

"Not true. You gave Paris back to me. At least you saved him in my memory. Most of all you stuck around when you could have run."

"Should have run."

"Could have. Should have. You stayed. It was a hard thing. Thanks."

"I wish it was Paris here." I didn't look at Hector when I said it. "I wish…"

"I know, man. You don't have to spill it all out to me. I know."

In the movies that would have been the moment that Hector racked a round into the chamber of the shotgun and one of us would say, "Let's go," or something like it. Life never goes like the movies. Hector already had a round of double-aught buckshot chambered, and I was already walking.

A little bell tinkled over the door when I shoved it open. Four men inside stopped laughing at the same time. Two of them froze. They belonged to the bikes outside. The one with the tattoo gun dropped it on a cluttered table and ran for the back door. I let him go. The man in the chair with his back to me would have jumped and run too, but he was only half out of the deep chair when I shouted, "Joaquin."

I couldn't see his face. I didn't need to. His understanding of his situation was carved into tense muscles and an artificially straight posture.

"You two," I said to the bikers. "Show me your hands."

They each put up their hands, palms up in surrender.

"The backs," Hector ordered.

The pair looked at each other.

"The backs of your hands." They complied. Hector let them run, but he kept an eye on them until the bikes rumbled down the road. "Clear."

All that time I kept my gun on Joaquin, and he stood as still as a pinned bug. "Can I turn around now?"

I shifted to my left, widening the line of fire between him and Hector's shotgun. "You can when your gun hits the floor."

Joaquin looked over his shoulder at me and then craned his neck to see Hector. Our separation made it impossible for him to shoot us both. He lifted his weapon gingerly and dropped it to the floor.

"I got something else to show you."

"I don't need to see your badge," I told him.

Joaquin's shoulders slumped.

"Badge?" Hector sounded incredulous.

"Joaquin here is the DEA man undercover with La Familia," I explained.

"Is that true?" Hector demanded.

"True enough." Joaquin turned slowly with his hands up in front of him. "See? We're on the same side."

"Which side was Gutiérrez on?"

"This guy?" Hector stepped forward with the shotgun level at center mass on Joaquin.

I reached out before he could react and grabbed Joaquin's right wrist. I twisted it around to show the new outline of a grinning skull with a mantilla comb.

"Things happen."

That was the last thing I needed to hear him say. I jerked him forward and let him fall face down in the tattoo chair. Then I raised my boot and put it in his back to hold him there. When I twisted his arm, he almost screamed. His fingers flexed open wide.

When I put the barrel of my .45 against his tattooed finger, he shouted, "No."

"Why not?" It was Hector asking, not me.

"I'm on the job. You can't do this."

"She was on the job." Hector bellowed the accusation. "Did she get to tell you that before you cut her tongue out?"

"I'm a federal officer."

"So was Cesar Barcia," I said it without anger or recrimination. Joaquin stopped fighting though. "You know that name."

"Who's Cesar Barcia?" Hector asked.

"Tell him." I gave the wrist another twist.

Joaquin grunted but said nothing.

"You remember him, don't you? He was a real funny son of a bitch, always laughing." I stepped harder into his spine and turned the wrist another inch.

"He was a friend of mine."

"You know what happened? Cesar Barcia begged me. After I broke his leg, he showed me his badge. *He* tried hiding behind it."

"What did you do?"

I stared down at Joaquin. His teeth were clenched, but the question was still on his face. Suddenly I wasn't proud of what I'd done. But I wasn't hiding either. "I broke his other leg. Then I broke his hand under my boot."

"You killed him?"

I shook my head. "I left him in the grave he made me dig for myself. I left him alongside others he'd killed. But he was alive." I flexed my muscles at the memory and turned Joaquin's wrist a little farther. "I left him a gun and a bullet. The coyotes were already howling."

Hector eased the pressure off his trigger finger. He took a sliding step back too. He was angry but not the same kind of man as me.

I was glad of that.

It didn't stop me from cocking my pistol. The barrel was still pressed to the first tattoo on Joaquin's fingers. It was still new and shiny. "For Bascom Wood?"

He didn't say anything. He didn't move at all. There was an energy in his eyes that I thought was an answer.

I lifted my gun and moved the barrel to the other finger. That one was red and angry-looking with the almost-complete skull inked there. "For Gutiérrez?"

Joaquin flinched.

I squeezed my trigger.

His digit disappeared into muzzle flash and a settling red mist.

The roar of the gunshot muted my hearing. Joaquin's screaming sounded like a power saw on the other side of a mattress wall. Hector said something. His mouth moved anyway. I couldn't make out any words.

"What?" I pointed to my ears and then at the writhing man on the tattoo chair.

"What do you want to do with him now?" Hector yelled over the screaming.

I hadn't thought that far ahead.

Joaquin passed out. At least he fell silent and stopped his thrashing around. That was good enough.

"Help me get him out to his truck," I told Hector.

Together we tossed him in the bed and shut the gate. Hector cuffed Joaquin's undamaged hand to a tie-down ring. I rifled his pockets until I found keys.

"Where to?"

"Are you hungry?"

Hector looked at me like I'd introduced him to Frankenstein's monster brought to life in my basement. Then he shook his head. "I don't think I'll ever be hungry again."

"That's the time you most need good food and people around."

"People?"

"Being alone is the worst thing at a time like this."

"What is a time like this?" Hector asked, looking around as if he was surrounded by ghosts. He may have been. "Do you mean the time of dead friends? Or maybe it's the time of brutality and violence?"

"All of it. And more."

"More?"

"Things can still get worse. Who makes the best barbecue in town?"

Hector stared at me like I was a crazy man. Eventually, though, he said, "Tubby."

TWENTY

I didn't know if the trip was hard on Joaquin. I didn't ask. Not that it would have mattered. He was still unconscious when I arrived at Tubby's BBQ. That or he had woken and passed out again. The trip was fast, and I took the corners none too gently.

I glanced in the truck bed. The red paint did little to disguise the pool under the body. And Joaquin's clothing appeared as if he'd rolled around on a slaughterhouse floor.

Tubby was aptly named. He was a huge black man with a lively smile and an ever-present scent of wood smoke about him.

"I need your help," I told him as he checked the meats in the smaller of two huge smokers.

"How can I help the police today?" He sounded willing but wary.

"They say you're the best in town."

"Ain't that big a town." He said it dismissively. "Now tell me," he said, turning paper-wrapped brisket on the grate. "How can I help the police? And keep in mind, my chief, the historical difficulties between the black business owner and the Anglo-centric authorities."

That I had to puzzle out. It took a second, but I finally said, "This isn't a shakedown. And if you ever get one while I'm around, we can smoke a new kind of meat."

"Fair enough." Tubby nodded but kept his eyes on his work. "Now, as long as I ain't turning over my hard-earned cabbage to the man, what can I do for you, Mr. Chief of Police?"

"We lost an officer today."

Tubby stopped fiddling with meat. He closed the smoker door and gave me his full attention. "Go on."

"It's been an awful day for a lot of folks. It's been a horrible one, as a matter of fact." I might have choked a bit, but I let it be because of the smoke. "I want the cops working for me to be fed. I want them to be together, not hunkered down at home or alone wondering..."

Tubby squared his shoulders and started to say something.

I stopped him by asking, "How much?"

"How many?"

"Anyone that shows up. Cops. Citizens."

He nodded like he had made an important decision and then jerked his head over at the bigger smoker for me to follow. The door was heavy steel, and even with welded-on counterweights, the big man had to push hard to lift it. Within were two hogs. Not cuts of meat—these were the entire animal splayed open and wrapped in chicken wire. They smelled amazing.

"This'll get us started," he said.

"We'll need beer."

His eyes lit up. "'Course you will."

"And potato salad?"

His grin was brighter than his eyes. "Best you ever had. And beans, roasted corn ears, cracklin's, broccoli-and-cheese casserole, and maybe a few other things. When you want it?"

"As soon as you can get it over to the station." I pulled a wad of bills from my pocket and counted out $2,000. "Keep it going as long as people are hungry. If the bill goes over that, see me."

"You got it, Chief. Glad to help."

* * * *

I was on the phone with Sunny Johnson telling her what was happening with Tubby and the food coming to the station when I saw Joaquin in the rearview mirror. He tried to stand. It didn't work out very well. When I hung up, he tried again. I twisted the mirror to get a better view.

Joaquin started shouting at me and wielding his injured hand like a college kid with an Occupy sign. He couldn't stand all the way. The cuffs required him to spread his legs wide and keep his back bent. People honked as they passed. He shouted into the wind and slung free-flowing blood from his nonexistent finger onto the back glass.

I jerked the wheel to the right and then hard back left. He went down, cursing loud enough I caught a few words. He stayed down the rest of the way to the motel.

I parked, and Joaquin lifted his head above the truck bed to scream at me and at anyone else he saw. He kept demanding that someone call the DEA.

I stepped down from the cab and said, "I'm not sure this is the place you want to be playing the DEA card."

"You're a dead man," he said, finally not screaming.

On the motel balcony, I stopped in front of my room to stare out to the southward dirt and sky. Old Mexico. Looking at anything at that moment was like peering through the wrong end of a telescope, distorted and distant. The day seemed to have gone on long enough to turn me into a fossil bone in the desert. Joaquin was right. I was a dead man. He was wrong about the timing. I had to wonder, Have I ever been alive?

Introspection and feeling sorry for yourself only go so far before the world sticks in its nose to remind you that none of us is that important, even in our own lives. Lenore appeared, climbing the stairs at the far end of the building. She wasn't looking at me. Her eyes were watching Joaquin, who had gone silent as he gaped at her.

I opened my room door but didn't go in. Lenore was on the balcony and walking slowly, but deliberately, right to me. "You picked up a stray," she said. "You're a good one for that."

"We all have to be good at something."

"That's not my experience."

I'd been fooling myself thinking I could ease into it. "About Simon Machado—"

"About Simon or about what I did?"

"I figure they're tied together."

"You don't understand nearly as much as you think you do."

"There's no arguing that."

"Why don't you go?"

That surprised me. "Where?"

"Anywhere. Run."

"I can't."

"Why? The way I hear it, you're not much of a cop. La Familia will turn you. Even your daddy thinks so."

"Turn me?"

She stepped away from me and through my open door. As she went, she mimed counting cash. Lenore folded the imaginary bills and tucked them away, saying, "Put you right into their pocket."

"They don't always win." I followed her into the room.

"They don't have to. They never stop playing."

"There's nothing special about them, Lenore. They're criminals. Killers."

"That's where you're wrong. You've seen Eladio. They are vampires. The suck the blood of peasants and gringos. La Familia de los Muerto lives in death and darkness, and you can't fight them."

"Mexican vampires?" I almost laughed. "I've seen that movie. What kind of hold do they have over you?"

"Ownership."

"We can stop—"

"Simon gave me to you. Not once but both times. He would be happy if I bent over right now and let you do anything you want. I wouldn't say no. I would spread. I would suck you and let you finish anyplace—anyway. Is that what you want? To have what he gives?"

"Make your own choices."

"He gave me to your daddy too."

All the breath disappeared from my chest.

"Buick grunted and sweated over me for hours. Then he pissed with the door open and sent me away. He said thank you to Simon."

My muscles were paralyzed. No air could come into my lungs.

"Will you thank him?"

It seemed to be impossible for me to speak, but I heard myself saying, "I'll kill him."

"For me? Or because of your father?" She shut the door.

TWENTY-ONE

My gut was acid and my legs trembling when I got back to the red truck. I had been unable to convince Lenore to come with me. I had convinced her of nothing. She had convinced me that she knew darkness better than I did. We'd both been in our own graves. I'd gotten out.

If Joaquin had been shouting, I would have gotten into the truck without a thought. He was quiet. That got my attention. Before I could ask, my nose grabbed on to the scent of cigar smoke.

While I had been inside talking to Lenore, Simon Machado had been outside talking with Joaquin. From the looks, it hadn't been a pleasant conversation.

"What happened?"

"Fuck you," he spat back but without venom.

"Machado was here."

Joaquin flipped me off with his missing finger.

"What'd he say?"

"What do you think he said? He'll kill you for this."

"You tell him you're a cop?"

"Stackhouse won't let you keep me. And once I kill you, I'll be back in La Familia and bulletproof."

"I wouldn't be betting on his batting average if I was you." I opened the truck door and tried not to show the trouble I had climbing in. "Let's go for another ride," I said and then slammed the door before he could curse me again.

* * * *

A hundred people had already gathered at the police station when I pulled into the parking lot, and they kept coming. Tubby was there with hogs on display. He had a trailer with a smoker behind a truck loaded with compartments both heated and chilled.

Some of the arriving vehicles were laden with folding chairs and tables. I saw two church vans pull up with more furniture and food. Cops and civilians were helping to unload and set up.

Almost everyone stopped what they were doing to stare at the prisoner in the bed of the red truck. The word had gotten out.

Before the engine was stilled, Hector, Sunny, and another ten cops came out of the station house.

"Is that him?" Officer Sunny called to me.

"Yep."

"Just when I was about to give up..." Hector said.

"I don't know what you're talking about," I told him.

"I didn't think I'd see him alive again."

There wasn't an answer for that. I didn't even try.

"What are we going to do with him?" Sunny asked. Her question wasn't casual. Nor was it fully trusting.

"Lock him up," I answered.

"Then what?" she hit back. "Are you going to give him over to the feds?"

"If we turn him over to anyone, feds or state, he disappears."

"So?" Sunny pushed.

"So—I don't know."

Hector took the prisoner to lock him safely in a cell. As he went, Officer Sunny asked, "Do you think a party is a good thing?"

"A party? No. A wake? Maybe. Something to take a little bit of the edge off a horrible day? Sure. Beer and barbeque? Can you say you don't need it?"

"That all sounds fine. But this feels like a funeral."

"Well…we should all have a send-off like this."

An hour later people were eating and drinking as a cloudless sky drained of light and color. Tubby's was the best barbeque I ever had. That may have owed something to the company and how good it was to be surrounded by people who didn't want to kill you.

I had tossed my well cleaned paper plate into the trash and was wondering if I could stand another beer, when two people who didn't quite fit flowed out of the crowd to seek me out. Simon Machado was dressed again like a country music star from 1969. He was wearing a black suit with embroidered green cacti. The green silk shirt matched perfectly. On his feet were hand-tooled boots that cost more than most people's cars. They were matched to the gun belt on his hip. In the holster was a revolver, hand scrolled and nickel plated. As bold as he looked, his light dimmed beside Lenore. She was dressed in an embroidered black skirt and white peasant blouse. Her hair was tied with ribbons, each in a different, brighter color. Through her eyes shone a charged light, electricity that crackled with energy.

Machado pushed her forward with a hand on her ass, and Lenore twirled for me, showing off the clothes and…something more that I was too blinded or too foolish to pick up on.

"You're beautiful," I said.

She smiled warmly, joyously.

A *snick* of sound, derisive and superior, came from her handler's mouth. Simon pulled a cigar from the inner pocket of his jacket. He bit and then spat out the tip before placing it in his mouth. The cigar bobbed and rotated in his mouth as he moistened it. That was when he looked at me and feigned a first notice.

Simon took the wet cigar from his mouth and turned it, butt end to me, and said, "I'm sorry. I should have offered first." He stared, white teeth showing, smug malice and hate. "Would you like a cigar?"

Before anything more could be said, Lenore interposed herself between us. She took my hand and put it on her breast before she pressed her whole body against mine. She was small at that moment. Her eyes were an animal's looking up at me. Lenore was a creature captured and on the edge of panic. She was also a woman, lovely and warm. Under the peasant top, she wore no bra. Her nipple was hard as a stone against my fingers. Beneath that, below skin and bone, her heart beat slower than I thought possible. It was a contradiction—one I had no capacity to understand. But I didn't take my hand away.

"Please," Lenore whispered up to my face. Her breath was warm. It caressed.

I breathed the scent of perfume and whiskey.

She moved her body against me. It was a gift of heat and license to take all the passion she represented. It was not a promise that her passions would be mine alone, though.

I snaked my hand from between our bodies.

"No, sir," I said, my voice thick and hushed. Then, stronger: "I'm not a cigar man."

Simon stuck the smoke back into his sneer. "This is a nice party," he said.

"It's not a party."

"It looks like a party."

"It's more of a wake. Something to remember a friend who has—gone on."

"She likes you." Simon pointed at Lenore, who was still pressed to my body while looking at my chest rather than my face. Then he lit his cigar. The flame exposed his face in a flickering orange that didn't touch his eyes.

"Not by choice." The words sounded cruel as soon as they left my mouth.

"We don't all have the same choices in life, amigo. Comprende?"

"I do. I understand very well. But that's the thing. We make the choices we have. Or they are made for us." I stepped back from him and, sadly, from Lenore. There was a fading heat where she had been pressed to me. It faded too quickly. I touched the brim of my hat and said, "You folks enjoy the food and the company."

"Tell me...*Chief*." his intonation managed to piss on the word. "Whose life are we remembering today?"

"You know that, Mr. Machado."

He didn't react.

"And you know I have your man, Joaquin, in a cell for the killing. He lost his finger in the fracas—the one he was just having decorated. But that's a small thing."

"How about—you give him to me?"

"Why would I do that?"

"An exchange of goodwill. A token of understanding."

"Mr. Machado, if there is one thing clear in this world, it's that you don't understand shit about me."

He puffed the cigar belligerently. Then Simon tilted his head back to exhale clouds of bluish smoke from under his hat into the deepening night. When his lungs were clear, he looked back at me to say, "You are doing a very nice thing here for one of your people." He turned to regard Lenore. She was staring at the sky, where stars were sparking. "You're a hard man." He continued and then shifted his focus back to me. "But even hard men have family."

I couldn't help but laugh at that. "My father? You're trying to leverage Buick Tindall against me?"

The confusion on Simon's face was perfect.

"You should have asked him how that would pan out before you showed up here." I turned and walked away. Three steps and I stopped. "But I tell you what." I turned and looked Simon Machado in the eye. "Come see me tomorrow. We have a few things to discuss, and you have a lot to learn."

He smoked and stared, giving nothing.

"We'll do it at noon."

"High noon?" he asked. "The cowboy cliché."

"Yep. High noon. At the tunnel entrance by the bank."

"Why would I do this?"

"Not just you. Bring your brother."

"Again, I ask why we would do such a thing."

"It's where I'll be. It's where Joaquin will be. Stackhouse and his boys will be there too. It's time you find out who your enemies are and why none of your plans for tunnels and banks are going to work out."

"Then look for us at noon," Simon said. He reached out and grabbed Lenore by the back of the hair and pulled. "Vamos, puta."

"Hey." I shouted loud enough to draw attention from the entire crowd. I hated to hear any woman called a whore. Without realizing it, I had put my hand on the butt of my pistol as well.

Simon took his hand from her hair and held it up for me to see.

"Lenore?" I asked.

She looked from the ground to me. Her gaze held my eyes but never stilled. Then she closed them and turned away. She stepped slowly. The walk turned into a sashay as she worked her hips and flounced the skirt in her hands.

Machado gave me an exaggerated shrug, "Choices, hey?" He turned and caught Lenore, putting his hand possessively on her ass as they went.

It wasn't twenty minutes later when Darian Stackhouse and his DEA crew showed up in their big SUVs. They parked on the street. As a group, they marched straight into the parking lot full of civilians. Every man was bearing automatic weapons. The crowd moved aside, a wake peeling off the bow of a tanker. Or a battleship.

"Turn him over," Stackhouse ordered as he approached. First shot across the bow.

"Who?"

"You know who."

"Hey." I pointed. "You got a new badge."

"Hand my man over, and we'll go away."

"Correct me if I'm wrong—but wouldn't a man of yours be a federal agent? A cop?"

Stackhouse didn't speak, but the big "fuck you" was blazing in his eyes.

"We don't have your man. We have, in custody, a murderer. A cop murderer and member of La Familia de los Muerto drug-trafficking organization." I sucked my teeth and then spit at the ground in front of Stackhouse's boots. "But don't go away. We want you to stick around. Have a beer and some food. Think about the life of Officer Bronwyn Gutiérrez."

"You know who he is."

"*Think* about her life. Consider it. Consider it real good."

Stackhouse held his ground and gaze. The other men, how-ever, looked away. None of them backed up, but they weren't happy to be reminded about Gutiérrez.

"You know you have to kick him loose." Stackhouse's voice was a measured calm, smooth as a flat line. That was scary.

"Hector," I called without looking away from the big man in front of me.

"Got you covered," he called back. "*All* of us got you covered."

"Everyone," I shouted out. "The man in front of me is Darian Stackhouse."

He looked around like a politician judging the mood of his crowd.

"He's a federal agent with the Drug Enforcement Administration," I went on, shouting to the gathered citizens of Lansdale. "He is the leader of a DEA Special Operations team."

When Stackhouse turned back to me, the blaze in his eyes was dimmed.

I finished up in a normal voice, "Let's all hear what he has to say about our prisoner."

"You're going to give him over one way or another."

"Yep," I agreed, speaking low and only to him. "If you want him tonight, bring a court order."

His eyebrows went up in a surprised arch.

I almost laughed. "See? I can be reasonable. But you don't want courts involved, do you?"

The surprise slid off his face.

"Or you can get him tomorrow at noon."

"What's the deal?" he asked, awfully eager.

"No deal. Tomorrow at noon. At the tunnel mouth."

His eyebrows crept up again.

"The one on this side of the border."

"What do you want?"

"I told you. No deals. Show up. We'll talk things over. I'll leave Joaquin and walk away."

He looked around. One by one he polled his men by eye contact. Stackhouse turned back to me and said, "Barbeque smells good."

"I changed my mind about that. You're not welcome."

TWENTY-TWO

Things settled down. The night unwound to a pleasant melancholy braced by food and beer. I offered Tubby more cash. He didn't take it. People pitched in and cleaned up. It was the ending of the gathering that most brought out the loss for me.

Guilt—I wrapped the feeling around me, feeding it beer and stars and the utter assurance that if I were Paris, Gutiérrez would still be alive.

"You should go home and sleep." It was Officer Sunny. I hadn't even noticed she was there.

"Who's going to sleep tonight?" I didn't wait for an answer. I crossed the lot over to where I had left the red truck parked.

There was a man waiting. I smelled the cigar smoke before I saw him. It wasn't Simon Machado. It was just a hulking form leaning over the truck hood, blackness within shadow, until the cherry on the cheap cheroot flared and showed Buick's face.

"You should have asked Machado for a good cigar," I said. "He likes sharing them."

"I never acquired the taste." He pulled the smoke from his mouth and examined it. "This is good enough for me."

"What are you doing here?"

He hesitated, working the cigar in his fingers. If it was to distract him or me, I couldn't tell. When he reached whatever point he was waiting for, Buick flicked the ash and said, "I've got one last chance."

"For what?"

"To get you on the payroll."

"After trying to kill me?"

Buick put the cigar back into his mouth. "Dead or paid. No one cares. What's happening calls for predictability."

"And I'm not predictable?"

"You never have been. I remember a time when—"

"Don't do that," I said. "Don't try to go all *fatherhood* on me."

"Anyway, I told them it wouldn't work."

"Why didn't you do that the first time? With Paris?"

"It was different with him. He wasn't the saint you think he was."

"You already said he wouldn't take the money. Are you saying something else now?"

"This is a nice truck," he said, running his hand over the smooth metal. "I like red."

"Is that an answer?"

"No. It's a chance to take the question back."

I looked at him and waited.

"The problem with Paris was one of timing, not character."

"I don't believe that."

"Yes, you do. He was a lot more like me than you ever were. I think he would have taken the money. Not at first. But he would have worn down. He never had your steel or your sense of outrage about things."

"I don't know what that means."

"It means you were a hard boy. And a hard young man. And you've grown into a hard bastard just like your old man."

"The key word being 'bastard.'"

"That's one key on a whole big ring. One your mama never dwelled on."

"You weren't there when she cried at night."

"Yeah, I was. A lot more than you know. And I was there when the cryin' was over you."

"Whatever."

"No. Now you seem all hard pressed to talk this out, let's do it."

His words were a challenge. I was dead set not to back down, but I did look away before I asked, "How do you do it? How does a man have two families?"

"By making the easy choice every time. By being selfish."

"Words are easy."

Buick pushed himself back from the truck and stood straight. He pulled the cigar from his mouth and dropped it. Then he waited for me to look at him. When I did, he said, "Shame."

I thought he was telling me I should be ashamed. I opened my mouth to shout my answer back at him.

"I was ashamed." He muttered the words.

I closed my mouth.

"Not of you or your mother. I was ashamed of myself. I was ashamed of the secret and then of not keeping it." He took a step to the front of the truck, and I took one back. Buick stayed where he was, but his hands moved like a man carving his own thoughts into words. "Can you understand that, boy? Most of my life was built on shame. But it never stopped me."

"Where's the reason in that, Buick?"

"Reason? Hell, there's no reason. There's no excuse."

"That's too easy."

"Easy?" His hands reached out again, but my father kept his feet planted. "What's easy? There's just...what is."

"Then why are you here? You didn't believe you could bribe me. The best explanation you have for all the mess in my life is that 'it just is what it is.'"

"You want things straight?"

"It would be nice for once."

Buick quickly came around the front of the truck. He surged forward too quickly for me to back away or put up my hands. He stopped with his face only inches from mine. I saw something of a wound in his eyes. It wasn't there long.

"I'll tell you this, Longview—looking at you is like looking at myself. A few years back, maybe. And I'm not talking about the outside, the bitter cast to your face or the concrete in your eyes, not the way you stand or the way you walk—we all three shared those. I'm talking about what's under all that. You're cocky at the expense of better judgment. Hell bent to have things your way, you bull through the lives of other, better people. You are me, boy."

"No. I'm not." I stepped back, putting a little distance between us. It wasn't enough.

"You're hard cast in an old mold, you from me and me from my daddy and he from his. On and on, probably back to Cain."

"You think that's true—make your offer. Try to buy me for La Familia, and see how that works out."

"I didn't come for that. I came to ask you to let all this play without you. Walk away. Have a chance at a life."

"Why?"

Buick deflated, and it was his turn to step back. "Because I've already lost one son to this, and I don't want to lose you both."

"It was your life that led up to this. Every part of it—every thought and action—brought Paris's murder a step closer."

"You think I don't know it? You think I don't live it in my heart and my bones? But what about the lives after his?" The old man backed away until he pressed against the truck fender for support. He fiddled at his pockets looking for a new smoke and then gave up and looked squarely at me again. "All your life you blamed me. I guess rightly so. I was responsible for the boy. But for the man, you have no one to blame but yourself."

I suppose it was a weakness, the kind of character flaw that Buick had talked about, but right then I needed to strike back at him. I asked, "Did you know that Paris was gay?"

"Of course I did."

I felt nothing but shame for asking and for having not known. "Get off the truck." I reached out and jerked the door open. The dome light created a cone of illumination that seeped through the windows. Buick looked old in the faint light. "I have things to do."

"You're not going to run, are you?"

"What do you think?"

He slapped his hand on the hood. "Listen to me."

I came back around the open door and faced him. "I'm listening."

"You're in it now, boy. These people—La Familia—they ain't the forgivin' kind."

"Neither am I."

"It's not about you. Don't you get it yet?"

"Talking to you is like chewing glass, Buick. Spit it out, or step aside."

"That little lady. The pretty girl with the tattoos." He said it like a confession. "They don't take things out on you. They take it out on everyone around you. Then you."

"Lenore."

"That's what they do. They suck all the life out of everything you touch."

"Like a vampire." I recalled Lenore's description.

"Call it what you want. They burn the fields, leaving you in the middle of the char to think about it. Then they come for you. Maybe you can save her if you disappear. Maybe it's too late."

"I'll kill Simon Machado."

"He's not the one to worry about. He works for his brother. Simon is a rabid dog on a leash. Eladio is the one who plans and orders."

"He looks like a skeleton."

"Cancer's eating him up, slow."

"I can speed things along."

Buick shook his head slowly. "It wouldn't be the punishment you think. His mind is sharp and cruel, but the man is resigned to death. He welcomes it."

"Fine by me," I said, imagining things worse than death.

"She was his, you know."

"What're you talking about?"

"The pretty girl."

"Lenore." I said her name like a warning.

"Whatever you call her, she was his. Eladio bought her for a few pesos at gunpoint when she was a little girl. He raised her to be his. When the cancer took his hard-on, he shared her out to his brother."

"To you."

"To me. And to you too. To anyone he wanted to compromise or control."

"That's where they'll start? With Lenore?"

"That's where they started."

TWENTY-THREE

whipped the red truck through streets and onto the highway, flying on asphalt. I called Hector.

In the black distance, the motel sign blazed in Easter egg colors. The pastel neon hit me like party balloons tied to a gravestone. Pushing the truck harder, I recognized something hopeless in the speed. There was not a chance in the world that Lenore was safe. This brutal life simply did not work that way.

Still…

Hope. It's a bitch.

Vacancy—the fluid pink word shone in front of the two-deck Desert Drop Inn. It was an innocent announcement that I read as a cruel joke. I slowed down. When I hit the parking lot, I was going something over seventy and slammed down on the brakes. My headlights projected my spin on walls and railings and closed doors.

One door was open and flickering with soft internal light. Mine.

The truck tires stopped screaming, and I ran. At the end of the motel building, approaching the stairs and dark concessions corner, I pulled my weapon. To make the turn and clear the machine cove, I slowed. Then I was running up the stairs again.

I stood in my room with my arms hanging loose. They were useless. My hands were lead shapes with no life in them. The gun I had gripped so tightly fell to the floor. Everything. Every feeling, thought, memory, and wasted desire of my life was coming back through my eyes.

The light in the small room was from forty or fifty candles flickering at their own rhythms. Illumination was a burden the scene bore sadly. I tried to see—and not see—the walls and blood that marked them. In my bed, Lenore was facedown. Her blood, still wet and vibrantly dark, soaked the sheets and spilled out onto the carpet. The blood was nothing. Lenore's hair, matted and wet to the point of being glossy, was bundled and set aside over her shoulder. Someone had been careful to keep it away from the work the blade had done.

A fly buzzed, and suddenly my ears worked again. An instant later my lungs gulped air, and I could smell dirty, wet copper. I retched at the scent. My gut kicked my spine again, and I doubled over. The smell was a thick miasma as physical as a knife in the belly.

Candles flickered and smoked. The smell got worse.

Steeling my heart and my timid guts against the odor of death, I looked into the nearest glass-jar candles. It was like peeking behind the robes of a dozen saints who were not who they claimed. Each candle was wet on the inside with melted wax and trickles of Lenore's blood.

I backed away, stopping at her naked feet. I wanted to touch her. I wanted to take her up and hold her. Even in death, though, I had the feeling an embrace would cause her to suffer more.

There was a spot behind the knee of her right leg that was clean. Her skin was still warm looking there and unstained by blood. That was where I concentrated looking.

Concentration was wasted effort. I stared at that spot but saw only the vicious outline of her flaying. The line ran from her neck down her ribs and waist until it curled around the soft shape of her hips and returned. All that skin was gone. All the beautiful art and words of her body had been stripped away and taken.

When Hector arrived, I was outside the room, bent over the railing. I was shaking with a rage that roiled in my gut. My mouth was open, waiting for the heaving spew that never came. Sunny Johnson showed up and put a blanket over my shoulders. It was a nice thought—that I could be soothed or comforted. That I could have the normal reactions.

I left the blanket hanging off the railing.

* * * *

That second drive was slower. My eyes were glazed with revenge. More than once I caught myself in the wrong lane. One time I realized I was staring at the speedometer. It read zero. I was stopped sideways in the highway with no idea how I had gotten there.

Eventually, though, I made it to Tubby's.

The big man was still cleaning up after a busy night and already tending the meats for the next day.

"Chief?" I could tell by the look on his face that it wasn't the first time Tubby had tried to focus my attention. He was holding out a beer. When I took it, he asked, "What can I do for you?"

I held the bottle up and savored the feeling of cold wetness in my hand. I pressed it to my face, soaking in the chill. It seemed for a moment I could get drunk by osmosis, but that was wishful thinking. I turned the beer up to my lips and swallowed it all. As the last suds spilled over my chin, I gasped to catch my breath.

"How much for that?" I pointed at a spread hog sitting on the grate.

"You want another hog?"

"One that you haven't put on the smoker yet."

"You want a whole hog? Raw? Whatcha got goin' on?"

"I can't tell you," I said, trying hard to look sincere and noncrazy.

"Oh," Tubby nodded sagely. "You want some of them can't-tell-you hogs."

"Yeah."

He nodded again and then said, "Hunnert bucks a carcass. Wholesale price."

"You got it." I offered my hand. Tubby pushed another beer into it.

* * * *

I took a six-pack and the hog with me when I left Tubby's. My head was a little clearer since I was traveling with the windows open to the night air. I went west out of town, past the bank building and the Border Crossing. When I sailed by the gates of the gun club, I hit the horn, blaring my presence even though no one could tell who was at the wheel.

Beyond that, the road degenerated, and I left it behind in favor of the dirt. I was on the same path I had taken that day after I'd made such a scene in the Border Crossing with Gutiérrez. That day I had been tired and angry, and I had ended up in Big Bend National Park to sleep in my truck. Sleep was the last thing on my mind now.

Hitting the high beams, I caught the green flash of ground-level comets. Coyotes scattered, tracking me with the reflective lasers of their eyes. I was glad for their company.

Spinning the wheel, I turned the truck, backing it up onto the flat plateau that overlooked the small valley. In the starlight, clumps of mesquite, juniper, and pecan trees were motionless demons. They witnessed, without commenting upon, my rite. Under them, the tiny stream had only enough water to make holes of reflected stars in the ground. The little valley was a place of power at night. I was there to harness it and sacrifice to it.

Dropping the tailgate, I reached in and grabbed the hog by one of his trotters and pulled. I couldn't see it, but I knew his skin was tracked with flakes of Joaquin's blood from the truck bed. The thought pleased me. His blood added depth to the offering.

I didn't stay to watch. I knew what would happen. I didn't drive back to the motel either. I went instead to the police station. There were still quite a few off-duty officers milling around. They looked at me like I was a ghost visiting their home. Maybe I was. I was a tired ghost, though, and avoided questions. I locked myself in my office and put my head down on the desk.

TWENTY-FOUR

Sleep would have kept me bound in its embrace much longer but for the demanding beat of knuckles on the door. It was Hector.

"Here," he said, shoving my own phone at me. "You dropped this…on the floor." He didn't need to say what floor. As soon as it touched my hands, it rang again.

"Thanks." I dropped it in my pocket.

"You're not going to answer it?"

"In a minute." I wiped at my face with my palm and then tried flicking crusts of sleep from the corners of my eyes. "How are you doing?"

"How am *I* doing?"

"Yeah. You. Everyone. Things."

"Where did you go last night?"

"Away," I lied. I think he knew it was a lie, but Hector held his tongue. "I needed—separation."

"Okay. I can understand that. Sunny's worried about you. Hell, we all are."

"Nothing to worry about." I wondered how much of a lie that one was. "Not anymore."

"Right."

"What time is it?"

"Almost eleven."

I patted the phone in my pocket. "Let me handle this, and then I'll get cleaned up."

"You should switch that around. You smell like you got drunk with a roadkill dog."

"Hog."

"What?"

"Never mind. I'll be out in a minute." I shut the door.

The phone rang again.

If I needed another indication of how screwed my life was, it came when Milo asked, "You doing okay?" instead of cursing at me.

"I'm fine," I answered.

The silence on the line judged me harshly.

"What do you want?" I said.

"Just an update and a warning."

"You've been calling all night. I don't imagine it was about the update."

"You knew I was calling all night?"

I took a long breath that cleared nothing and then filled Milo in on everything that had happened since we had last talked.

"It's time to get you out of there." Milo didn't curse or push. He didn't spin anything, and he didn't sound like I had fucked up. The statement worried me.

"Why?"

"It's time."

"Now? All of a sudden—*now* it's time?"

More silence from his end.

"You mentioned a warning," I reminded him.

"We've been thinking…"

I'd never seen or met Milo face to face; still, I was imagining him looking at the ceiling and gathering thoughts that didn't come easy.

He tried again. "We've been working this as a rogue thing. We—I thought it was all about the SOT getting off leash and working on their own."

"They're not."

"There's pushback."

"What's that mean?"

"It means there are questions—pressures—coming through official channels, from Homeland and from unofficial—official channels."

"You're saying what's happening here is legal?"

"No. I'm not saying that."

"Then what are you saying?"

"I'm saying it's time to get you out of there."

We talked for a few more minutes, circling the same black hole. I began to think that maybe Milo's phone was being monitored. If someone was listening to his conversations, how hard would it be for them to spy on mine? I disassembled the smartphone again and dropped it into the drawer with Stackhouse's badge.

I opened my door. Before Hector could say anything, I asked him, "Do you have a rope?"

"What kind and how much?"

"I don't care what kind, but fifteen or twenty feet ought to do it."

"There's a twenty-five-foot length of nylon tow rope in my trunk."

"Would you put it in the bed of that red truck outside?"

"I will if you change."

Hector was right; my clothes smelled vaguely of dead animal. I should have cleaned up or at least washed my face. Instead I went down the hall to our holding area.

Joaquin was holding his wounded hand against his chest. He looked as terrible as I smelled. His hand was bloody and black. Some of the darkness came from stippling, burning powder that had been injected into his skin from my gunshot. Some looked like creeping infection. The finger had not been attended to. That didn't bother me a bit.

The jailer cuffed him behind the back and chuckled when Joaquin winced. I checked him out and took him to his own truck.

"Are you going to throw me in the back again?" His question was pissy but without a lot of power. I doubted he'd slept at all.

"Nope. You get to ride up front with me. We can talk."

"I don't have anything to say to you." He clumsily climbed into the cab, and I closed the door behind him.

"I figured you would say that," I said, once I was seated and the truck was in gear. "It's why we're going someplace before the big meet-up with your people."

"Where?"

"I noticed you didn't ask which people."

"What are you talking about?"

"You're going to have a choice."

He looked at me, mistrustful and angry, but he didn't ask.

"Your cover is intact. You can go back to La Familia. *Or* if you think you've had enough, you can go back to Stackhouse."

"You're cutting me loose?"

"Such as it is."

"What's that mean?"

"It means I don't think much of either choice you have. But they're your choices. You deal with them."

"Why? And where are we going?"

"Now, that's the big question, isn't it? Why?"

"You want information."

My answer was to give him my biggest grin. Then I turned off the highway and headed up to the bluff with the trailer park development.

"Why are we going up here?"

"Room."

"What room?"

"Room to talk. And room to move around."

"Open the window," he said. "It stinks in here."

"I don't notice it anymore."

"Are you taking me someplace to work me over?"

"You've seen too many movies."

"Bullshit."

"Are you a runner? How's your cardio?" I pulled the truck off the road and onto the graded plain that waited for more trailers. Dust swirled around when we stopped. "Come on," I said as I jumped out, even though I knew he couldn't open the door.

"What do you want to know?" Joaquin asked desperately as I pulled him out. As soon as his feet hit the dirt, I dragged him to the back of the truck.

"What have you got?"

"Just tell me what you want."

"Nope." I dropped the tailgate. The rope was neatly coiled behind the fender well. "You see, I don't think you're properly incentivized yet. Know what I mean?"

"What's that for?"

"It means I don't trust you to tell me anything straight without you knowing how much it is in your interest to do so."

When I secured one end of the rope around the trailer hitch, Joaquin got an idea of why. "No."

"Yep."

"Ask what you need to know."

"Run first; then talk." I pointed at his boots. "Those are going to be tough going. You should have worn some running shoes."

"What the fuck?"

"Leather soles and a riding heel. At least you won't be running on the street. Might be hard on the ankles, though."

"You're crazy. You can't do this."

"Tell me something."

Joaquin shut up. The wild, wounded-animal look remained in his eyes.

"Did anyone ever once say that about Gutiérrez?"

"What?"

"You can't do this." I pushed the free end of the rope through his belt and fixed the hook over it. "Ready to run?"

In the truck, I looked at the rearview mirror. Joaquin was scrambling up onto the bumper and trying to climb into the bed of the truck. I dropped the transmission into gear and hit the gas. He flipped backward, and his feet kicked to the sky as the truck lurched forward.

I yelled out the window, "Better get up quick. It's time to go."

He probably didn't make it up to his feet. I didn't wait at all before letting the truck amble on. I couldn't see him, so I knew he wasn't running.

After a few feet, I stopped and shouted out, "Better get up and ready. This next one won't be slow."

Joaquin could have been a dust devil. When he popped up, the dirt shook from his clothes and swirled in the breeze. "What do you want?" He screamed the question.

"I want you to run." I pressed the gas pedal and kept speeding up. I didn't stop until he fell.

Joaquin rolled to the side where I could see him and then stayed on his knees. "I give up," he shouted at me.

"I don't," I said out the window and then pulled my foot from the brake. The truck rolled.

Joaquin stood on shaky legs. He trotted.

It was easy to tell when he was getting tired. The rope lost its slack and jerked him at the waist. Each time it happened, it took longer for him to catch up and get the tension out of the line.

"That's only jogging," I called back. "Let's get to the running." I sped up. He made it a few stumbling steps and then went down again. I stopped. "Are you getting it yet?" I shouted out the window. "You understand that you're not on the cop side anymore?"

"You can't." He screamed the words as he scrambled back to his feet.

I touched the gas, and the line popped tight. Joaquin was jerked facedown into the dirt.

I didn't drag him far or over cactus, but I wanted him certain that I would.

"I can," I shouted back to him. "The only question is, do you believe I will?"

He didn't answer. I got out and went to the rear bumper of the truck. Joaquin was lying in the dirt, panting like a fat dog in July. Fresh blood stained the dirt on his face where his nose had gotten bloody.

"Yeah, you get it now, don't you?" I asked, standing over him. "You're not a cop. You're not a fed. You're a piece-of-shit criminal. And you're not dealing with a police chief. This is between us, criminal to criminal. ¿Lo entiendes?" I spat some grit from my mouth. "Yeah, you understand."

We had a long talk.

TWENTY-FIVE

The officers of the Lansdale Police Department arrived at the tunnel site first. Hector was in charge. I'd asked him to bring everyone available, and he had said, "Try to keep us away." I could have kissed him for that.

The construction workers were surprised to see so many cops show up all at once. No one put up a fuss when they were told the workday was over. After that, Stackhouse and his crew showed up. They took position by the contractor's trailer. The Machado brothers, both of them, along with a dozen armed men, arrived next. Buick was with them. They set up closest to where the workers had parked their trucks and vans.

I arrived with Joaquin tied into the bed of the truck about five minutes after noon. I wasn't the last. I stayed in the red truck with my windows down talking to Joaquin until I saw the last car drive up and park between two police cruisers.

"Looks like it's time," I said to Joaquin.

He had nothing to say. That was fine. I was tired of hearing him anyway. Pulling him from the truck, I let him drop like a sack of potatoes to the ground.

The feds and the criminals watched him rise on wobbling Bambi legs without a word. When he was up and moving in front of me, I pointed over at Stackhouse and then at the Machados. They each moved to meet us where the plastic tarps gaped in front of the tunnel. Buick came but stayed a few steps behind Eladio.

"You got us here," Stackhouse was the first to talk. "What's it all about?"

"Doesn't anyone want to know about how poor Joaquin is doing?" I asked.

No one did.

"You talk a lot," Simon Machado said. "You make big noises, and you get people killed." He stared at me, sucking his teeth, waiting for a reaction. When I didn't say anything, he added, "We're tired of it."

"Me too," I said. "That's why it's almost over."

"I am very curious about this," Eladio Machado said. His voice sounded like old bones grating. "What is it you think is almost over? I'm yet to see an ending."

"You will."

"I think everyone's sick of your bullshit," Stackhouse said. "You wanted to talk. Let's get it over with."

"Fine. Here's the sad truth. This"—I gestured to the tunnel opening, then the bank, and then in a broad circle that I hoped indicated everything around—"all of this is over. It stops, and all your big deals"—I looked at Stackhouse—"to control the drug trades, to siphon off the cash, to keep Mexico under the American thumb." I turned to the Machados. "And your deal. The exclusive franchise to import drugs, to bank and launder cash—" I stopped talking, wanting the fact that I knew the big picture to sink in. Then I said, "All of it. Over."

Agent Darian Stackhouse was the first to find his voice. "I don't give a flat fuck what you think you know but—"

"Betrayal," I said, cutting him off. "Bad deals and betrayal. That's how wars are started."

"You have said this before," Eladio Machado mused. "I think you are trying to stir a pot that is not as hot as you think. ¿No es verdad?"

"Let's work it out," I said. "Way I see it, there are two parts at issue. One." I held up a finger and then pointed it at Stackhouse. "The failure of your project to control the drug trade and profit from it."

"You have no idea what the Homeland Security Act will allow me to do to someone like you." Stackhouse sounded as though he was already imagining breaking me on a rack.

"You're right," I answered. "I don't." I turned to where the last car had pulled in and waved at the occupants. Mr. and Mrs. Toomey got out. Mr. Toomey came to join us.

"Here you go," Mr. Toomey said, handing me a sheaf of papers. "It's all taken care of."

I took the pages and separated the two copies and then handed one over to Stackhouse.

"What's this?"

"This is notification of annexation."

"What the hell?"

"Yep. Bureaucracy can be our friend. The City of Lansdale has annexed the land from the city limits to the far side of the Gun Hills Hunting Lodge and Private Club. All of the properties within the new city limits are subject to building inspection for codes violations and tax assessment."

"You can't do this." Stackhouse didn't sound as sure of himself.

"We just did."

"It'll never hold up in court."

"Who cares?" I gestured around the work site. "Do you want all of this laid out in court? Do the people you're working for?" I gave a quick look to Mr. Toomey, and he walked back to his car.

Eladio Machado laughed. I think it was a laugh. It sounded more like wind blowing dry leaves. "Do you think we will simply let this old man stroll through our grounds looking for things to use against us?"

"No," I said. "I think you're going to be busy."

"With what?"

"Payback."

Buick spoke. "You don't have to do this. Not any of it."

I looked at my father. "I don't blame you, Buick."

"For what?"

"Anything. From here on out."

He looked around at the gathered men. "I'm interested in seeing how long that is."

"The payback is for number two." I held up my fingers again and waved them at the Machado brothers. "The failure of La Familia to protect itself from becoming the DEA's whipping boy for when this whole thing blows up."

"Eladio is right, I think," Simon said through his constant sneer. "You stir and you stir waiting for the pot to boil. I think maybe you forgot to light the fire, eh?"

To Eladio, I said, "I'm assuming you know Buick is working for these guys every bit as much as you."

Simon didn't seem to appreciate being snubbed. He spread his suit jacket and put his hands on his hips. The gesture put the nickel-plated revolver on display. He answered the question. "Your father is a go-between. He has been useful."

"But a man, even a man working both sides, has to be more on one side than the other. Am I right?"

"What are you doing?" Buick asked. He spoke slowly.

Simon shifted his gaze to look at Buick. There was new suspicion.

"My father is a bad man. But I just realized that he's only bad. Not evil. Not a monster." I turned and spoke directly to Buick. "You tried to get me to take money, to get on the payroll."

He didn't answer. He didn't look around. My father stared at me, waiting.

"Whose payroll?" I asked him.

His eyes shifted quickly toward Stackhouse.

I followed his look and said, "I thought so."

"You're just making a bigger mess, boy." Buick told me. "What do you hope to get out of it?"

"You can't stay now," I answered him. "You're out of La Familia no matter what. You can get away."

"You can too. Walk away. We'll go together."

I didn't say anything to that. Buick seemed to understand. He patted at his pockets, finding one of the cheap cheroots, and then stuck it, unlit, into his mouth. "Yeah," he said, agreeing with my silence. He turned and walked back to stand beside one of the SOT vehicles.

"Is there a real point to all this?" Stackhouse jumped in. "Or are we waiting around for you to work out more of your daddy issues?"

"Well, yeah." I addressed Eladio again. "I've got a point. And it has to do with trust. And who you let into the family."

"I'm listening," he answered for himself, the words rasping out.

"There was a man. You lost track of him a couple of weeks back. Always seemed to be laughing. His name was Cesar Barcia."

"It's time you stopped talking." Stackhouse's voice was low and cold.

I ignored him and told Eladio, "Ask Agent Stackhouse why he's worried."

Eladio turned his attention to Stackhouse. Simon inched his hand closer to the pearl grips of his revolver.

When no one said anything, I went on. "Barcia was DEA."

"Accusations are easy, and you toss them out like rubbers at a whorehouse." Stackhouse challenged me. "I say he wasn't a cop. At least not one of mine."

"You remember the last time you saw him?" I asked Eladio. "You sent him yourself to kill my brother, Longview. I've been wondering, was that about sending a message to Buick or about taking over the Guzman Cartel?"

"Both," Simon answered. His sneer showed tobacco-stained teeth.

"Cesar Barcia is the man who cleared out that house and left your men dead."

"Bullshi—"

Eladio stopped Stackhouse by raising a hand. I noticed that Simon's hand was on his fancy pistol.

"I would like to hear this," Eladio Machado said. His voice had a new life to it.

"Barcia lost his badge, and it was in the house, wasn't it?" I was talking to the Machado brothers, but each of them was focused on Agent Stackhouse. "Think he did it alone? The way I hear it, that house was shot up bad. How much did they get away with? A little over a million, right?"

"These are dangerous accusations," Eladio said.

"Yeah. That pot's ready to be stirred now, isn't it?"

"You have more?"

"Buick was working both sides, but everyone knew it. The real breach of trust was for Agent Stackhouse to have a snitch— someone you trusted within La Familia, wasn't it?"

Since we had been standing there, Joaquin had stared silently at the ground. He'd heard enough. He looked up at me and said flatly, "You're a motherfucker."

"What if they had two snitches in place?" I asked. "People you trust, working for the DEA. And it's not about reporting your crimes. It's all about setting you up for the fall if things go wrong."

"Who?" Eladio's voice was creaky as an old door but full of anger.

"Joaquin here is free to go. I'm not holding him for anything. It'll be interesting to see who he runs to, don't you think?"

Joaquin shouldered past me and bolted for Stackhouse.

Fast as an old-time gunfighter, Simon Machado pulled his shining revolver and started firing.

We all scattered like dandelion fluff in a hurricane, except for Joaquin. He fell hard with three bullets in his back.

TWENTY-SIX

That's how wars start. And I was fine letting it happen. When the shooting started, I ducked back and held my hands up to the Lansdale police, shouting, "Hold your fire."

They showed remarkable restraint. Officer Sunny pulled other cops together around the Toomey's car for protection. Hector rushed forward to join me and kept his shotgun ready as we retreated to the line of police cruisers.

The SOT and La Familia held nothing back. Stackhouse's men moved into the fray laying down suppressing fire and then advancing in teams. Their weapons were full military versions, and they were trained.

La Familia fighters were not as skilled, but they were motivated. One started up a car and moved it in to cover Simon as he half carried Eladio.

Stackhouse shot the driver of the car. La Familia fighters ignored the dead driver as they formed up in two groups. One screened the escape of Simon and Eladio. At least three of them died doing so. The other group set up behind the car and kept up a brutal spray of streaking bullets.

I heard the blast of a shotgun and caught sight of Connors, the treasury agent on the right side of the SOT line. He fired, and another man advanced. I saw Connors nod to his teammate once he was set. The other man fired, and Connors advanced. He only made it a couple of feet before his throat blossomed with red. The treasury agent thrashed on the ground only a moment before he was gone.

Behind the blocking car, another vehicle rolled back, throwing up a dirty cloud on the bare ground. Some of the SOT fired blindly at it for a moment before giving up. Several La Familia men broke cover to get between the car escaping with the Machado brothers and the SOT. They all died.

A new wave of return fire crashed against asphalt and body armor. That time it engulfed us. Bullets popped holes in the sheet metal of the Lansdale police cruiser. Glass from shattered windows rained on us and scattered like shiny teeth on the ground. The cops shot back. For a few furious moments it was us on the side of the SOT, fighting the cartel forces. It would have felt good if I wasn't worried about my officers.

One of the SOT rolled a grenade under the car La Familia was using for cover. I saw it skitter and hop to a stop. One of the cartel men reached for it. It was only a flash-bang, but it went off in his hand. A blinding charge of yellow light and disorienting noise burst from under the vehicle.

Bart Ganz, the big DEA agent I knew from the pool table, broke left, darting behind a van to come out on the open flank of the men remaining behind the car. He pinned the men down while the rest of the SOT finished the job. No one surrendered.

Simon and Eladio got away. But they were almost the only members of La Familia to do so. Stackhouse lost Connors and two other men who were wounded.

When the last gunshot sounded, Darian Stackhouse turned to march across the lot. He strode straight up to me and centered his weapon on my heart from about five feet. Behind me, the weapons of cops raised. They were all aimed at him.

Slowly, probably much slower than he expected, the other members of the SOT approached behind Stackhouse. Their weapons were ready but held down. Still, it seemed like Stackhouse was determined to have his revenge—at least until Buick walked between the cops and SOT. He moved right up beside Stackhouse and raised a nickel-plated .357 under his chin.

"You may be willing to take the chance that cops won't shoot you down," Buick said. Stackhouse's jaw flicked up, trying to get away from the weapon under it. "Are you willing to take that chance with me?"

He wasn't. Stackhouse lowered his gun and stepped slowly away from the one my father held. As he rejoined his team, she shouted over, "It's your mess. You clean it up." The SOT took their dead man and wounded and piled into the SUVs. They left.

"Where do you think they're going?" I asked.

"Nowhere," Buick said. "They will be right here until something changes."

"You don't think something has changed?"

"Some people are dead. Some plans are screwed up. Nothing has changed."

"It will," I said. "Until then, come with me." I took my father over to where Hector was pulling blankets from the back of a cruiser to cover bodies. "Hector, meet my father. Paris's father."

Hector's eyes widened with surprise and questions that I didn't let him ask.

To Buick, I said, "This is Hector Alazraqui. He was the only person at Paris's funeral."

They shook hands but said nothing. It was as if there were a fragile, invisible wall between them each feared to breach with questions.

"We need to break into teams," I said to my father. "Hector here is in charge of the shooting scene—evidence and getting bodies to the morgue. Something you have a lot of experience with."

Buick puffed up. "I do," he agreed, talking to Hector. "Would you take a little help?"

Hector relaxed and almost smiled. "I was thinking to get the bodies covered first." He pointed to a patch of parking lot with no cars and no dead men on it. "And thought we could make a command post there."

"That's good," Buick agreed and then pointed to the road. "But if you set up there, the ambulances can line up and load up. Everything can be logged, and nothing goes without a tag."

I left them talking and collected Officer Sunny Johnson. I put her in charge of exercising our annexation order and trumped-up charges against the Border Crossing. She closed the bar for not having a city liquor license.

It was Sunny who came up with the idea of running the girls out of the cribs because they had no connection to city plumbing. It was also her idea to call state social services and nonprofit agencies that helped women escape from trafficking. She was also responsible for seizing some of the Machado's worker's mobile homes and providing the girls and their children with places to go. Sunny was an amazing cop.

* * * *

That night I ate dinner—carne asada and cold beer—with Hector and Sunny at Ernesto's taqueria. I had showered before, but the scent of death still lingered. I wasn't certain it was simply the smell of the hog I'd taken out to the desert.

After dinner, I went next door for a fresh haircut and a shave. I got the same splash of scent that I'd been given that first night I had come to town. A man should have a signature scent, I decided.

The sandalwood and cedar helped when I picked up the second hog from Tubby. That time I had the sense to show up with a plastic drop to keep the juice of a dead pig off my clothes.

Tubby offered a beer. "I think you need it," he said.

He was right. What I was up to was hard, troubling work.

With the cold beer bottle sweating between my thighs, I drove out to Big Bend and to the same level spot I'd been the night before. Last night's hog was nothing more than ratty, scattered bones and flies. Even at that, there were still a few coyotes slinking around. They kept watchful eyes on my truck as they bit through bone to get at the moldering marrow within.

I opened the door and stepped out. Suddenly the coyotes were invisible. They weren't gone. I knew that. I was simply unable to see them. That didn't mean there was no sense of them. I could clearly feel the gaze of each animal. It was as if they had disappeared, leaving only eyes behind, like a pack of brutal, scavenging Cheshire cats.

That lasted as long as it took to pull the new hog out and drop it into the dirt.

I folded up my tarp and tied it with a bit of string I'd brought for the purpose. The long end of the string I tethered to the same tie-down I'd secured Joaquin to. Once things were tidied up, I drove the truck back and turned it to shine my headlights on the carcass.

The lights and truck kept the coyotes back from the hog for a few minutes. After the first brave animal slipped forward for a taste, their fear was gone. It was what I wanted.

For two hours, I listened to Merle Haggard and watched the beasts rend the pig to bone.

* * * *

It became almost routine. My days were spent finding the bodies of men. Mostly they were La Familia cleaning its own house. One man I recognized as a member of Stackhouse's team. There were a couple of Hispanic men with tooled belts and boots with long pointy toes found with holes in them made by military weapons.

My evenings, once it was dark enough, were occupied by bringing hog carcasses to the coyotes. They came to expect the feeding and didn't care that I remained close by and watched.

That routine lasted for three days while the fighting between La Familia and the SOT, and my feeding sessions, grew more violent.

I had no contact with Milo. He tried. Paris's phone remained disassembled and locked away. When he called the station line, I had him put on hold. While he waited, I went for beer.

On the third evening, as the sun faded and the heat flowed into the empty sky, the conflict became open war. The gun club grounds erupted with a firefight. The Lansdale police responded to the edge of our jurisdiction and watched. There was no response from county or state law enforcement.

I hoped the two sides, the criminal and the corrupt, would take care of each other. No such luck. The fight ended with an anticlimactic retreat of the big SUVs used by the SOT. I imagined them licking wounds and bragging about the damage they'd inflicted.

That night the coyotes didn't even wait for me to get the hog out of the truck before they stalked around. Their numbers had swelled from the few to at least fifty snarling beasts. They circled close as I worked, ready and dangerous.

The next day two bodies were sent to the Houston morgue. They didn't go through our department. They were members of the SOT.

Stackhouse showed up when I was eating dinner at Ernesto's with Sunny and Hector. Buick was with him.

"You need to fix the hell you started," Stackhouse said without preamble.

"I didn't start anything," I said. "I ended up in the middle of your storm."

He bolted forward like he was going to rip my head off. Buick was the one who stopped him. He put himself between us and faced Stackhouse down. Then he turned to talk to me.

"We have an opportunity," Buick said.

"I'm not interested."

"Hear things out. This is a way to get what you want and for the government to get what they want."

"What is it I want?" I asked him.

"To make better choices than I ever did." He stared down at me, waiting for a response I didn't give. "Or to finish the job you started."

"Those two don't line up." I pushed my plate of tamales away.

"You want people to keep getting killed?" Stackhouse demanded.

"Depends on who they are."

Buick held up his hands for a pause. "All you gotta do is talk to the Machados. They won't talk to anyone from DEA."

"You want me to—"

"To go up there." Buick was adding a little extra emphasis to his words. "Just you. To talk."

It took a second, but I understood the opportunity he was presenting between better choices and finishing what I had started. "Talk about what?"

"A new deal."

"Why?" I turned my gaze back to Stackhouse. "You wouldn't be here asking me if something hadn't changed."

"The FBI," he answered. "Your boy, Milo Janssen, has them involved. If we don't settle this, we're all going down in the same flush."

"Classy." I turned back to Buick. "Do you think they'll talk to me?"

"Yeah." Buick pulled a cheroot and stuck it in his mouth. "I think they'll listen." He lit the smelly little cigar. "The way they see it, you're an asshole. But you haven't lied to them." He glanced over at Stackhouse.

"When?" I asked, hoping.

"Go over now. Get something started and the shooting stopped," Stackhouse said. He sounded a little desperate. "Then we can fix things. We can all get what we want."

I looked back at Buick. "What do you think I should do?"

"Are you asking my advice?"

"Yep."

"I think you should leave. I've said it before—walk away."

"The better choice?"

"You know it is."

"And if I don't make that choice?"

"Who am I to judge?" He bent over the table, placing both hands on the top, and then looked straight and level into my eyes. "But anything you do, do it all the way."

TWENTY-SEVEN

Before going to the gun club, I stopped at Tubby's. I paid him for a hog but told him to keep it. He handed over a beer without comment. I held it in my hand and stared at the bubbling amber lit by the inferno red of the smoker's open firebox.

Tubby used an old shovel to arrange coals.

"You got another one of those?" I asked him.

He jerked a thumb over his shoulder toward a barrel against the wall. It bristled with the burned and rusted ends of rakes and shovels. I went to the tools and hefted a shovel.

"You want it," he said. "Take it. Don't worry about bringing it back."

Something else caught my eye. On one of the posts that supported the roof was a wire hanger on a nail.

"Mind if I take your hanger too?"

* * * *

No one stopped me when I drove onto the gun club grounds. It wasn't surprising since the iron gate was warped and pushed to the side. There were men at the main door. They led me in without comment.

At the glass doors of the inner sanctum, they demanded my weapon. I refused. No one was surprised or angry. They were tired of everything. One man grabbed my arms from behind as another put a gun to my temple. A third man pulled my pistol from the holster. He looked more bored by the exercise than angry. He opened the door, and I was led in without my .45.

Simon sneered.

Eladio wheezed, but his eyes were alive.

"We're here to talk," I said. "The feds think things can get back to some kind of working relationship."

Eladio nodded and smiled as if I had told a joke he was politely acknowledging. "What do you think?"

"I think you can't trust them anymore than they can you."

"Would you like a drink?" As soon as the question was out of his mouth, Eladio looked away. His expression was the kind they would have called "inscrutable" in old novels.

"How do you keep holding on?"

He didn't look at me. Eladio kept his gaze focused someplace over my head. He did smile though. "Because I must."

"If ever a man looked ready to let go, it's you."

Simon sucked his teeth and flipped the tail of his silk jacket aside to show the shiny revolver.

"That's a pretty gun," I said.

"We each have our appreciations," Eladio said. "The lust for things is not that different from the lust for women, I think. They are both a holding on. A possessiveness."

"You think that's what I want to talk about?"

"Yes."

"No."

"It's the only thing you want to talk about," he insisted. "Pretty Lenore." Eladio lifted a shaking finger and pointed to a spot high on the wall above my head.

I looked and wished I hadn't.

Mounted, framed and illuminated by a soft spot of light, was what looked like parchment. It wasn't. Ink on the skin made a crucifix that bore a bleeding Christ. Those were made of shades of gray. Blood, in red, poured out to become roses and skeletons.

At the bottom was a colorful band of grinning skulls. Between them was a tattooed poem in Spanish.

One line stood out to me: "In my bed the shadow resides— each side of my eyes."

She believed that her bed was a grave—death, both before and behind her eyes. I understood how she could see herself as both a victim and a tool of death. It wasn't parchment. It was the skin taken from Lenore's back.

Simon expected me to go for my gun. He was ready for that. He wasn't prepared for me to grab his brother by the loose collar and lift him off the couch.

In my rage, Eladio Machado had no weight. But he was the perfect shield. I shoved him against his brother, and when the fancy revolver peeked from under the bony arm, I turned it to the side and jerked Eladio higher. Under his frail body, I lifted my knee into Simon's crotch. As soon as it connected, I twisted at the shoulder and threw my weight into Eladio's chest.

The one brother, thin as bird's bones, fell aside. The other brother sneered at me again right up to the instant I shoved the barrel of his own revolver into his mouth.

I pulled the hammer back. "Don't move," I ordered, quiet but hard.

Reaching behind and into my back pocket, I pulled out the coiled bit of clothes hanger I had taken from Tubby's. With my mouth and free hand, I unwound the wire and then hooked it over my right wrist. It was just long enough to wrap around Simon's head and back to the pistol. The end went through the trigger guard and locked us together.

When it was done, I asked him, "Understand?"

He nodded as slightly as it was possible.

"Good." I inclined my head down at his motionless brother. Simon bent with me as I pulled Eladio up. Left handed, I hefted him over my shoulder. "Out to my truck," I ordered.

The gunmen in the hall quickly read the situation. They had the sense to not even raise their weapons. Or maybe they didn't care anymore. As long as they stayed out of my way, I didn't worry about it. I pointed at my .45 sticking from the belt of the man who had taken it. Then I shoved my hip out. He got the message and put my weapon into the holster. He didn't even give me a dirty look.

Outside, I tossed Eladio into the truck bed without being gentle. Simon went with me to the driver's-side door and carefully slid over the low console.

It was a quick drive over to the flat spot overlooking the little valley. The coyotes were gathered with expectation.

I made Simon lie in the dirt while I released the hanger wire from around his head. When I turned to lower the truck tailgate, I wasn't worried that he would jump and run. He could see the glowing green eyes and hear the growls as well as I could.

"Start digging," I ordered as I tossed him the shovel.

I patted Eladio's face, trying to revive him.

"Big man," Simon said. He used the shovel to sweep away some pig bones. "You feel pride in doing this?" His shovel bit into the dry earth.

"Nope," I answered. "You've got mostly sand and loose dirt. This should go quick."

"Why bother with a grave?"

"Because you gave me one. I'm just returning the favor."

"What are you talking about?"

"Never mind. I think your brother is waking up."

Eladio was rousing.

"Are you going to make him dig his grave too?"

"We only need one grave."

"Why?"

I pulled the revolver from out of my belt and pointed it at a cluster of coyotes getting close. I fired, and they scattered. The noise got Eladio a little closer to full consciousness. "I'm glad you could join us," I told him.

Simon had worked at the ground with little self-deceit. The grave was still very shallow, but it was about the right size.

"Why?" Simon demanded again. "Which of us gets the grave?"

I raised the revolver and flipped the loading gate open. One by one I used the plunger to remove the spent casing and four live rounds.

"You awake, Eladio?" I patted his face a few more times. "You with us?"

Simon stopped digging and raised the shovel.

I aimed the revolver at him.

"You going to shoot me? Wouldn't that ruin all your fun?"

"I wouldn't kill you." I gave him a moment to work that over. "A leg wound would be worse than killing you outright in this situation. Don't you think?"

He spat.

"Dig."

"I always knew a bullet in the desert would be my ending," Eladio said. His gritty voice had taken on kind of a delirious sing-song. "That is what I was waiting for."

"You think you're better than us?" Simon spat again to show his opinion of that.

With my .45 in my right hand and the revolver with one bullet in the left, I helped Eladio down from the tailgate. Coyotes were crowding around again. I didn't drive them off.

"That's enough," I told Simon. "Toss the shovel away."

He threw it hard at a bunch of creeping coyotes. They yipped and retreated with tails tucked under.

"Get out of the hole," I ordered. With the .45 I pointed to a spot beside the grave. "Kneel."

"You don't have to do this, amigo," Simon said. The plea was hopeless and without force. He went to his knees.

"You too," I said to Eladio and helped him down.

The brothers faced each other from about eight feet.

"You are no better than we are," Simon said.

"I'm exactly what you are," I told him. "That's why it happens this way."

I reached over Eladio's shoulder and put the revolver in his hand. "One bullet," I said. "Your choice."

Without hesitation, seemingly without thought, he raised the weapon and shot his brother in the heart.

"I chose," he said. "I get to live."

"No. You get the grave."

I pulled Eladio up by the collar and threw him into the shallow hole.

If it had been Simon, I would have shot him in the knee. I didn't think Eladio was going to get very far. The coyotes already smelled blood.

As I walked to the truck, I realized that something, finally, was easy.

* * * *

Milo showed up the next day. He didn't come alone. There were cadres of lawyers and investigators from every three-letter branch of the government you could name.

I was right: Milo Janssen was a black man. But if I had guessed any more, I would have been wrong. He was older than I thought. Gray dusted his short hair. Deep lines made deltas of skin at the sides of his eyes. His muscles were softened with a layer of desk-earned fat. That took nothing away from the power in his eyes and his carriage. Even though there was a stew of federal agencies around, there was no doubt Milo was in control.

I kept reporting to the office as chief of police of Lansdale, Texas. A week later I was surprised to find no one had kicked me out. I asked Milo about it over tacos and beer.

"That's a tricky question. Isn't it, Longview?" His brown eyes were bright. They had humor but no laughter in them.

"You know?"

"You think I'm an idiot?"

"No."

"It's good to understand each other."

"When did you know?"

"You never fooled Gutiérrez."

"Wait." I almost spilled my beer. "You were in contact with her?"

Milo took a drink but managed to shake his head with the mug at his mouth. When he set the glass down, he was looking right into my eyes. "The man she worked for—worked for me."

"Did she know that?"

"I haven't had a beer this good or this cold in a long time." Milo lifted the mug again and took another long, slow drink.

I let the news and his refusal to tell me more sink in. Once he set the beer down, I asked, "What happens with me now? With Longview, I mean."

"With Longview, nothing. And Paris—you did what was needed," he said. "The job is yours as far as the DOJ is concerned. Keep it or don't. What do you want?"

"I haven't thought about it."

"I don't believe that." He pushed a big bite in his mouth and chomped. He chewed quickly, keeping his eyes on me. It was a knowing gaze.

"What makes you sure?"

He set the taco down and wiped his mouth. "I talked to your old man."

"What did he say?"

"He said he was signing on to work for you and get this department back into shape. He said you asked him."

"There might have been a discussion about that."

"Uh-huh."

"How long are you sticking around?"

"I'm not. No point. I'll be gone tomorrow or the next day." He took another big bite.

"How can that be? What was going on here was huge. You can't figure the whole thing out in a week."

Milo nodded, smiling around his chewing. After washing the taco down with beer, he said, "There won't be any figuring things out. Our government won't incriminate itself." He wiped grease off his fingers and dropped the wadded napkin. "What began as a secret operation that no one wants to claim is quickly becoming a multiagency program. That's how you hide things in the bureaucracy. You embrace them and give them your full retroactive support."

"I don't believe it."

"Oh, believe it. In a very short time, everything that happened here will have been a part of a fully authorized exercise in border, currency, and trade security. Even the Mexican government is already claiming to have been involved from the start. That might even be true."

"What about the people? What about Stackhouse?"

"It turns out that Darian Stackhouse is no fool. The people he took his orders from were well protected, but he'd documented everything. Things that were never written down, Stackhouse had the sense to catch on camera or audio. He doesn't come out well, but he will be coming out."

"What about—"

"All the hard-core bad guys, except maybe Stackhouse, are dead. Mostly you did that. What more do you want?"

"I don't know. Just—more."

"Ain't that always the way?" Milo took another swallow of beer and then asked, "So you think you can handle it?"

"What?"

"Staying here and doing the chief thing?"

"Are you kidding?"

"You're a fighter," he said. Then he waved a hand around us. "The fight's over. Parking tickets and Saturday-night drunks will be harder in the long run."

"We'll see."

That night I purchased a hog from Tubby. There were still a lot of secrets, and secrets need to be fed, or they eat you up. I went out to the small valley as a half-moon rose. The coyotes knew I was coming. They were there to greet me, snarling and circling, waiting and ready.

ABOUT THE AUTHOR

Robert E. Dunn was born an Army brat and grew up in the Missouri Ozarks. He wrote his first book at age eleven turning a series of Jack Kirby comic books into a hand written novel. Over many years in the, mostly, honest work of video and film production he produced everything from documentaries, to training films and his favorite, travelogues. He returned to writing mystery, horror, and fantasy fiction for publication after the turn of the century. It seemed like a good time for change even if the changes were not always his choice.

In addition to DEAD MAN'S BADGE, Mr. Dunn is the author of the horror novels, THE RED HIGHWAY, MOTORMAN, and THE HARROWING, as well as the Katrina Williams mystery/thriller series, A LIVING GRAVE, A PARTICULAR DARKNESS, and the upcoming A MOMENTARY LIFE.